# LISTEN TO YOUR HEART

# ALSO BY KASIE WEST

P.S. I LIKE YOU

LUCKY IN LOVE

LISTEN TO YOUR HEART

MAYBE THIS TIME

PIVOT POINT

SPLIT SECOND

THE DISTANCE BETWEEN US

ON THE FENCE

THE FILL-IN BOYFRIEND

BY YOUR SIDE

LOVE, LIFE, AND THE LIST

FAME, FATE, AND THE FIRST KISS

LISTEN
TO
YOUR
HEART
KASIE WEST
POINT

ISBN 978-1-338-21006-4

10 9 8 7 6 5 4 3 2 1 19 20 21 22 23

Printed in the U.S.A. 23

This edition first printing 2019

Book design by Yaffa Jaskoll

THIS ONE'S FOR
THE DAYDREAMERS

# CHAPTER 1

The sky was perfectly blue. Not a single cloud marred its surface. I lay on my back on the seat of my WaveRunner, my feet up on the handlebars. I let my hand drift down to the water and skim along the surface.

"You're teasing me, aren't you?" I asked the sky. "Today of all days." I pulled my phone out of my pocket and took a picture of the sky. I posted it online with the caption *In denial*.

My phone rang and I startled, nearly dropping it into the lake. I sat up and answered.

"Hello?"

"Kate. Where are you?" Mom asked.

"Um . . ."

"It wasn't a hard question," she said, a smile in her voice. "Out on the lake, huh? You have to leave for school in twenty minutes."

"Ugh." School. I'd been trying to pretend it didn't start today. If my school were in Lakesprings, the town where I lived, it wouldn't start until after Labor Day. But there weren't enough permanent residents in Lakesprings to support a school. So my high school was thirty minutes down the mountain in Oak Court. Oak Court didn't care about lake season.

"Come on," Mom said. "It's your brother *and* your cousin's first day of high school. Don't make them late."

"I'll be right there," I said. I hung up and powered on the WaveRunner. Just then, another WaveRunner passed me by, sending a spray of water over my entire right side.

"Hello! Distance!" I shouted. I hated when people who clearly saw me drove too close.

I wiped off the screen of my phone on my left sleeve, tucked it back into the pocket of my board shorts, and steered back toward the marina.

Mom was waiting on the dock as I pulled up. People often said I looked exactly like my mom. Not really what a sixteen-year-old wants to hear when her mom is forty. But I knew what they meant. We both had long, light brown hair, easy-to-tan skin, and hazel eyes, which was really just a fancy way of saying brown with a little bit of green in them.

"Fifteen minutes now," Mom said, giving my wet swimsuit a once-over.

I flashed her a smile. "I just have to change. I'll be fine." I pulled up to the dock and she reached for the WaveRunner to tie it off.

"This one is rented out starting at eight a.m.," I told her.

"Does it need gas?"

"Probably," I said. "I can fill it."

"School, Kate." Mom gave me a side hug.

Sometimes school felt so pointless when I already knew what I wanted to do with my life—run this marina with my parents.

"Okay, okay." I kissed her cheek. "Thanks, Mom."

"Have a good day!" she called after me.

I walked across the street, around the corner, and through the front door to our house. A short person ran past me, followed closely behind by another little kid screaming, "Uncle Luke said it was my turn!"

Here is the thing about our living arrangements: My grandparents grew up in Lakesprings. They owned both the marina and the five acres of land across the street from the marina. When they decided to retire, they gifted the marina and the land to their three kids, who then divided the lot and built three houses next door to one another. My aunt and my uncle, who had other jobs, sold their shares of the marina to my parents, who had already been managing it. And that is how we ended up with a marina we ran while living on a family commune.

I rushed down the hall to my bedroom and quickly changed into clean shorts and a striped tee. I ran a brush through my hair; it was still damp, but it would dry on the drive to school. Then I grabbed my backpack and hurried out of my room.

My younger brother, Max, was waiting by the front door with his backpack on.

"You ready?" I asked him.

"So ready," he said drily.

"Where's Liza?" I looked around for our cousin.

"Not here yet."

"I'll go get her."

I walked outside and turned right. Our house was in the middle, sandwiched between Uncle Tim's house to the left and Aunt Marinn's to the right. My aunt and my uncle were each married, and each had a bunch of kids.

I knocked on Aunt Marinn's front door. Nobody else in the family felt that knocking was a necessary step before entering a home, but I hung on to that courtesy, hoping others would follow my example. When nobody answered, I sighed and walked in.

"Liza!" I called. "We have to go!"

My fourteen-year-old cousin appeared at the door in a cute sundress and a cloud of fruity fragrance.

I coughed. "What is that and did you shower in it?"

"It is Mango Dreams and it will fade." She tossed her blonde hair and pulled me by my arm out the front door like she had been the one waiting on me.

Max was already in the passenger seat of my car. Liza climbed in behind him and squeezed his shoulders. "Freshman year!" she cried. "This is the start of a new chapter where anything is possible!"

"Sure," I said. Or it would be exactly the same as the year before—a placeholder until summer.

⁂

The first bell was ringing as I pulled into a parking spot at the high school. Max and Liza were out of my car faster than I'd ever seen them move. They were already halfway across the parking lot by the time I'd locked the car and stashed my keys in my backpack.

"Late on the first day of school?" Alana said, walking over to me and hooking her arm through mine.

"I'm not late yet. And you didn't have to wait for me."

"What kind of best friend would I be if I didn't?"

"The kind that wants to be on time."

"We're juniors now. Bells are arbitrary," Alana declared, pushing her sunglasses up on top of her head.

"I think you said something similar last year."

Alana shrugged as we walked into the building together. "You can't expect me to remember the things I say."

Sequoia High was exactly what the name implied—a high school that stood in the middle of a lot of sequoia trees. It was one big building, three stories high. The cafeteria and library were separate, though, so we did get a taste of freedom and fresh air occasionally during the day.

This year, Alana and I had managed to score three of our six classes together, including first period, which was probably the real reason she'd waited for me. As we headed down the hall, my phone buzzed in my pocket. I waited until we were sitting in History class, listening to Mr. Ward talk about expectations for the year, before I pulled my phone out.

Hunter had posted a first-day-of-school picture online. It was a selfie of him and his sister standing outside their new house. Well, *new* was relative; they'd been there for three months now, since they moved when school got out last year. Beneath the picture, he'd written *Wish us luck*.

He looked . . . happy. His dusty blond hair was styled off his forehead and his blue eyes shone. I clicked on his profile and scrolled through his old posts until I found his first-day-of-school picture from last year—the two of us standing by his car. I was staring up at him, my eyes squinting with a smile. He was looking at the camera. His caption read: *I fished this girl out of the lake to join the rest of us at school*. I had forgotten I'd gone to the lake before school last year, too.

Alana cleared her throat and I looked up, thinking Mr. Ward had called me out. He was still writing away on the board. Alana lowered her brows and nodded toward my phone, clearly wondering what was up. I mouthed *Nothing*, and x-ed out of Hunter's profile. I needed to stop. I was over Hunter. We'd said we'd keep in touch but over the summer he slowly stopped responding to texts and emails until I had to admit defeat. I put my phone away and tried harder to listen the rest of class.

"What were you looking at on your phone?" Alana asked after the bell rang and we were walking down the hall to our next classes. "You were staring at it dreamily for like ten minutes straight."

"I was not. I was just looking at everyone's first-day-of-school posts."

"Yeah right," she said. She probably wouldn't have let the subject drop so easily if something at the end of the hall hadn't captured her attention. She gasped.

"What?"

She pulled me to the side, out of the flow of traffic. "Do you know Diego?" she whispered.

"Who?"

"Diego Martinez. From last year?"

"No, I don't remember him."

"Really? I could've sworn I mentioned him once . . . or five hundred times. Remember when I had to do a stint in Math lab last May? He was the tutor. He was dating that Pam girl so I couldn't pursue him but . . . No?" Alana asked when I was clearly still searching my brain. "He snuck his puppy into school once because his mom had gone out of town and couldn't watch her. And he got away with it."

"Are you making this stuff up?" I asked. "Because I don't remember any of these things."

"It's because he's not lake stock, isn't it?" Alana asked, putting her hands on her hips. "You don't even *try* to know the city kids."

We called them "city kids" even though Oak Court didn't really qualify as a city. It boasted only fifteen thousand people. But that was thirteen thousand more than Lakesprings.

"So not true!" I argued. "I don't try to know *any* kids. You know I hate people."

Alana laughed because she knew it was at least partially a joke.

"I remember the guy with the nose ring you talked about—Duncan," I said, tilting my head to one side. "And there was someone else named Mac . . ."

"Okay, I get it. You proved my 'lake' theory wrong."

Her theory was kind of right. I didn't spend a lot of time in Oak Court. I preferred the lake over all else. "It's not city versus lake," I said. "It's the fact that you talk about a lot of different guys."

"I appreciate them. Is there anything wrong with that?"

"No. I was just explaining to you why I might not remember *this* one."

"Even though I talked about him five hundred times?"

"You didn't. *That* was Brady, the guy who lit a sparkler in the cafeteria for you on your birthday and got detention for a week."

Alana was the kind of girl who guys did things like that for. She was tall and curvy with dark hair and nearly black eyes. She was Polynesian and had stories about growing up in Hawaii that everyone loved to listen to, like Hawaii was some alternate universe. I loved her stories, too, so I didn't blame them.

She waved her hand in the air. "Brady is so last year." She took me by the shoulders and pointed me toward the end of the hall. A guy with shaggy dark hair stood in front of a locker. "*He* is so this year," she said.

"This is the bring-a-puppy-to-school guy?"

"Yes. Diego."

"I thought you said he was dating that Pam girl." I had no idea who Pam was, either. I was just repeating information.

"Apparently they broke up over the summer."

"Okay, I have made a note. Can we go now?"

"First, you have to tell me what you think."

"Of what?"

"Of him."

"Why?"

"Because you're my best friend and if I'm going to devote all my time to thinking and talking about a boy, I want your approval."

I laughed. Alana never asked for anyone's approval. I patted her on the cheek. "That's sweet of you to make me feel needed."

"No, I'm serious. What do you think of him?"

"You're asking me to assess him from fifty feet away based on zero knowledge?"

"Based on initial impressions and the puppy story."

I narrowed my eyes at the boy, as if that would give me better insight into who he was. "I think he takes an inordinately long amount of time at his locker."

As if he heard me, Diego retrieved a book, shut his locker, and whirled toward us.

Alana still stood behind me, a vise grip on my shoulders, making it more than obvious we had been staring at him. He met my eyes with his soft brown ones, and then his gaze shifted to Alana. Now that I could see his face I understood why Alana was willing to devote hours to thinking about it. He was cute. Wavy brown hair, light brown skin, big eyes, high cheekbones, full lips.

"Hey, Alana," he said as he walked by, acting like this was the most normal thing in the world. Like girls lined up at the end of hallways to watch him exchange books in his locker all the time.

Then he was gone. Alana released my shoulders and I faced her.

"So? What do you think?" she asked.

"I think that was really embarrassing."

"No, about him. I want your advice."

"Yes, he's cute. Plus, it was obvious by the way he said hi that he's halfway to falling in love with you. I approve."

She smiled. "Thanks." The late bell rang, signaling that it was *really* time to get to our second-period classes.

"See you at lunch," I called, waving as we parted ways.

"See you. Oh, and don't forget we have our podcasting class last period!" Alana said, waving back.

"How could I?" I groaned. "I still can't believe you talked me into it."

Alana shot me a triumphant smile before turning and racing down the hall.

# CHAPTER 2

"You've been listening to Sequoia High's premier podcast. For teens, by teens, about teens. The only podcast recorded in a high school. At least as far as we're concerned. School's out, but can you listeners smell the scent the six hundred teens left behind? There's nothing quite like the mix of hot Cheetos, body spray, and sweat. We seniors will miss it almost as much as you'll miss us. But don't you worry, next year's podcasting class will be here to outdo us, or totally screw it up. Can't wait to see which. Peace!"

Ms. Lyon turned off the audio with a dramatic button push and then faced the class. She was petite, with large eyes that were even larger now in excitement.

"And that was last year's very last episode," Ms. Lyon said. "You all have a lot to live up to. I know it's the first day of school, but our audience is hungry. We've had more episodes downloaded this summer than in the previous two summers. Our podcast may be a toddler, just starting its fourth year, but it's gaining momentum. It's up to you all to keep that momentum going."

Alana and I exchanged a look. This was too much drama

for the first day of school. "What have you gotten me into?" I whispered.

Alana had begged me to take this class with her, as our required elective. She'd even filled out the application for me, telling me it would be amazing. "Podcasts," she'd said, "are like instant entertainment in the palm of your hand. Prerecorded, downloadable talk shows on pretty much every subject in the world."

She'd really said that. Like she had been hired by the inventor of the podcast to sell the concept far and wide. When I wasn't buying, she'd added that I could learn soundboard or editing or some skill that I could use in my everyday life. It seemed better than pottery, so I gave in.

"Your assignment for this week," Ms. Lyon continued, "is to come up with our podcast topic for the year. Each of you needs to turn in one suggestion. Check the website as the topics come in, because first posted equals first claimed. I won't accept repeats. We will vote from the entries. My only rules? The topic can't be something previously done and it has to be teen-centric. After all, this is the podcast for teens, by teens, and about teens."

A hand shot up to my right.

"Yes . . . ?" Ms. Lyon looked at the seating chart she had filled in after we'd sat down at the beginning of class. "Mallory."

"What were the other themes?"

"Ah, glad you asked. I'd hoped maybe you all had done your homework and caught up on previous years' episodes, but alas, I expect too much."

I hadn't listened to any of the episodes, but apparently others had.

"I know all three themes from the last three years. I've been listening since freshman year," a girl to my left piped up.

"Great . . . !" Ms. Lyon scanned the seating chart again.

"Victoria," the girl filled in for her.

"Victoria. That's the kind of enthusiasm I like. Why don't you come and write the topics on the board?" She held out the dry-erase marker and I thought maybe Victoria would say she'd rather not. That's what I would've said. But she stood up and took the pen with confidence. She even narrated as she wrote.

"The first year they did inventions. They researched different inventions by teens and shared them on the show. They also let teens call in to talk about things they were working on, or failed inventions, which was entertaining." Victoria turned around and smiled. "My favorite invention from that year was the Pick Your Outfit app." I wondered if Victoria was in Drama. She seemed perfectly comfortable standing up there like she had prepared this presentation for the class.

"I liked that one, too," Ms. Lyon said.

"The second year was famous teens in history," Victoria continued. "It was fun listening to stories of people our age doing interesting things in the past, like ruling nations or robbing banks. But overall that year, in my opinion, was a bit of a flop. It wasn't interactive enough. People didn't get to call in. It was all just talk talk talk."

Alana let out a grunt from beside me. "I think that dry-erase marker is going to her head," she whispered.

I was surprised that Victoria was admitting any sort of negativity about past shows to the director herself, our teacher. She had power over the gradebook, after all. Ms. Lyon's eyebrow shot up.

Victoria continued, "But thankfully, last year's class raised the bar with opposing opinions about controversial court cases featuring teens. People got to call in and voice their views on the cases. Did they have researchers for that one?"

Ms. Lyon nodded. "They did. You will all contribute to the show in some way, from researching to editing to sound checking to equipment. There are many aspects to recording a podcast. You will all learn them this year."

I wondered how Ms. Lyon had learned about podcasting. She seemed older, late forties maybe. Podcasting couldn't have been around when she was in college.

"Speaking of jobs," Victoria said, still holding the dry-erase marker, even though she had finished writing. "I would like to be one of the hosts."

"I'll be assigning the appropriate people to that role, along with everyone else's positions, next week." Ms. Lyon held out her hand for the marker and Victoria passed it over. "The highest priority right now is finding the best possible topic." Ms. Lyon swept her hand to the side, gesturing to the board. "These are off-limits, but everything else is fair game. Be creative, think outside the obvious. You must submit a topic by Friday."

Several groans sounded in the room.

"I don't need complaining about something as important as the topic," Ms. Lyon said. "And I hope all you complainers know that the lab hour for this class is after school once a week. A third of you will be in the production lab on Wednesdays. The other two-thirds in the postproduction lab on Thursdays." She clapped her hands twice, then tapped the board. "Did you all forget to bring notebooks on the first day? Write these topics down. Then you can take the remainder of class to brainstorm new topic ideas with your neighbor."

The sound of backpacks being unzipped and notebooks being opened filled the room. I wrote down the off-limit topics, then turned toward Alana.

"Any ideas?" I asked.

"None," she said.

"I kind of thought the topics were assigned."

"Me too. I mean, what class would actually pick teens through history?" she said quietly.

"That one sounded interesting to me."

"Really? I thought I knew you." She wrote the word *History* on my blank page, then put a giant *X* through it.

"We should do something about the lake," I said, drawing a stick figure riding her *X* like a wave. "Teen wakeboarders or lake folk tales."

"Ah. There it is. I do know you after all."

"It's a good idea!" I protested.

"You really think the city kids would vote for that?"

I glanced around the room to see how many Lakesprings students were in the class. That's when I noticed Frank Young in the back row. I scowled. Frank's parents owned half of Lakesprings and wanted to own all of it. They'd been trying to buy the marina out from under my parents for years. It sat on prime property that they'd been eyeing for a high-end hotel. Since my parents weren't selling, the Youngs had been attempting to force them out—conservation studies, code violation reports, the list went on and on.

"Did you see him?" I hissed.

"Yep. I'm surprised it took you this long," Alana said.

"Did you know he was going to take this class?"

"How would I know that?"

Frank was sitting next to Victoria. He doodled in an open notebook while she talked about topics.

"I think music would be cool. That hasn't been done before," she was saying.

"There are a million music podcasts. Not to mention the radio stations that actually play music," Frank responded.

"She's taking this very seriously," Alana said, obviously overhearing Victoria as well.

I forced the scowl off my face and took a deep breath. I wouldn't think about Frank. Maybe we could just ignore each other in this class. That could work well.

"Probably because she wants to host," I told Alana. "I could see caring a lot more about the topic if you have to talk about it for the next however many weeks."

"I wouldn't mind hosting," Alana said.

"You'd make a good host." It sounded like torture to me.

"What job would you want?" she asked.

I shrugged. "Research, I guess."

"Here's hoping we get our first picks." She tapped her pen against mine in a writing-utensil toast.

The bell rang, and I shoved my notebook into my backpack. I stood up, and someone knocked against my shoulder as he walked by.

"Hello. Distance," Frank said, and kept walking.

"Excuse me?"

"At least you stayed dry this time," he threw back over his shoulder, and then exited the classroom.

For a second I was confused, but then I remembered the lake that morning. *Frank* had been the guy on the WaveRunner. He had sprayed me on purpose. An entire year in the same small class as Frank Young was not going to be fun.

# CHAPTER 3

When I got home from school, I stopped by the kitchen, where Mom was stirring a pitcher of iced tea.

"Does Dad need me at the marina?" I asked.

"No, it slowed down this afternoon."

My eyebrows popped up. "So does that mean there's an extra WaveRunner I can take out?"

Mom laughed. "You are determined to spend all your earnings on gas, aren't you?"

"Yes, you should just pay me in gas from now on."

She opened the fridge and pulled out an apple. "How was school?"

"Not bad."

"Your junior year might be your best one yet."

"You say that every year."

"I like to think positively." She turned on the tap, washed the apple, and handed it to me.

"Thanks, Mom." I left the kitchen just as Max entered, and Mom started asking him about his first day of freshman year.

As I headed down the hall to my room, my phone rang and I pulled it out of my bag.

"Hey, Alana. Miss me already?"

"We need to brainstorm more podcast topics," she replied.

"Why? We just had class. And the assignment's not due until Friday."

"Topics will get picked fast. The longer we wait, the harder it will be. And by the way, have you listened to any of the podcasts I told you about?"

I opened my bedroom door and let my backpack slide down my arm and onto the floor. Then I plopped down onto the beanbag in the corner, biting off a chunk of apple. I looked across the room at my big poster of a wakeboarder creating an arc of spray. It reminded me that I wanted to be out on the lake. "I've been busy."

"You know you can listen to podcasts while you go on your WaveRunner."

"I know, I know. What's your favorite? I'll listen to it."

"I like the funny movie review one, ooh, or the funny food review one. Or there's this first dates one that is awesome."

"So all of them?"

"Pretty much."

My cousin came into my room then with a loud, "Ughhh."

I gasped in surprise, nearly choking on chewed-up apple.

"What happened?" Alana asked.

Liza's strong citrus scent followed her in. "It's Liza. She seems happy."

"I am *not* happy," Liza said.

"Oh, you just smell happy, I was confused."

"You need to get over this problem you have with my perfume."

"Are you having a conversation with me or Liza?" Alana asked from the phone.

"Sorry, you," I told Alana.

"I have a problem," Liza said loudly.

"Did Liza say she has a problem?" Alana asked.

"Yes."

"Put me on speaker."

I sighed but complied.

"Hey, Liza," Alana said. "Tell us your problem."

"My mom wants me to go to tutoring at that center by the grocery store in town," Liza said with a frown.

"Okay . . ." Alana said.

"Once a week, after school. To 'get ahead of the problem,' she said."

"What problem?" I asked.

"You know, my grade problem."

I didn't know. "You have a grade problem?"

Liza shrugged. "I lack motivation when it comes to homework." She used two fingers to stretch a piece of gum out of her mouth.

"And going to the tutoring center is a bad thing?" Alana asked. "What's wrong with forcing yourself to do homework once a week and having help readily available?"

Liza twisted the gum around her pointer finger, then

scraped it off with her teeth. “I’m a freshman. Think of my reputation.”

I wasn’t sure what reputation she was referring to, but I understood what she was saying. “Who is going to know about this?” I asked. “Anyone that’s there is also getting tutored.”

Liza gave an epic eye roll like I was the most ignorant person in the world, and sat down on the edge of my bed. “It’s by the grocery store. Do you know how many people from our school go to that grocery store?”

“No, I don’t.” I rarely went to the grocery store in Oak Court. We had a small market in Lakesprings and even though it was owned by the Youngs, it was more convenient than the alternative.

“I don’t, either,” Liza admitted, “but I’m sure it’s a lot. Someone will see me.”

Alana’s voice rang out from the phone. “Why don’t you talk to your mom and see if you can prove to her that you’re willing to do homework on your own? Tell her that she can check the school website every week and the first time that it shows a missing assignment, you’ll agree to her tutoring plan.”

Liza sat forward with a smile. “That is an excellent idea, Alana. You give the best advice. Thank you!” She hopped up and ran out of my room, apparently to share this idea with her mom that second.

“You’re welcome,” Alana said to my empty room.

“She’s gone,” I said.

"That girl is funny. But hey, my mom just got home from work and is patiently waiting to talk to me."

"Okay. See you tomorrow." I ended the call and went to my dresser for a swimsuit. When I turned around to shut my door, my mom stood there, leaning against the frame.

"That's not a bad idea," she said.

"What's not?"

"Checking the website to make sure your homework is done before you have lake time."

"Nobody suggested *that* as an idea."

She winked. "I made a couple of modifications. I heard you telling Alana that you have something due this Friday."

"It's just a topic for the podcast. No big deal."

Her face brightened. "How was the podcasting class? Did you love it?"

Alana had sold my mom on podcasts last year as part of her strategy to convince me. "It was okay."

"Give it a chance. It might surprise you."

"Do you wish you could take the podcasting class, too, Mom?"

"Funny. So you have to think of a topic for the show?"

"Yes." I dropped the apple core into the small trash bin under my desk.

"What are your ideas so far?"

"I have none. Alana and I will figure something out."

"How about fashion advice?"

I looked down at my plain old shorts and striped tee. "Is that a hint?"

"Not at all. I'm just trying to think of something teens might be interested in."

"Leave it to the actual teens," I said with a smile.

"How about, 'What's in Your Lunch?' Exposé-type news stories of what's happening around the school."

"Mom, I love you, and thanks for trying, but no."

She pointed to the swimsuit I still held in my hand. "Well, you better think of something fast, because no lake time until you do."

I let my mouth fall open as she walked away. "Since when?"

"Since now," she called back as she headed off down the hall.

*Crap.*

My brother walked by my door. "Max!" I shouted in desperation.

He backtracked so he stood in my open doorway.

"Do you have any ideas for a podcast?" I asked him.

He thought for a second. "Hmm. Gaming? Comics?"

"Any mainstream ideas?"

"Lots of people like both those things," he argued.

"I know, but the show has to have mass appeal." Actually, maybe that didn't matter. Ms. Lyon didn't say it had to appeal to a wide audience. She just said it had to be original. "Maybe I *should* suggest lake myths. Or lake sports."

Max shrugged and walked on.

I threw my swimsuit on my bed, pulled out my laptop, then logged on to the website for Ms. Lyon's class.

I was surprised to see that there was a list of ideas already there. People had beaten me to it! And I was even more surprised to see that one idea listed was: *lake stories.* I growled. Had Frank submitted that? Was there someone else from Lakesprings in the class? The entries were anonymous on the site (only Ms. Lyon could see who had entered what). If I wrote in *lake sports*, would that be too close to *lake stories*?

Liza came barreling back into my room and flung herself on my bed. "She said no!"

"What?"

"My mom. She says tutoring is nonnegotiable for at least the first quarter of school. I even told her *you* would tutor me."

I frowned. "Why did you tell her that?"

"Because the other thing Alana told me to say wasn't working."

I rolled my eyes.

"I start next week," Liza said glumly.

"I'm sorry, Liza. But it won't be that bad, right?"

"My *mom* walking me to my weekly tutoring session?"

"I can take you."

Liza scrunched her nose up like she hadn't thought of that idea and wasn't sure if it was a good one. "Okay. Yeah . . . sure. You're a junior now, after all. That makes you at least cooler than my mom."

"Thanks . . . I think."

"This might work!" And just like that, she was gone again. That girl was a ball of energy.

I scanned the list of topics once more. Not only was *lake stories* taken, but *comics*, *music*, and *fashion* were on there, too. Someone had even submitted the suggestion my mom had given, about exposés of high school life. And this was the first day! There'd be nothing left if I waited.

I tapped my fingers lightly on the keyboard. I just had to think of an idea. It wasn't like it would actually get used when the whole class had to vote. Maybe I could call Alana back and get her advice.

Advice.

The thing Alana had wanted about Diego. The thing Liza had wanted about tutoring. Wasn't that something teens were always looking for? Whether from their friends or parents or teachers? An advice show could totally work.

I typed in my idea. It was a solid one. Or at least original enough to count. I hurried into the kitchen to tell Mom I'd submitted my topic, and she gave me a thumbs-up. Within seconds, I'd changed into my swimsuit and was on my way to the lake.

# CHAPTER 4

The next day, at lunch, Alana and I discussed my topic choice.

"I like it," Alana said as we sat side by side on our usual bench outside. "The Ask Alana Advice Show." She placed each word in the air with her hand. "Triple A."

"That might be copyrighted," I said, sticking a straw into my smoothie.

"Either way, I'm voting for your idea."

"You don't have to," I said.

"I know. I want to. It would be fun to hear people call in with their problems."

I shoved her shoulder. "Be nice."

"Was that mean?" Alana asked as she unwrapped her sandwich.

I ignored her question because I was pretty sure she was joking and asked, "Have you thought of a topic yet?"

She let out an exaggerated groan. "No. Do you have any other ideas in that brilliant brain of yours that I can have?"

"I had a hard enough time coming up with mine!"

Alana's attention was drawn across the commons, her eyes

locked onto a target. I followed her gaze to see Diego talking to a group of guys. He held a can of Pepsi and a sandwich.

"How about Stalking 101?" I said. "How to get and hold the attention of your crush."

Alana smirked. "Don't tempt me. I'd be an excellent host for *that* topic as well."

"So if that was your topic, step one would be: Drag your friend to stare at him in the hall. Step two: Stare at him while he eats his lunch. What is step three, Alana?"

"You think I'm all talk and no game? Is that it?"

"I know you are far from *no game*. I've seen you in action. I'm just wondering how this particular one is going to play out."

"Step three, my doubting friend, is to make him think he's the one with the crush on *me*."

"And how is that accomplished?"

"Watch and learn."

Alana left me on our lunch bench with my smoothie. I watched her dig her phone out of her pocket. As she walked, she stared at the screen until she walked herself right into Diego. She jumped back, her hand flying to her chest as if startled. He reached out to steady her from the impact. She said something and he smiled and dropped his hand to his side. Then she started talking to another guy in the group. That guy shrugged. Alana said something else to the other guy, kicked his shoe playfully, and turned around and walked back to me.

"And that's how it's done," she said, sitting back down.

"I have no idea what just happened."

"I made my presence known but then made it clear I hadn't been walking over there to talk to him."

"Who was that other guy?" I asked.

"Bennett. You don't know Bennett?"

"I've heard of him. Never met him."

"Back to my city versus lake theory."

It wasn't that I wasn't social . . . well, okay, it was a little bit that.

"I blame this all on Hunter," Alana continued, taking a bite of her sandwich. "He hoarded you to himself for nine months and then had the audacity to move."

I played with my straw. "He didn't want to move. He had to because, you know, his whole family was moving and without them he was kind of homeless. But I'm over Hunter. That was last year. Why are you bringing up things that are in the past?" I asked.

That might have sounded a little defensive considering I had been checking Hunter's online statuses all day—a pic of him eating popcorn for breakfast; a pic of a sign that said *Everything is bigger in Texas*; and a pic of a stack of textbooks.

"Because Hunter is the most recent thing I *can* bring up," Alana pointed out. "Your love life has been as dry as these pine needles." She kicked a pile of rust-colored pine needles by our feet.

I put down my smoothie. "I haven't found anyone as interesting as Hunter."

"As interesting as Hunter?" Alana smirked. "That guy could put babies to sleep just by sitting there."

I bristled. I didn't think Hunter was boring. He was mellow. And quiet. "I like mellow and quiet."

"How is this mellow, quiet guy going to find *you* is the question," Alana said, raising her eyebrows. "You post just enough online to prove you exist but are vague enough that nobody ever gets to know who you are."

I was private. There was nothing wrong with that. "I don't know, there's a thing called talking," I pointed out.

"You? Going out of your way to talk to someone? Huh. Well, maybe you can listen to my podcast to learn tips." She grinned.

I laughed. "Okay. And I'll tell you when I find someone interesting."

The sound of a throat clearing had me whirling to my right.

Diego stood there. Had he heard that entire exchange?

"Hey, Alana. You dropped this earlier." He held up a key on a silver surfboard key chain.

Alana, obviously not prepared for this encounter, stuttered out, "I—I . . . oh," without taking the key.

Not as flustered as Alana, I smiled. "You are a lifesaver," I said. "She would've had to climb in her second-story window without this. Not that she hasn't done that before."

Alana recovered quickly, stood up, and held out her hand. "I'm very practiced at that climb." This was true. Alana had been locked out of her house more times than I could count. It used to be because her parents hadn't made her a key and the keyless entry on the garage door was broken. Now that she had a key, she usually forgot it.

"Maybe you should put your key somewhere more secure." Diego placed the key in Alana's palm and then closed each one of her fingers over it. His hand gripped her closed fist for a beat before he let go.

Alana lifted one side of her mouth into a half smile. "Yes, I need a better system." She put her key into her pocket.

Wow, they were both really good at flirting.

"I don't think I've met you before," Diego said, probably feeling me staring at them.

"Oh." Alana placed a hand on his arm. "This is my best friend, Kathryn. Lakesprings zip code. Kate, this is Diego."

"Hi," I said, not sure what more I could add to that single word.

"Do you go by Kathryn or Kate?" Diego asked me.

"Both, weirdly enough."

"Kathryn has lots of variations."

"Kate's the only other one I like," I informed him, perhaps a little too emphatically.

"Got it."

"Oh, look!" Alana said. "There's your brother, Kate. We were looking for him. We have to go." She turned and walked casually in the direction of my brother.

"Um . . . sorry," I said to Diego, feeling like Alana left a little too suddenly. I gathered our lunch stuff and shoved it in a brown paper bag. "We have to . . ." I stood up and pointed toward Max.

"Off to search for someone *interesting*?" he asked with a wink. So he *had* heard our exchange before. No wonder Alana liked him. He was as confident as she was.

"Yes . . . I mean no. It was nice to meet you."

"You too."

I caught up to Alana. "What was that?" I whispered.

"Trust the master," she said as we kept walking toward Max. "I had to be the one to leave first."

"Okay. And the dropping your house key thing?"

She smiled, and I realized Diego's surprise appearance had really been part of her plan. She was good.

We made our way to where my brother, in his too-baggy jeans and overgrown brown hair, was walking down the path toward the library.

"Maximillian!" Alana called, and flung her arm around his shoulder.

"Hi," he said.

"Whatcha doin'?" I asked.

"Returning this book to the library." He held up a book about programming.

"You're returning a library book the second day of school? Did you check this out the first day of school?" Alana asked.

"Yes. It's not what I thought it was."

"The first clue should've been these numbers on the front," Alana said. "You might want to find the books with dragons or swords on the cover."

"I hadn't considered that," Max said, straight-faced, and I smiled.

"I think your brother is mocking me," Alana told me. "Freshmen aren't allowed to mock upperclassmen. It's in the handbook. But I'll let you get away with it because you're adorable."

Max blushed. "Much obliged," he said. Then he stopped at the door to the library. "Are you guys going to follow me in here?"

"Are we embarrassing you, Maxie?" I asked.

"Yeah, kind of."

"Really?" Alana said. "Two hot juniors hanging out with you is embarrassing?"

"One is my sister."

I stepped back and pulled Alana with me. "We'll leave you alone to go meet your friends in the library. Have fun."

"Yeah, thanks."

"Your brother is funny," Alana said after the door swung shut behind him. "If I were a freshman, I'd be hanging out with my older brother and his friend all the time."

"You don't have an older brother."

"This is a hypothetical situation I'm using to prove a point."

"Maybe we're just not as cool as we think we are." I linked my arm through Alana's and led us away.

"Impossible," she said. Then she brightened and added, "I think I am going to submit dating dos and don'ts as my podcast idea."

"You should." And given what had happened with Diego, she'd be the perfect host for that topic as well. "I bet that will win."

Her eyes sparkled. "I think it might."

# CHAPTER 5

"And the winning topic is . . ." Ms. Lyon paused dramatically.

It was Monday again. The first week of school had been uneventful, except for podcasting class, where we got to hear about all the different aspects of producing a podcast. It was surprisingly fascinating. Over the weekend, we'd had to vote online for the topic. I'd happily voted for Alana's "dating dos and don'ts" idea.

So I was stunned when Ms. Lyon took her marker and wrote *Advice Show* across the dry-erase board.

"Kathryn Bailey, please stand."

I bit my lip and slowly rose to my feet.

"Congratulations! Your idea earned the most votes from the class."

"Uh, thanks," I said, feeling my face flush pink.

"What I didn't tell you all when giving you this assignment," Ms. Lyon continued, adjusting her glasses and smiling, "was that the person who submits the winning topic will automatically be one of the hosts."

"What?" I blurted out. "No. I can't."

Ms. Lyon laughed. "You *are* in a podcasting class, Kathryn. You didn't think you might have to do some speaking?"

It hadn't even crossed my mind. "I think other people would do better at that particular part of the process." My heart raced. I wasn't qualified to give advice to anyone.

"Like me," Victoria said.

"Yes, like Victoria," I agreed. "She should do it."

"I'm glad you think so," Ms. Lyon said. "Because Victoria will be your cohost."

Victoria smiled triumphantly.

My eyes locked with Alana's. She looked hurt.

"Or Alana," I said quickly. "Alana would be an excellent host."

"I've already assigned all the jobs," Ms. Lyon explained, picking up a sheet of paper from her desk. "I will post them on the board momentarily. Once I have, please, in an orderly manner, come check them out. Then look for the corresponding binder on the back table. Two people are assigned to each task. Our first show will be Wednesday after school. This is so exciting!" With a flourish, she used a magnet to stick the piece of paper to the board.

I was still on my feet but I didn't move as the rest of the class stood and jostled around me. Nobody said anything as they made their way to the list. Not even Alana. Something lit a fire in me and I pushed my way through the class.

"I really think you picked the wrong student," I told Ms. Lyon when I reached her. "I only got the idea for this topic because Alana gave some great advice to my cousin. *Alana* is good at advice. I'd like a different assignment, please."

Ms. Lyon shook her head. "Kathryn, the harder you fight me on this the more I realize it's exactly what you need to do. You obviously applied to this class for a reason."

Was *Alana forced me to* a reason she would understand?

"But I wanted to learn about behind-the-scenes stuff," I explained. "Maybe the hosts can switch after two weeks like the rest of the jobs do?"

Ms. Lyon shook her head. "Sorry, but hosting has to be consistent for the listeners. You know it's the one job that doesn't get to switch. But you'll learn about every element of podcasting in class along with the others." She glanced past me. "Now, it looks like Victoria already has your binder. I need you two to get to know each other so you can work well together on air."

There was something about Ms. Lyon's stance and the firm set of her jaw that let me know I wasn't going to talk my way out of this.

I slumped and turned around, catching sight of Alana. She had her binder and was sitting next to Frank Young. Did that mean he was her partner? This was getting worse and worse.

I rushed over to my best friend. "What did you get assigned?"

"I start with marketing," she said, flipping through the binder.

"With him?" I asked, under my breath.

"He has a name and you know it," Frank said.

Frank was the kind of guy who might have been cute if not for his personality. His blue eyes looked sleepy in a laid-back way and he had one of those dimples in his chin. His nose was larger than average and crooked, but that gave him a rugged look. He wore his brown hair short around the ears but long and full on top.

"I try to forget your name daily," I said.

"It's the name that's going to be on your marina soon so it will be easier to remember."

My insides boiled. "You wish."

Alana held up her hand. "Stop," she said. "Yes, I'm paired with Frank. Did you see this lovely contract in the binders that we have to sign? It basically says that even though Frank is a jerk, I have to get along with him."

"*I'm* the jerk?" he said, narrowing his eyes.

Alana scrunched her lips to the side as if actually thinking about that question. "Yes."

Frank had proven his jerk-hood many times. But fighting over this in class wasn't going to get any of us anywhere, so I swallowed my words like I often did to keep the peace.

"Marketing?" I said instead.

"We're in charge of the podcast's social media accounts and trying to get people to call the phone lines while we're recording," Alana explained.

"You'll be good at that," I said.

"Thanks," she said.

"I'm sorry." I knew that despite her smile, she was disappointed. "You know I don't want to host."

"I know. It's okay, though. You'll do a good job."

"I'll do a horrible job and we both know it."

She let out a little laugh. "You'll be fine, Kate."

Frank scoffed beside her.

"Shut it, Frank. She will," Alana said. Then she turned back to me. "You better get over there before your partner has a coronary." She nodded her head toward Victoria.

I looked over to where Victoria sat, holding up the binder and waving it at me. "If I could give you my job, I would," I whispered to Alana.

"I know. But there's nothing you could've done. Go figure out how you're going to work with Victoria and I'll stay over here and try to figure out how I'm going to work with this." She smacked Frank's arm and he looked up from where he had disappeared into his phone.

"What?" he asked.

Alana rolled her eyes at me. "Wish me luck."

I scrunched my nose. "Me too."

I didn't know much about Victoria aside from the fact that she was a senior, that she'd studied every episode of past podcasts, and that she apparently binged other podcasts all the time. So she was basically an expert. I sat down in the desk next to her.

"Finally," she said.

"Hi. I'm Kathryn."

"Kathryn? Hmmm. We'll have to work on that."

"What do you mean?"

She pointed at the first page in the binder. "We need to come up with a catchy name for the show and after the name we always say, 'with your hosts, Victoria' "—she pointed at herself—" 'and' . . . you."

"Kathryn."

"I think 'Victoria and Kathryn' is too much of a mouthful. We should shorten your name. 'Victoria and Kat.' "

"I don't go by Kat."

"Why?"

Mainly because people couldn't help but add "kitty" before it. "I'm just not a Kat personality. I can do Kate if you're looking for one syllable."

" 'Victoria and Kate,' " she said, trying it on for size.

" 'Vic and Kate'?" I offered.

"Ew. No," she said, dismissing that idea with a flick of her hand. "Victoria and Kate. That works."

"Okay."

"And what should the show be called?" Victoria asked, jotting down a note. "Maybe something like 'Bring Us Your Problems.' "

I felt overwhelmed. "I didn't think this idea would even be picked!" I blurted. "I mean, what qualifies *us* to solve anyone's problems?"

Ms. Lyon must've been standing close by because she answered my question. "Absolutely nothing. In fact, you'll need to read a disclaimer at the beginning of each show explaining how you're not licensed therapists, these opinions are just opinions, etc., etc."

I nodded.

"Ms. Lyon?" Victoria asked. "What do you think of calling the show 'Bring Us Your Problems'?"

Our teacher tilted her head to the side. "I think it can be edgier. Shorter."

"Like 'Not My Problem,'" I said quietly, offhand.

Ms. Lyon pointed at me. "Yes, I love it. That's it."

"Oh. Um, okay," I said, surprised. I'd never intended for any of my ideas to be so popular.

Victoria curled her lip. "Won't that discourage people from calling? If we tell them it's not our problem?"

"You'll figure it out," Ms. Lyon said, and walked on to a different group.

Victoria tapped her pen on her notebook while staring at me and I realized she was waiting for me to figure out the conundrum I'd created with my title.

"What if we ask the listeners what issues they have that have been greeted with the words 'not my problem'?" I suggested.

"Good idea," Victoria admitted grudgingly. She jotted down another note. I realized I should probably be taking notes as well, and I grabbed my notebook from my bag.

"So obviously I'll be the lead host," Victoria said. "Since I'm the senior and you didn't even want to do this. You can chime in during the show with things to back up what I'm saying."

That actually sounded like something I might be able to handle. "Okay."

"Maybe there are problems you can each specialize in based on your experiences." Ms. Lyon's voice sounded from over my head. How did she keep appearing out of thin air? I turned around to look at her but she was already gone.

"That's kind of creepy," I said. Alana would've agreed, and laughed with me about it.

Victoria just said, "What is?"

"Nothing."

"Anyway, I'm older, so I might have more experience in most areas. What problems might people call in about?" Victoria asked.

"Um . . ." I tried to think of things I'd listened to friends and family complain about in the past. "Parents, maybe?"

"True. Are your parents still married?"

"Yes."

"Then I'll mark myself as the expert on parent problems. Mine are divorced and it was ugly."

"Okay."

"Relationship problems will be high on the list. Advice about love and all that. How many relationships have you had?"

"Just one," I said, blushing and thinking of Hunter.

"Okay, me again." She put her name down.

"I can give good advice about the lake," I piped up.

"The lake? You think people will want advice about the lake?"

"I don't know. Maybe? Like the best time of day to visit or where to take a date or . . ."

I could tell by the look on her face that she didn't think anyone would ever need advice about the lake, but she said, "Sure," and wrote it down on her paper. "I play basketball and run track. So sports advice is all me."

The rest of class went pretty much the same way. Fashion, homework, teachers, friends, she gave those all to herself. The only other one I got was siblings because she counted my cousin situation as unique.

I was pretty sure our list-making had only reinforced Victoria's initial idea that she would lead the advice and I would back her up. Again, I was fine with that arrangement. The less talking I had to do, the better.

The bell rang. Victoria packed up her bag fast and was out the door before I'd even stood. The tension that had tightened across my shoulders released and I took a deep breath. The fun class Alana had promised was turning out to be more stressful than I'd anticipated.

Alana joined me. "I'm going to kill him."

"Frank?"

She nodded. "I can't believe I have to work with him."

"I'm sorry."

"Not your fault. Let's get out of here. Want to go get milkshakes at the diner?"

"I wish I could but I promised Liza I'd take her to her first day of tutoring. Tomorrow after school?"

"Deal."

We walked several more feet in silence. My insides felt close to unraveling. "Advice is your thing, Alana. How am I going to do this?" I asked, kicking at the ground.

She took me by the shoulders and looked me in the eyes. "You got this, Kate. Advice can be your thing, too. People are just looking for understanding and a solution."

I let out a single laugh. "Yeah, exactly. I'm not good at either of those."

"Just don't think about it too hard. It will come naturally to you. Imagine you're sitting around talking to me."

I nodded and gave her a hug. Then we separated to our own cars.

My cell phone dug into my hip when I sat down so I freed it and threw it on the passenger seat. I stared at it. I wanted to text Hunter—tell him about the craziness that happened today. He'd understand why I didn't want to speak on air about things I knew nothing about. But he hadn't even answered my text from last month. Why would I text him again? I was sure that if Alana's topic had been picked for the podcast, *letting go of someone who has already let you go* would make the Top Ten list of dating advice. I stuck my key in the ignition and turned.

# CHAPTER 6

"Is she gone?" Liza asked. We had parked outside of the tutoring center, but as soon as I turned the car off, Liza had thrown her head down between her knees. I was surprised she hadn't smacked her head into the dash in the process.

"I have no idea who you saw, so I don't know."

"A girl my age and her mom going into the grocery store. Didn't I tell you this would happen?"

"You know, Liza," I said. "Having a tutor is not a bad thing. A lot of people I know have had tutors over the years."

"Well, nobody I know has, so I don't believe you."

"Okay. I think the coast is clear now."

She poked her head up slowly and looked around. "Good. Let's walk fast. You can walk fast, right?"

"Yes, I have the ability to walk fast. But I thought the whole point of me going with you was that it wouldn't be so bad to be seen with me."

"Yeah, I've decided you don't hold that much power. Nobody at school even knows who you are," she said, and flung herself out of the car.

By the time I caught up with her, she was at the door.

When she opened it, a loud bell rang, announcing our arrival. There was a tall counter in front of us and behind that a large room with long tables. Along the back wall were small cubicles. An entire side wall was full of windows, which made the atmosphere bright and airy. If it had a view of the lake, I would've wished I had brought my homework so I could sit at one of those tables and work. But we weren't in Lakesprings. The windows faced a parking lot. Not that Oak Court didn't have nice views. There were lots of trees; we were in the Sierra Nevadas, after all. This just wasn't one of those views.

A guy walked out of a back cubicle, in between the tables, and came to the counter.

"Welcome," he said.

He and I both recognized each other at the same time.

"Kate."

"Diego," I said. "I didn't realize you worked here."

"You come here?"

"My cousin. I'm here for my cousin." I pointed at her to verify my statement.

"Oh, now you understand the embarrassment of it all," Liza said under her breath.

I ignored her. "Are you her tutor?" I asked.

Diego looked at a schedule on the counter. "No. Tommy is her tutor." He called out over his shoulder, "Tommy! Your client is here."

"See, you're a client," I said quietly to Liza. "That's fancy."

"Too late. Now I know how you really feel."

A tall guy with long brown hair, wearing a band T-shirt, came out of a back room. Liza straightened up beside me.

"Tommy, this is Liza," Diego said.

Tommy smiled big. "Nice to meet you. We only have an hour today, right? Let's slay your homework."

Liza nodded and followed him to a long table by the window.

"Tommy is great. She's in good hands," Diego said as my gaze lingered on them.

"Does Tommy go to Sierra High?" I asked, feeling a little silly for asking. If Alana were here, she'd tease me about her lake versus city theory.

"No, he's a freshman at Fresno State."

I nodded. Fresno—and its college—was about an hour farther down the hill.

"Oh, okay. Am I supposed to . . ." I looked around. To my right, there were chairs that formed a small waiting area.

"You can sit. Or come back in an hour."

"I told her I'd stay." I backed up and lowered myself into a chair.

Diego continued to stand behind the counter like he was guarding it.

"You don't have to babysit me. I'll read a magazine or something." There were stacks of magazines on the coffee table beside me. I searched the spines for my favorite water sports one but didn't see the standard green color.

"Full disclosure," Diego said. "Those magazines are like

three years old. So if you want to find out which celebrities were dating three years ago, be my guest."

"That was exactly what I had hoped to find out today. It's serendipity." I plucked a magazine from the table. But it wasn't celebrity gossip. It was a skating magazine. I raised my eyebrows and showed Diego the cover.

"Not serendipitous, after all," he said.

"Who contributed this to the mix? You?" I reassessed him. He didn't seem like the skater type, but really nobody seemed to fit into types anymore.

"That would be Tommy. You were trying to decide if it was me, though? You have quite the analyzing stare."

"Really? That obvious?"

"Yes, kind of a squinty-eyed, silent judgment thing."

"I'll work on that."

He smiled. "I didn't say it was a bad thing."

"So are any of these magazines your contributions, then?" There were five stacks of them, ten deep.

"Yes, I've brought a few."

I nodded.

"Can you figure out which ones, silent judger?" he asked.

"You're asking me to judge out loud? That won't end well."

He laughed. "Give it your best shot."

I shrugged. This could be fun, to get to know the guy Alana liked. If they ended up dating, I'd have to hang out with him, too. I might as well make an effort. "All right. Let's see . . ." I spread out the first stack. It consisted of a home decorating magazine, a cooking magazine, several celebrity gossip issues, a magazine about bodybuilding, one on science, one on traveling, another about scouting, and finally woodworking.

I stood up and walked over to Diego.

"Uh-oh, she's in the game now," he said.

"Let me see your hands."

"My hands?"

"Yes, your hands. Hold them out."

"Um . . . okay." He held them out, palms down. He had nice hands, with long fingers and well-trimmed, clean nails.

"Flip them over."

"Flip them over?"

"Are you going to repeat everything I say?"

He smirked and flipped his hands over.

He had a few minor calluses on the pads of his fingers but otherwise his hands weren't worn or roughed up. I walked back to the table and moved the woodworking magazine off to the side. I also moved the bodybuilding magazine over because he didn't have the body of a weight lifter. He was well built, but more lean and toned than beefy.

"Should I be insulted about that last move?" he asked.

"For sure," I said. I dug into the other pile of magazines, which added some new options: fishing, entertainment, sports, parenting (which I quickly added to the discard pile), gaming, music, and cars. "I'm impressed with the wide variety of three-year-old magazines you keep here."

"We have a diverse staff, who apparently don't know how to throw things away."

I laughed. "Are these magazines you still read today, or are they from thirteen-year-old Diego's life?"

He squinted at the stacks. "Two I still read today . . . online. One is from my younger life."

I pulled out the scouting magazine. "Younger Diego," I said, plopping it in the middle of the table with confidence.

"That was an easy one."

"True."

Now for the hard ones. I pulled out gaming, fishing, cars, sports, and science and stared at the covers like they could tell me who had spent time reading them. I remembered Diego's clean nails and moved cars off to the side. I looked up at him again and took in his face. His skin was naturally tan, but I could see a lighter line of skin just under the collar of his shirt that showed some of his color was from spending time in the sun.

"This is intense," he said, shifting under my gaze.

I dropped my eyes, realizing I was being obsessive about something he had probably thought was just a lighthearted game. "Um, the fishing is one, and the gaming, I guess, for the second," I said in a rush, and then leaned back in my seat and tried to make up for my intensity by being the picture of chill.

A slow smile lit up his face, like he knew exactly what had just happened in my head. But he couldn't know that, right? I maintained my relaxed position.

He came out from behind the counter and picked up the fishing magazine. "You were right about this one." Then he picked up the gaming. "But when you gave up halfway through because you got embarrassed, you failed the second one."

"I didn't get embarrassed."

"You totally did. You were like Sherlock one second and a person embarrassed to be Sherlock the next second."

I laughed. "You couldn't think of a contrast to Sherlock, could you?"

"I couldn't." He pointed to the four remaining magazines. "But . . . since none of your final selections were right for my second one, Sherlock, I won't make you guess for real."

He sat down in the seat next to me, riffled through the magazines, and pulled out the cooking one.

"Really?" I asked.

"I know, it's like I'm a tiny bit interesting or something."

I rolled my eyes. "For the record, I never said you weren't interesting. But I know you walked in on the middle of a conversation between me and Alana. Perhaps it will be your lesson on eavesdropping."

"Fair enough."

"So you like to cook?"

"I do."

"That's cool." Alana liked to cook, too. She specialized in Hawaiian dishes, but she loved all different kinds of food and trying new things to eat. As with a lot of things in my life, I didn't go out on a limb with food; I preferred to play it safe.

I wondered if Alana knew Diego cooked. I'd have to tell her. "I didn't realize how much insight the magazines someone reads can give into that person's life," I mused out loud.

"Really? What do you now know about me based on these magazines?" Diego asked, raising his eyebrows.

I tapped my fingers against my lips. "I know you like alone time, to think or ponder or speculate on the world, away from people. Maybe you're a bit private."

"Because I like to fish?"

"Yes."

"What if I go fishing with a bunch of friends?" he challenged.

"Do you?"

"No."

I smirked. "And cooking . . . that says to me that you like to try new things. You like to experiment and you have an adventurous side." I really wasn't sure about any of this. I was making some major generalizations based on very little knowledge.

"Impressive," he said. "What about you, Kathryn? Any magazines on our table that you read?"

"Aside from outdated celebrity news?"

"Aside from that."

The phone behind the counter rang, and it took a moment for either of us to react to it. Then it was like we both realized at the same time that Diego worked here. I pointed to the phone while he simultaneously hurdled the coffee table, slid around the counter, and picked it up.

"A-plus Counseling, Diego speaking." After a moment he said, "She must be off exploring somewhere." He rolled his eyes. "No, I got it. Dora and Diego are cousins. Yep. It was funny. How can I help you, sir?"

I cringed. Diego turned to the computer on the counter and began scrolling through some screens and typing. "How about Wednesdays at four thirty?" He waited for a response. "Okay, I have you on the schedule. Thanks." He hung up the phone and looked at me over the counter.

I bit my lip. "Full disclosure in the spirit of honesty?"

"Okay," he said warily.

"I thought of Dora when I first heard your name."

He laughed. "I'm glad to know you are unoriginal. Thanks for clearing that up."

The phone rang again and he gave me a smile and picked it up. "A-plus Counseling."

I got my phone out of my pocket and texted Alana: You'll never guess who I'm staring at right now.

She texted back right away.

Alana: Someone famous?

Me: Only famous in our world.

Alana: Like a local newscaster or something?

Me: No! Do you even know what they look like?

Alana: Who then?

Me: Diego.

Alana: You're stalking him? For me? I appreciate it!

Me: He tutors at the counseling center where Liza goes.

Alana: Awesome! Now you have a legit reason to spy on him and give me intel.

Me: Yep. I already found out that he likes to cook. I think you should challenge him to a cook-off as a way to spend time with him outside of school.

Alana: Good idea. I will try to work that naturally into a conversation.

Me: I have faith that you can do just that.

Alana: Hey, find a way to say something nice about me while you're there.

Me: He's on the phone now, but as soon as he gets off, I'm on it.

Alana: Thank you!

Only he didn't get off. Two more phone calls came in. While he was on the third call, Liza came around the counter to where I'd been sitting.

"I'm done," she said.

"Already?"

"It's been an hour."

"It has?"

She raised her eyebrows, looked at Diego and then back at me.

I stood and pocketed my phone. "Do you need to schedule your second session?"

"Nope, they're every Monday at the same time."

"Okay . . . I guess we should go, then." I gave one last glance at Diego, thinking I could wave or something, but he had his elbows on the counter and was glued to the computer screen. He didn't even look our way when the bell on the door signaled our departure.

Once outside, I asked, "So how did it go?"

"It wasn't bad. Tommy is nice," Liza said with a small smile.

I gave her a hip check. "Older guy, huh?"

"No, it's not like that. Whatever."

However it was or wasn't, Liza didn't seem to be as concerned about who might or might not see her on the way back to the car. So Tommy must've said something to make her realize going to tutoring wasn't a bad thing. I'd have to thank him for that next time. Because Liza wanted me to come back with her again. And I would. For her.

# CHAPTER 7

"He likes to cook?" Alana said when I called her as soon as I got home.

I shut my bedroom door to keep my little cousins out—not that a shut door would stop them—and filled her in on the interaction I'd had with Diego.

"See, isn't he amazing?" she said. "And I can ignore that fishing thing. That's more a solo activity anyway, right? I knew we were meant to be."

"I haven't fished in forever," I said, flopping down onto my beanbag chair.

"Even you, lover-of-all-things-lake, know it's boring."

"I didn't say that."

"Now, we need to somehow use these tutoring sessions to my advantage. He and I have established we are good at flirting with each other, but flirting doesn't always lead to a relationship."

"Really?" I said. "He's passed the Alana test? He's ready to move past the crush phase?"

"Yes! And we need a plan before you go to Liza's next session."

"Okay. Let's work on that."

My door flew open and the handle banged into the wall, most likely adding to the dent that was already there.

"Kate!" Cora cried, dashing inside.

Cora was my youngest cousin. She was four and a half and right now had chocolate all over her face.

"Did you eat pudding?" I asked.

"What?" Alana responded. "No, but that sounds delicious."

Cora was now circling my room, running her hand along the walls.

"Not if you saw it in its current state," I told Alana. "I have to go before this ends up all over my stuff."

"Okay, see you at school."

"Cora, come here." I scooped her up and took her to the bathroom across the hall. "Did Aunt Maggie give you pudding or did you get this yourself?" I held her up to the sink, turned on the faucet, and used my hand to scrub her face.

"No, I got it myself cuz I'm four."

"That's what I thought. You need to stay at the table when you're eating, Cora."

"I did! But then I finished."

She had me there. I dried her face with a towel. "Well, good thing you're so sweet." I plopped her back on her feet and she took off like a windup toy.

I sighed and went back to my room. I really wanted to take a WaveRunner out. But I knew there was something I'd been putting off for too long. I needed to listen to more past episodes of the school podcast. Wednesday was coming faster than I wanted it to, and I didn't feel ready.

* * *

Listening to old podcasts only served to let me know how horrible I was going to be at hosting. The past hosts were so outgoing and clever and quick on their feet. I was not any of those things.

On Wednesday, Ms. Lyon stood in front of the production crew in our school's recording studio. She was giving us a summary of how the day would go. I kept eyeing the big glass window to my right. Soon, I would be sitting behind it.

"This is the *school's* podcast," Ms. Lyon was saying. "So even though we encourage callers and listeners from the whole community, we are expected to promote school activities. Sequoia High's big fall fund-raiser is coming up in about a month. The Fall Festival. After your opening, talk that up a bit. Okay?" She looked at me and Victoria.

"Sounds good!" Victoria said, hopping to her feet. "Can we start now?"

I had hoped Ms. Lyon would want to prep us some more. Unfortunately, she nodded and gestured toward the door to the sound booth. Victoria bounced through the door and took her place on one of the stools waiting for us.

Alana, who'd been sitting next to me, whispered, "You should probably follow her."

"Should I?"

She gave me a playful shove.

I stood up and walked through the door. The recording studio was mostly used for the music classes, and I looked around at the guitars, a keyboard, and a set of electric drums. The only thing Victoria and I needed were the microphones that stretched from the floor to above our heads and then angled back down again. A pair of big headphones rested on the stool. I picked them up and slid them on as I sat down.

The remaining class members stared at me through the glass. On their side was a big soundboard, a couch, phones, and a few computers. Mallory and a guy named Jed were manning the phone lines. Two other students sat behind computers, ready to fact-check or do research when called upon. Alana sat on a rolling chair with a laptop and Frank sat on the far side of the couch, scrolling through his phone. I was glad Alana's first assignment was on the production crew. I wasn't looking forward to when she'd switch jobs and have a different lab day than me.

"This is so exciting," Victoria said from beside me.

I turned toward her and my headphones slipped off the back of my head. They were too big. I adjusted them. Victoria's headphones seemed to fit perfectly. She wore bright pink lipstick, as if the listeners would actually see her. She had dressed up as well. She was in a bold cotton sundress and had straightened her normally curly dark hair. I was just wearing my standard wardrobe of shorts and a T-shirt.

I swallowed the lump in my throat that was surely going to make me sound like a frog for this recording. Maybe they could fix it in the editing process the next day.

Alana pushed a button on the long board in front of her, and her voice sounded in my headphones. "I sent out the tweet for phone calls. The lines will be ringing off the hook soon."

"Yes, they will," Ms. Lyon said. "You ready, ladies?"

"Definitely," Victoria said.

Apparently they could all hear us without us needing to push any buttons because Ms. Lyon said, "Good."

I hadn't answered, but that didn't seem to matter.

Alana held up her notepad to face me. On it, she had written *Want to switch?*

I knew she still wished that she was the one with the headphones and the microphone and I was the one with the podcast's Twitter account. I would've switched places with her in a heartbeat if I could've. I nodded at her and she smiled and lowered her notepad.

Ms. Lyon pointed at me. "And we're recording." She let go of the button and pushed another.

My stomach lurched. Victoria leaned into her mic a little and said, "Hello, Oak Court! Welcome to our first podcast of the year."

Ms. Lyon pushed the button again. "You don't need to scream into the mic, Victoria. It will pick you up just fine. Enthusiasm yes, screaming no. Our editing team can edit a lot out, but let's not make them edit for volume." Ms. Lyon pushed the recording button again and pointed our way.

Victoria tried again, her enthusiasm undiminished.

"Hello, podcast listeners. We're your hosts, Victoria and Kat. Welcome to *Not My Problem*. Have you heard that phrase before? Have you tried to share your angst and woes with friends and they responded with their version of 'it's not my problem'? Well, people, for the next thirty minutes, we are going to make your problems our problems. We are here as your listening ears, your sympathetic shoulders to cry on. Figuratively, of course."

It was now my job to read the disclaimer. I leaned forward and my mouth hit the mic with a thump. "Oops."

"It's okay, we'll fix it later," Ms. Lyon said. "Keep going."

I backed off the mic slightly. "Actually, my name is Kate." That needed to be clear from the start. "And as a side note, we are not professionals." My hands were trembling as I read off the notecard we'd prepared with Ms. Lyon. "Whatever views we express today are our own opinions. If you do feel like you have an immediate problem that needs professional help, please call 911 or any of the other emergency numbers we have posted on our website."

Yep, the lump in my throat absolutely made me sound like a frog.

"And just some additional Sequoia High info," Victoria said. "The Fall Festival is coming up. Most of you know what that means, but for you freshmen, who may not, the festival is a week of fun school activities, followed by a football game and an amazing carnival that takes place Friday night in the school parking lot. There are games and snacks and rides. You have five weeks to ask a date and get your tickets!"

Victoria was a natural.

Now was the time in the show when our first phone call was supposed to be waiting for us. Both Victoria and I looked at the board on the other side of the glass. It was ominously free of blinking lights. Mallory, at the phones, shook her head and shrugged her shoulders.

"We'll edit out the silence," Ms. Lyon said into our headphones. This was one of the benefits of a podcast, she'd told us in class last week—editing. This couldn't be done on live shows.

I glanced over at Alana, who mouthed, *I posted on every site.*

I nodded, grateful she was trying.

"Before we'd ask any of you to share your problems with us, however," Victoria said smoothly, "what kind of hosts would we be if we didn't participate? Right, Kat?"

"Kate."

"Kate. Okay. Lay it on our audience. What is the biggest thing you're struggling with right now?"

I swallowed hard. "Right now?"

"Yes."

"Um . . . having to host a podcast when I don't like people very much."

Alana covered her mouth with a laugh I couldn't hear. Victoria's laugh was not silent, on the other hand. It was a big, happy laugh that would probably sound perfect on the air. "You are too funny. Well, here we go, first bit of official advice on our baby podcast. Take a deep breath. Let it out. Relax your shoulders. And remember, only the entire student body and the greater Oak Court city area will be listening." She was born to host a show. "I bet even Lakesprings is listening. Kat is from Lakesprings, everyone."

"Not helpful," I said. I tried to relax my shoulders.

Victoria smiled. "No, but really, you'll do great. And they, whoever *they* are, say that the more you practice something that scares you, the easier it gets. So after twenty-four more shows, you'll be a pro just in time for our podcast to be over."

"Thanks, Victoria." There were still no lights on the board. "Your turn. What is your biggest problem right now?" I asked.

"Aside from having a cohost who doesn't like people?" she said with perfect comedic timing. Were we on a sitcom, the laugh track would've sounded.

"Yes," I said drily. "Aside from that."

"My biggest problem in life right now is being a size sixteen in a world that values size twos."

And this was just proof that I was going to be horrible at advice. I had no idea what to say to that. I was surprised she was already being so open with our listeners. Impressed, but surprised.

"I guess we need to work on changing what the world values," I ventured.

"I agree," she said. "Oh, looks like we have a phone call."

My heart skipped a beat. I zeroed in on that red blinking light through the glass. Mallory gave us a thumbs-up.

"Hello, you're our very first caller on *Not My Problem*. Tell us your name and your problem," Victoria said.

"I'm Doug," a guy said. "And my problem is with the local pizza place. I ordered a pizza there the other day and they were very skimpy with their toppings. I called them back to complain and they said, not my problem. But it *is* their problem. It's *their* pizza place. Are you one of those programs who will show up at businesses and demand answers from them?"

"No," I said.

"Doug, is it?" Victoria asked.

"Yes," he said.

"We feel your plight."

*Plight?* I mouthed to Alana, and she bit back a smile.

"Next time you go into the pizza place," Victoria continued, "maybe ask for a manager and see if they will give you a discount due to your bad experience. And tell them about your penchant for lots of toppings. I think telling someone before the pizza is made instead of once it's already in your living room is the best way to go."

Were we really giving advice on pizza toppings? I couldn't believe this. I could feel the eyes of the entire production group on us. This podcast would go down as the worst in the history of this class. Ms. Lyon would use us as examples of what not to do for future classes. I wondered if we'd have to change topics after this first podcast. Maybe just changing the title would work. The title was my stupid idea, too.

I tried to focus. Was Victoria still talking to this pizza guy? No, she was wrapping it up now. "Thanks for calling in. Good luck on your next food quest." The phone line was disconnected and she looked at me. "When I'm hungry, I'm always the most irritable. I could totally understand how he was feeling."

"Yes, the plight of the undertopped pizza," I said.

"I could go for a pizza right now, undertopped or not," Victoria said. "Yum."

I smiled. Ms. Lyon pointed at the microphone as if to say a smile could not be heard. I tried a small chuckle. It did not go well.

The phones were eerily silent again. I knew Ms. Lyon said we could edit out all this dead air but if there weren't any other calls, there would be nothing to fill the dead air with. I looked to Alana again for reassurance but she was no longer at her post. I searched the small room and my headphones slipped off the back of my head again. I readjusted them. A red light blinked; a new call was coming through.

"Hello," Victoria said, when the call was patched through to our headsets. "You're on *Not My Problem.*"

"I have a problem," a girl said. The voice seemed vaguely

familiar but affected in some way. Like she was trying to disguise it.

"What's your name, caller?"

"I'd rather not say."

"Okay," Victoria said. "A mystery. I like it. Do you like mysteries, Kat?"

If she called me Kat one more time, there would be no mystery as to what my fist would do to her face. Okay, fine, there would be because I'd never punched anyone in my life. My thoughts talked a big game. "I do like mysteries," I replied. "And it's Kate."

"So what's your problem, caller?" Victoria asked.

"It's about my friend."

I gasped. The caller was Alana. I almost blurted her name into the mic, but I managed to hold my tongue.

Victoria gave me a sideways glance but said, "Okay. Tell us."

"I have a friend, my best friend in the whole world, and I fear she's not over her ex. He moved away and hasn't kept in touch with her at all, despite her efforts, and she still can't move on."

I could both kill and hug Alana at the same time. She'd seen our podcast crashing and burning and she was helping me out. But on the other hand, she was choosing her helpful moment to shed light on the problem she knew I had. Clever girl.

"That's a hard one," Victoria said.

"Not hard at all," I jumped in. "Give your friend some time. She obviously really liked her boyfriend and now just wants to take a break from love for a while. What's wrong with that?"

Victoria widened her eyes at me, obviously surprised at my forceful response when I'd been so quiet up until that point.

"Maybe you can set your friend up on a date," Victoria offered. "Show her that there are other fish in the sea."

"I don't think that's necessary," I said. "Your friend is probably perfectly capable of finding her own fish when she's ready to eat fish again."

"Nobody said anything about eating fish, Kat," Alana said.

Even though she wasn't in front of me, I could practically see the teasing glint in her eye as she used the name I hated. I'd forgive her for all of this, because she was totally saving me right now. She was saving me, even though she would've loved to have been sitting where I was sitting. She really was the best friend ever.

"You're right, *dating* them is worse," I said.

"Well," Victoria said, "you know what they say. The best way to get over someone is to start loving someone else."

"Who says that?" I asked.

"We'll be quoting 'they' a lot around here, so get used to it." Victoria winked at me.

"I personally like the saying: 'time heals all wounds,'" I said. "Just be her friend."

"I'll always be her friend," Alana said.

"I'm sure that's all she wants," I said.

"You're right. Thanks for the advice!" Alana said.

"You're welcome," Victoria said. "Thank you for calling in."

A few moments later, Alana slipped back in the room and took her seat. First, I narrowed my eyes at her, but then I mouthed *thank you* and she smiled.

The red light blinked again and I jumped a little. Some static came over my headset, which I was learning meant the call had been put through to us.

"You're on *Not My Problem*," Victoria said. "What can we help you with today?"

"This is like an advice podcast?" a woman's voice asked.

"Yes, it is," Victoria replied.

"Advice from high school students?"

"Yes," Victoria said. I wasn't sure how she could keep a smile on her face when the cynicism in the caller's voice was so obvious.

"What qualifies you to give advice?" the woman asked.

"Absolutely nothing," I said.

Victoria gave her practiced laugh. I wondered if it really was practiced. Had she rehearsed a routine in the bathroom mirror the night before like I had? "We don't claim to be experts," she said after her laugh. "Just hoping to offer objective opinions and open up discussion."

"Good luck with that," the woman said, and hung up.

And that was it. No more calls came in. We waited out the hour of allotted time for lab and Ms. Lyon powered down the equipment. I left the recording booth feeling weak with relief that it was over. For now.

"Okay," Ms. Lyon said when Victoria and I joined the rest of the group on the other side of the glass. "In tomorrow's lab, the editing team will get this cleaned up. We're going to list this podcast as an intro instead of an episode. I don't think we'll be able to get more than fifteen minutes out of it. Then in class, we'll brainstorm some ways to get more people calling in. Hopefully, once people hear the first podcast, they'll get the idea." And as if I didn't already suspect the whole thing had been a train wreck, she confirmed my fear by adding, "It's fine. It wasn't that bad."

Frank, who had somehow ended up standing closer than I wanted, said just loud enough for only me to hear, "No, it was worse."

I put my hand to my forehead and groaned. Maybe the best thing to come of this would be that I'd get fired.

# CHAPTER 8

"I don't want to hear how you thought it was fine," I said to Alana as soon as we were out of the room and walking down the wide hall.

"I wasn't going to say that at all. That was awful. You kind of sucked."

"Hey!"

"It was more that nobody real called in. You sucking was secondary."

I pushed open the door at the end of the hall. The heat of the day mixed with the scent of pine hit me at once. I stopped for a moment to breathe it in. It smelled a little like the lake and that helped release my tension.

"Thank you for saving us at least a little bit," I said, glancing gratefully at Alana. "You're the best."

"Of course." She paused. "And you know, I really do worry about you, Kate. And the stuff with Hunter."

I grabbed her hand and squeezed. "I love you but I don't want to talk about Hunter."

"I know."

"No, really."

“Okay, I promise I’ll stop after this one question—I was right, wasn’t I? You really are still hung up on him. I suspected, because you haven’t looked at another guy in months. But I thought maybe I was wrong.”

“I’m one step past hung up on him. I was hung up on him over the summer, now I’m . . .”

“Hung *down* on him?”

I laughed. “Off the hook but still touching it?”

She shook her head. “Well, instead of touching that hook, you can help me in my romantic endeavors.”

“Are you still coming to Liza’s tutoring thing with me on Monday so you can hang out with Diego there?” I asked as we headed to my car. This was the strategy we’d come up with after several discussions.

“Would that be too obvious?” Alana asked, twirling a strand of her dark hair around one finger.

“A little, but when has that ever stopped you?”

Alana laughed. “Okay. Since you are now the expert advice giver, I’m going to listen to you.”

“Funny. When does the podcast get posted online, anyway?” I asked.

“Friday.”

“Oh joy. Can’t wait for my debut.” It wasn’t like nobody listened to the podcast. It had actually built up quite a loyal following. I had two days to pretend this would all go away.

The wind whipped through my hair and pounded at my ears as I practically skidded across the lake on the WaveRunner. I knew I was driving fast, maybe too fast, but it felt good. I loved being out on the lake, doing something I was good at. I didn't feel stupid or out of my element or judged. I felt strong and confident. I felt free.

Well, except for the fact that I wasn't supposed to be out here. I was supposed to be cleaning this WaveRunner. A bucket of soapy water sat on the dock about twenty minutes behind me. It was nearing sunset and there was actually a whole row of WaveRunners I was supposed to clean. But as I'd stood on the dock, holding the bucket, I knew I needed this more.

I released my hold on the gas and the vehicle slowed to a stop. I put my forehead to the handlebars and let the tension melt out of my shoulders and back.

The way I felt now—relaxed and happy—was worth the look on my dad's face as I pulled back up to the dock thirty minutes later. But not necessarily worth the fact that I realized he held a towel in his hand and had obviously just done my job.

He sighed. "Kate, I know the siren call is strong, but sometimes I wish you could resist."

"I needed a break."

"You always need a break."

"That's not true. I work here a lot."

He let out a small chuckle. "I wasn't talking about here. I meant the things waiting for you at the house—homework, chores, responsibilities."

I couldn't argue with that. "I'm sorry."

"Hurry home. Mom said you were supposed to have your homework done before going out on the lake."

"I know. Sorry." I probably should've been more sorry. I hung up the keys and made my way home.

* * *

The next two days passed in a blur. Before I knew it, it was Friday afternoon, and I was pacing the floor of my bedroom. Liza and Alana sat on my bed, staring at me. The three of us had just finished listening to the first episode . . . or intro . . . or whatever Ms. Lyon was calling the thing. The editing team had done a good job editing out the silence at least.

"I thought you hated being called Kat," Liza said. The editing team had also edited out every time I corrected my name.

"I do." But my name was the least of my worries.

"It wasn't *that* bad," Alana finally said, echoing Ms. Lyon's words from Wednesday. Anytime someone has to say something isn't that bad, that just proves the opposite.

"You were funny," Liza said.

"For sure," Alana agreed. "You played the snark to Victoria's straight. It almost seemed like you two meant to play it that way."

"You used the word *almost*." I sank to the floor and pulled my knees to my chest.

"You sounded a tiny bit froggy, but otherwise you were okay, Kate," Liza said, playing with her blonde ponytail. "I don't understand why you're freaking out."

"Thanks, Liza."

"Did your group come up with any ways to get more callers?" Alana asked.

In class today, Ms. Lyon had split us into different groups to try and brainstorm ideas.

"Not really." I sighed from my spot on the floor. "My group was too busy giving me advice on how to be more charming and likable on air."

"Oh yeah, what kind of advice did they have?" Alana asked, shifting on my bed.

I thought back to their shouted suggestions. "One was to smile while I talk. Then I would at least *sound* happy."

Liza screwed her lips up into a smile. "Does that really work? Do I sound happy right now?" she asked us.

"You sound like a robot," Alana said. "You're supposed to both smile *and* move your mouth."

"Is that possible?" Liza practiced it a few times, whispering different words with a smile pasted onto her face.

"What about your group?" I asked Alana. "Did they come up with brilliant plans for more calls?"

"No. They're thinking that once the first episode airs, more people will call in."

"Based on what, exactly?" I asked, feeling defeated. "My winning charm?"

"Based on wanting to be on a podcast, I guess." Alana shrugged.

I tapped my bare feet against the floor. "Maybe we'll have to assign all the people who are in Thursday's postproduction lab to call in on Wednesdays with fake problems," I said, remembering how Alana had called in. "They can work on their voice manipulation and acting skills."

Alana scooted off my bed and came to sit on the floor next to me. She put her arm around my shoulder. "Look on the bright side."

"There's a bright side?"

"It can't get any worse than that episode, right? It will only get better from here."

"You just totally jinxed it. Next week someone will call in about undercooked meat at the local hamburger joint."

"Or they'll want you to help them with math homework," Liza said in her robot smile voice. Then she checked her phone. "Oops, my mom just texted that it's dinnertime. I'll see you guys later." She bounded off my bed and was gone.

Alana squeezed my arm. "You are being too hard on yourself. Let's forget about this stupid podcast for now, okay?" She pulled me to my feet. "It's Friday. We are going to find something amazing to do."

# CHAPTER 9

"This is Mr. Young's hotel," I whispered to Alana half an hour later. We stood outside the metal gate that led to the pool and hot tub. "Are you trying to make him hate my family *more*?"

"You think Mr. Young mans each and every one of his properties on a Friday night?" Alana waved her hand through the air, her big brown eyes sparkling with excitement. "Please. Besides, he owns all the hotels in town. So it's not like we have a choice if we want to go hot tub hopping."

This had been Alana's amazing plan for Friday night. The two of us wore swimsuits under our shorts and tank tops, and we were ready to sneak in.

"Mr. Young doesn't own Sierra Inn," I pointed out.

"True," Alana said. "And that's why Sierra Inn doesn't have a hot tub."

A couple headed down the path toward us and Alana pulled me out of the way. "We forgot our key," she said when they reached the gate.

They used theirs to let themselves in and held the gate open for us.

"See, easy," she said under her breath. "Think of this as what Mr. Young owes you for all the trouble he causes your family."

I looked around. Lights strung overhead reflected off the wet, stamped concrete. The pool was lit a bright blue and the hot tub bubbled with white steam. Pine trees hugged the back side of the fence, like towering guards. The moon rested just above one, as if the tip of the tree had pierced it and held it in place. The whole atmosphere was gorgeous and I could see why people came to Lakesprings for honeymoons and family vacations and weekend getaways. What I didn't understand was why anyone ever wanted to leave.

Alana and I stepped into the hot tub and I slid into a corner, letting the heat work at my muscles.

Alana nudged my foot with hers. "See, I knew you needed this. You should never question my plans. They are always perfect."

* * *

That night, after Alana dragged me to three more hot tubs, I lay on my bed decompressing. As much fun as I had with my best friend, I liked my alone time, too. That reminded me of a text Hunter had sent me months ago. I pulled it up on my phone.

It's okay to gain your energy from silence, he'd written. Silence isn't static.

I smiled. Hunter got me. No, Hunter obviously didn't get me, because he'd stopped texting me ages ago. I should've just deleted all his texts and his contact info and unfollowed him on social media so I could stop torturing myself. But I didn't delete anything.

My bedroom door was nudged open and Uncle Tim's dog walked in. He was a big dog, some mix that included Great Dane. Of course he came straight up to where I was lying on my bed and stuck his nose on my cheek.

I covered my face. "No, CD."

My cousins and I called him CD, short for Community Dog, because he spent so much time in all of our houses. I didn't even remember what my uncle had originally named him two years ago.

"Come on," I added, "you're in the wrong house." I rolled off my bed and stood up. CD followed me out my door, outside the house, and into the backyard. I walked to the right, stopping at my uncle's back sliding door. I gave a cursory knock and waited ten seconds before I slid open the door, pushed the curtains aside, and directed CD inside.

My uncle sat at the kitchen counter eating a bowl of cereal. He looked up when I appeared and a smile lit his face.

"Kate! Hey."

"Hi, Uncle Tim. CD thought I needed a friend tonight."

"Ah, sorry about that." Uncle Tim patted his leg. "Come here, boy."

I'd started to leave when my uncle called me back.

"Do you want some cereal?" he asked.

"It's eleven o'clock at night."

"And?"

I shrugged. "And nothing, I guess." I pulled out the stool next to him and sat down. He got me a bowl and pushed over the milk.

"How's the new school year so far?" he asked as we ate together. Uncle Tim's kids were my younger cousins; they were all still in preschool or elementary school.

"Decent," I answered, my mouth full of cereal. CD, curled up beside my uncle's feet, began to snore.

"And your brother? Is he adjusting to high school well?"

"I think so. He hangs in the library and reads."

"Sounds about right. And why are you hanging out at home on a Friday night?"

"I wasn't. Alana and I went out and now I'm back." I hoped Uncle Tim wouldn't ask me what we'd done. I didn't like lying, but I would never tell my uncle about trespassing on Mr. Young's properties. He'd be disappointed, maybe worried. My parents always said we needed to maintain a squeaky clean reputation, never give the Youngs ammunition.

"You seem down," my uncle said in his thoughtful way.

Despite Alana's attempt at distracting me, my brain was still wrapped up in my major fail at hosting. Thinking about struggling through a year of something I never wanted to do in the first place wasn't sitting well.

"How do I convince my podcasting teacher to let me switch jobs?" I asked my uncle, turning to face him. "She's really stubborn, but I feel like the entire class wishes that would happen."

"Ah. Yes."

My heart sank. "You listened to it, didn't you?"

"I did."

He didn't finish that sentence with: *you were great* or *you were funny*. Instead he said, "You'll get better. And don't worry, the class will come around."

Ouch. "Yeah . . . maybe." We finished our cereal in silence. I stood up and dumped the remainder of my milk into the sink.

"Don't stress about it, Kate. Success doesn't happen without some failure."

I turned back around to look at him at the counter. "That's one of those things adults say that really means nothing, isn't it?"

He laughed. "I stand by it."

"Thanks."

I wanted to believe him. But his statement implied that success *always* came after failure. I knew that wasn't true. "Maybe I should just drop out of the class," I mused out loud. "Take pottery instead."

"Your mom wouldn't like that. She's excited that you're taking this class."

"I know." I rolled my eyes. "She's all into podcasts thanks to Alana."

Uncle Tim laughed. "I think it's more that she wants you to find some new passions. Make sure you're living up to your potential and all that."

"But I already have my passion!" I protested. "I want to run the marina. Why are my parents suddenly acting like my caring about the lake is a horrible thing? *Their* lives are about the lake."

Uncle Tim nodded. "But there's nothing wrong with exploring some more options before making a decision about your entire future. That's all your parents want."

"Says the guy who has known he wanted to fly airplanes since the time he was five."

He smiled. "True."

I started to walk toward the door.

"But I minored in Biology because I thought cutting things open sounded fun, too."

I turned and walked backward a few steps. "You're weird."

He raised his cereal bowl to me. "Sometimes the path of least resistance isn't necessarily the right path. You can resist the siren call of the lake sometimes."

I stopped walking. "What?"

"What?"

"You were talking to my dad, weren't you? He used those exact words. Did you all sit around talking about me?"

"No."

I lowered my chin and continued to stare.

"They're just concerned about you, Kate."

I frowned. "They think I only want to run the marina because it's easy? Because I'm lazy or something?"

"They don't want you to choose your future by default."

"I love the marina. Maybe more than they do."

He held up his hands in surrender. "Don't shoot the messenger."

I grunted and marched to the door. "Fine. I won't quit the podcast."

At least, not yet.

# CHAPTER 10

"I thought Alana was coming with us today," Liza said as we pulled up outside the tutoring center on Monday afternoon.

"She's meeting us here."

Alana had explained to me that she didn't want to show up at Diego's place of employment without a good reason. I wasn't sure what good reason she'd come up with, but I'd learned long ago to just go along with Alana's plans. Things turned out better that way.

This time, Diego was at the front counter when Liza and I walked inside.

"Hey, Kate, Liza," he said.

Tommy came out of the back room. "Hi, Liza. You ready to get to work?"

She shrugged. "Not really."

Tommy laughed. "Well, too bad, kiddo. I get paid the big bucks to make you work." His gaze slid to me. "Hey, nice job on the podcast Friday."

I nearly choked on my own surprise. "Oh . . . you listened to that?"

"Yeah. You were funny."

"See!" Liza said. "That's what I tried to tell her, but she cried about how awful she was."

"I did not *cry*." My face got hot.

"Whined, whatever."

She had me there. "Yes, there was lots of whining."

"Well, I liked the podcast," Tommy said. Then he gestured toward the tables and led Liza away.

I bit my bottom lip and tried to avoid Diego's stare, which I could feel on me.

"You host the school podcast?" he asked.

"I know. I seem like the last person who should've been picked to be a host."

"I didn't say that."

I occupied myself with the magazines on the table again. There were new ones, I noticed. "It was a job forced upon me." I picked up one of the new ones, a fashion magazine, and showed it to Diego. "This another hobby of yours?"

"No. Do you like fashion?"

I threw the magazine down and sank onto the chair. "Not really." I opted for one of the three-year-old celebrity gossip magazines and began reading some articles. It was interesting going back in time for a bit. Some things seemed exactly the same and others were totally different.

I wasn't sure how long I sat leafing through that magazine and wondering if Alana would ever show up. But when I looked up again, Diego was typing into his phone. A picture was tucked into the clear case of his phone. My curiosity had me tossing the magazine back on the table and standing up to take a closer a look.

"Your family?" I asked. The photo showed Diego with two adults, plus two older guys and a girl I guessed were his brothers and sister. They were all good-looking, with similar wide smiles.

"What?" he asked.

I pointed. "The picture."

He flipped his phone over to look. "Oh. Yes. I like my family. Go figure."

I smiled. That was sweet. "Me too. Most of the time."

Diego went back to typing something, and I was just about to ask him what had his attention when Victoria's voice rang out over his phone's tiny speaker, broadcasting the podcast.

I gasped and without hesitating, I lunged forward tried to steal the phone from Diego. He held it out of my reach. Then *my* voice rang out from the speaker. I grabbed his arm and tried to pull the phone down. He laughed and twisted out of my hold.

"Seriously, Diego, this isn't funny. Please turn it off."

"But I want to listen."

"No, I forbid it." I had his sleeve now and I knew he wasn't taking me seriously because I was laughing, too. It was my nervous laugh, but a laugh just the same. How was anyone supposed to take me seriously when I laughed? Our collective laughter made it impossible to hear the podcast. But not impossible to hear the bell on the front door as it opened.

"Alana," Diego said, and I whirled around.

"Am I missing a good game?" Alana asked.

In the new silence, my voice sounded from Diego's phone. *"Having to host a podcast when I don't like people very much."*

"You don't like people?" Diego asked me.

"Only the ones that try to talk to her," Alana answered for me.

"Please turn it off," I said. This time my sincerity was obvious.

Diego lowered his phone and pressed the screen. The room went still.

"Thank you," I said.

"I brought you back your math book, Kate," Alana said. "I dropped it off in your car."

"Oh. Thanks." She hadn't borrowed my math book. Apparently that was the *really good excuse* she was going with.

"Ooh, fashion." Alana sat down, propped her feet on the coffee table, and started looking through the magazine.

"Two questions," Diego said as I backed out from behind the counter and took a seat next to Alana. "One, why do you feel like the podcast was a failure? And two, I thought you hated to be called Kat?"

"I do. All the times I corrected Victoria were edited out. And the podcast was a failure because hardly anybody called in."

Tommy yelled out from the back like he'd somehow been able to follow along with our conversation. "Just keep being funny and people will call in."

My cheeks went pink from his praise.

Alana casually stood, most likely to get a look at Tommy, but pretending it was to examine the art on the walls.

"Oh, really?" she mumbled when she sat back down. "Maybe that finger is about to come off the hook, after all?"

I answered just as quietly back, "No. Liza is crushing on him. He's off-limits."

"Anonymity," Diego said.

"What?" both Alana and I asked at the same time, turning our attention away from our private conversation and back to him.

"People aren't going to call in with personal problems if there's a chance the listeners will know who they are," Diego said, leaning his elbows on the counter. "I mean, I guess some people might. But you'll have a bigger chance at success if people can be anonymous."

"He's right," Alana said.

Of course he was, and I wasn't sure why I hadn't thought of that. Even Alana, the most outgoing person ever, had tried to disguise her identity when she called in. Part of it was that she didn't want the class to know she was bailing me out, but it was also because she didn't want everyone in the world to hear her problems . . . well, *my* problems.

"You're right," I said. "That's a great idea."

"Yes, it is," he said with a smirk. "You're welcome."

Anonymity. Like when people didn't put their real identities on their posts online. "Email," I said. "We need to let listeners email in, too. Some people don't like to talk on air, right?"

Diego nodded. "That's true. Email would help."

"Ms. Lyon is going to be impressed with our practical ideas." Alana freed a food magazine from the stack on the table. "Ooh. I love to cook."

"Me too," Diego said.

"Really?" she asked.

Diego's eyes went to me like he was wondering if I had told her this about him. I had, of course.

"Cool," Alana went on smoothly. "We'll have to exchange tips sometime."

"Like in a cook-off," I said.

She gave me a warning look, like she was working up to that.

"Is that a challenge?" Diego asked.

"Yes, it is," Alana said.

Diego grinned at her. "You're on."

Tommy and Liza appeared from around the counter. Tommy said, "If people are cooking, I can be available to do the eating."

"Ditto," I said.

Tommy pointed at me. "Kat and I will be eating partners."

"It's Kate," Diego said before I could.

"How come it's Kat on the podcast, then?" Tommy asked.

I sighed. "Long story."

"I like 'Kat,' " Tommy said. "It's edgy and makes you sound sure of yourself. It fits your on-air personality."

"You think?" I asked.

"Absolutely."

"I agree," Alana said. "You should definitely keep Kat for the podcast. Kat is snarky and sarcastic. 'Kate' doesn't fit that persona as well."

Liza hadn't joined us by the coffee table yet, just stood by Tommy, staring up at him with dreamy eyes.

"What do you think, Liza?" I asked.

"I agree with Tommy. Kat is cool."

Diego didn't give his opinion and I didn't ask for it. I'd always hated the name Kat. But I kind of hated the podcast, too. Maybe they fit together.

"Okay, time to go," I said.

Alana picked up her backpack and glanced around. "Since I *am* at a tutoring center, do either of you guys have a minute to help me with an algebra problem I can't get through?"

"I can help," Diego said, sliding down the counter to make room for Alana. She sidled up next to him with her book, their shoulders touching. Diego didn't move away. And that's how I left Alana alone with Diego. He'd fall for her before they could even solve for *X*.

# CHAPTER 11

I sat on the dock at the marina, wiping down WaveRunner number four with a soapy sponge. My phone was tucked into my board shorts and my earbuds were firmly in place. I was fifteen minutes into the *First Dates* podcast Alana had recommended I listen to, and I'd laughed approximately fifty times. That was about three times a minute. No wonder Alana had wanted me to listen to this podcast—it was good. And I needed to get better.

I was *going* to get better. Mainly to prove everyone wrong. My parents thought I was only choosing the lake and marina because it was easy? So I'd get better at the podcast and prove to them that I would still choose the lake. That way, they'd realize I knew exactly what I wanted, no matter what I was good at.

"I figure if I go on a first date once a week," Samantha, one of the hosts, was saying, "I can save approximately a hundred dollars a month in food."

"You never pay?" Tami (the other host) asked.

"I offer to pay for the second date. That saves me even more money."

"Why?" Tami asked.

"Because I rarely have second dates."

I giggled. The *First Dates* podcast, while making me feel worse about my podcasting ability, *was* making me feel slightly better about my dating life. And with my feet dangling in the lake, I always felt better. "I like this strategy," Tami said. "How has this not come up before?"

"We've been too busy talking about deworming cats and selling used cars and opening avocado-based food trucks," Samantha replied. Their dates always talked about the weirdest things, but that made the show hilarious.

"Good point," Tami said. "We've learned so much from our first dates. And from yours, listeners, so keep them coming, people. We feed off your misery."

Samantha and Tami were definitely better at playing off of each other than Victoria and I were. Well, better than me, in any case. Victoria was great. She could have joined right in with Samantha and Tami.

While the podcast went to commercial, I grabbed the folded towel next to me and dried off the seat of the WaveRunner. The sun was setting, throwing oranges and pinks onto the lake. I watched a large speedboat race across the water, pulling a skier behind it.

One of my earbuds was tugged from my ear and I whirled around to see my dad standing there.

"Hi," I said, taking the other earbud out as well.

He smiled. "Hey, welcome back to the real world."

"Sorry, were you calling me?"

He took his baseball cap off and ran a hand over his bald head. "What are you listening to?"

"A podcast."

"For your class?"

"Sort of."

"Are you done here?" Dad asked, gesturing to the WaveRunners.

"Almost."

"Okay. I locked up the marina. Will you just padlock the gate on your way out?"

"Yes."

"Thanks, kid."

I put my earbuds back in. I hadn't hit PAUSE, so it took me a second to get back into it, but that was all. Only a second. That's how engaging the hosts were. That's what I had to work on—being engaging.

* * *

I stared at the microphone. It loomed in front of me. I couldn't believe Ms. Lyon still wanted me to be the one talking into it.

"Remember, class." Ms. Lyon's voice came through my headphones, pulling my attention away from the microphone and to the group on the other side of the glass. "If you recognize the caller's voice, I expect you to maintain their privacy since we won't disguise it until edits. We must hold true to our reporting morals."

The day before, in class, Alana and I had suggested the anonymous calling and email options. Everyone had loved the idea, including Ms. Lyon. Alana had been talking up the podcast's new anonymity policy on social media ever since.

I adjusted my headphones.

Ms. Lyon turned a full circle. "We have someone checking emails, right?" she asked.

A girl named Jamie raised her hand.

"Great, let us know if any good ones come in. And I assume all the social media reminders have gone out?"

Alana held up her phone. "This new batch has been going out for the last thirty minutes."

"We already have two callers waiting," Mallory said.

"We do?" I asked, surprised.

"Then let's get started," Victoria said, her excitement obvious.

Ms. Lyon pressed the RECORD button. Then she pointed at us, our signal to start talking.

Victoria leaned forward. "Hello, listeners. It's Victoria and Kat here from *Not My Problem*. We gave you an intro teaser last week, and now we're here to sink our teeth into our first full episode. Right, Kat?"

I started to correct her, then paused. I remembered what Tommy had said, about how the name fit my on-air persona. Maybe I could be however I wanted to be on the podcast. Maybe I could be the voice that I forced to stay inside of my head most of the time.

"Well, I don't know about my teeth," I said, "but I'll sink something into it."

Victoria gave a trill of laughter. "How about you give a whirl at our disclaimer?"

"Right. We are not professionals. Not even close. So if you have a real emergency, please call 911 or any of the phone numbers we put up on our website."

"And speaking of our website," Victoria said, "we have a new email option for those of you who don't like to speak on air. We get it. You're shy but you still have problems. So type away and we'll try our best to help. It looks like we already have a caller on the line. Let's get started."

The crackling sound of a connected caller sounded in my ears.

"You're on *Not My Problem*," Victoria said. "We're listening."

"I'm anonymous, right?" was the first thing the girl said. "I sound like Batman or something?"

"Or something," I said because right now she sounded nothing like Batman or any other disguised version of her own normal voice. That would change in edits.

"Yes, of course. Nobody will know who you are. Complain away," Victoria said.

"It's about Mr. Grady."

"As in the Biology teacher here at Sequoia High?" Victoria said.

"Yes, that one. He is the worst teacher in the world."

I cringed and looked at Ms. Lyon. Our teacher didn't make a move to indicate we should stop Batman in her blaspheme. In fact, Ms. Lyon held her hand out to the side as if to say *continue*.

"In what way?" Victoria asked.

"He is horrible at teaching, goes off on personal stories throughout the class, and then expects us all to know the answers to the tests when he hasn't taught them."

"Have you tried telling him this?" Victoria asked.

"I haven't, but enough other people have that I know the result—harsher grading of homework. No, thanks."

"How about asking for a study guide for each unit?" I offered.

"Yes," Victoria agreed. "So during class while he's talking about his life, you can be filling out the study guide. Then if you have a question, just raise your hand and ask. Maybe it will get him back on track."

There was silence on the line and I thought the Batman girl was going to come back with how this wouldn't work. But then she said, "That's not a bad idea. Thanks."

When she hung up, Ms. Lyon said, "We'll edit out the name of the teacher."

That was probably a good idea, to avoid the students all having to deal with his wrath.

"There's another phone call," Mallory said. "She also wants to be anonymous."

"You're on *Not My Problem*," Victoria said to the caller. "What can we help you with?"

"Hi. My boyfriend wants me to meet his parents for the first time," the girl said. "And not just, hey, come over to my house and say hi. A formal dinner, at a fancy restaurant. A formal dinner? What does that even mean? Like there will be more than one fork and I have to pretend to like Roquefort?"

"What's Roquefort?" Victoria asked.

"It's a cheese. And it's gross," I said. I only knew this because my aunt was a caterer.

"Right?" the girl said. "So gross. I can't pretend to like that."

"Don't pretend," Victoria said. "You want his family to know the real you, not some made-up version. So be real."

"And don't order a cheese plate," I said.

"What should I wear?" she asked.

"Take a deep breath," Victoria said. She was right; the girl sounded close to panic. "Wear something you already own. Nice but not too flashy. Google some etiquette rules to feel more comfortable with the silverware. And then just be yourself. You sound absolutely charming to me."

"I do?" the girl asked, sounding surprised but relieved.

"Yes, you do. Very well spoken and nice," Victoria said reassuringly.

"Thank you."

"Good luck."

Victoria was going to be president one day, I decided.

Mallory shook her head, indicating no more calls.

I could see Jamie say something but couldn't hear her.

Ms. Lyon pushed the button, letting us in. "Jamie says we have some interesting emails. Kat, I'll bring you the iPad so you can read them." Now even *she* was calling me Kat?

Ms. Lyon opened the door and brought me the iPad, pointing to where the emails waited. There were two, each with no subject line, so I didn't know what to expect. I clicked on the first one and read aloud into the microphone.

"'Kat, I happen to like Roquefort. It is one of the best. Perhaps you should keep your uncultured cheese opinions to yourself.'"

I let out a groan. "Was that a cheese pun? Is cheese cultured or am I thinking of something else? Also, this isn't a live show. How does someone already know my opinions on cheese?"

Alana held up her phone, indicating she had been live tweeting.

Victoria spoke into the mic. "One of our fellow podcasters is tweeting this, Kat. You should've thought of the cheese lovers before you made such a bold declaration about cheese."

"For the record, I'm a little picky about food, so I'm not a good judge," I said.

"Let's move on to the next email," Victoria said, gesturing to the iPad.

I clicked on the second email and began to read out loud.

"'Dear Victoria and Kat, I want to ask someone to the Fall Festival, but I'm seeing all these elaborate invites and wondering how I can even compare. Some guy used sidewalk chalk to write his invitation out in ten-foot-tall letters on the parking lot and then sent his drone up to take a picture of it. Is that what my date is going to expect? Will she say no if I just simply walk up and ask her?'"

I finished reading and caught my breath. With the Fall Festival about four weeks away, I wondered if we were about to get lots of these kinds of questions.

Victoria gave a small hum. "I guess you have to know *who* you're asking. For example, I don't think Kat here would mind a simple proposal. But I, on the other hand, expect the ten-foot letters. Do you hear that, Brian?" She paused and added, "Brian's my boyfriend, listeners."

"Hey now," I said, even though she was very right about my preferences. "I don't think it's about the simplicity or complexity of the ask, but the thoughtfulness and sincerity of it."

Victoria nodded. "I'd agree with that. Brian, when you do the ten-foot letters, make sure you're sincere."

"We have another caller," Mallory said over the headset, then clicked it through.

"Hello, welcome to *Not My Problem*," Victoria said.

"Hi."

"What can we help you with today?" Victoria asked.

"I'm anonymous, right?" The voice was low and husky, almost like he didn't expect us to change it, so he was changing it himself.

"Yes, you are," Victoria said. "Do you have a problem you'd like to share?"

"Yes. It's about my family. They are so focused on my future and what it's going to take for me to get there that sometimes I feel like I don't get to live in the now. It's all about schoolwork, college applications, tests, and studying. I have no time for anything else. It's like they don't want me to have a social life at all until I'm done with *college*."

"Is there a question in there somewhere?" Victoria asked.

"How do I make my parents relax a little so that I can do something outside of school and work?" the caller asked.

"What about making a schedule?" Victoria offered, which I thought was smart. "Maybe you can block out times for studying and times for social things. They can't expect you to eat, drink, and breathe schoolwork."

"They probably can," I said. Sometimes parents expected a lot.

"So do you have advice, Kat?" Something about the way the caller said my name felt personal. And that husky voice of his wasn't helping, either. A shiver went through me.

"No. I mean, I don't know," I said. "But I understand when parents expect something different for us than what we want for ourselves."

"Is there a certain someone you're wanting to spend some time with, and these obligations are getting in the way?" Victoria asked the caller.

He coughed and stuttered for a moment then said, "No."

Victoria said, "That didn't sound like a no."

"Well, I do like someone, but this isn't about her."

"Does she know you like her?" Victoria pressed.

"No" was all he said. "But you've both given me things to think about. Maybe I'll try the schedule thing. Thank you." And just like that, he hung up. Victoria had scared him away.

Victoria fanned her face and mouthed *Sexy voice* to me. I agreed.

The clock on the wall said forty minutes had passed. We could definitely whittle that down to thirty minutes. Victoria must've noticed the clock too because she said, "That's all the time we have today. Thanks for listening! We'll be back next week, so if you were too shy to call today, please pick up your phone another time. We're not too scary. Well, Kat is a little scary but we keep her behind glass so you'll be safe." I shoved Victoria's shoulder and she laughed. "Until next time."

Ms. Lyon opened the door between the two rooms. "Great work, team. We're getting our legs under us. The postproduction crew will edit tomorrow. You're all free to go."

Alana grabbed my hand as we walked out of the recording studio. "You did better today."

"You think?"

"Much."

"Victoria does a good job. I'm just along for the ride." In fact, I barely hung on. If there was no Victoria, there would be no podcast.

But something else was bothering me, too. Something that was hanging in the back of my mind.

"Did you recognize the voice of that last caller?" I asked Alana.

"No, but he was changing it."

"I know."

"Did *you* recognize him?" Alana asked.

"Maybe . . . I think . . ." I bit my lip. "Was it Diego?"

"What? No."

"I think it was. And if it was, you know what that means, right?"

"What?"

"You heard him. He likes a girl. A girl he wishes he had more time for. He was talking about you, Alana."

Alana's eyes widened. "That's a big jump."

"Didn't you say you had a solid flirting session at the tutoring center the other day? The boy likes you."

"Shhh!" she hissed as if he might be lurking in the halls of school listening in.

I lowered my voice. "He said he wants to spend more time with a girl he likes, but his family is preventing it." I stopped suddenly, remembering the picture Diego had in his phone case.

"What?" Alana asked.

"Maybe it *isn't* Diego. He and his family seem close. He gets along with them."

Alana shrugged. "Just because you're close with your family doesn't mean you can't have disagreements."

"True," I said. "So you think the caller was Diego?"

"No. I was just pointing out a flaw in your logic. I still think you're making a big assumption."

"But if it's him, the time issue is probably why he hasn't asked you out. He knows he doesn't have time for a relationship right now."

"Maybe."

I still wasn't totally certain it had been him. But somehow I'd find out. Because if the caller was Diego, it was obvious that all he needed was a tiny push in Alana's direction. I could help with that.

# CHAPTER 12

Labor Day weekend was one of the busiest rental times of the entire year. It was like people realized the warmth was leaving, so they were trying to soak up every last minute of sun.

"Guess who doesn't have tutoring because of Labor Day?" Liza asked happily. She sat next to a rack of swimsuits in the marina shop, not helping at all. I stood at the register, behind the computer. Max was in the back, unpacking a shipment we had received that morning.

"You don't?" I asked my cousin. I found myself slightly disappointed. The plan was to help Alana with Diego, and the tutoring center had been a good place to do that. Plus, I wanted to see if I'd been right about the podcast call—if Diego was the mysterious caller. I needed a long period of talking to him to figure that out.

"Nope," Liza said, beaming. "Mom didn't even reschedule it for another day this week."

"Lucky you." I nudged her leg with my foot. "Aren't you going to miss Tommy?"

"Ha ha," she said but she looked at the floor, probably to hide pink cheeks.

My dad appeared in the open doorway. "Kate, will you check the position of WaveRunner number seven on the GPS?"

"Yep." All our power rentals had GPS units to keep track of them. Cell coverage on the lake was spotty and sometimes people couldn't call in to the marina if they got stuck. "It's in the cove," I said when I pulled up the location on the computer.

He sighed. "That's what I was worried about. It's an hour late. The next renter is here."

"It probably ran out of gas," I said, and Dad nodded. "Want me to go check on it?"

Liza hopped up. "I can stand at the cash register."

"Okay," Dad said.

We had a smaller, older WaveRunner that had aged out of our renting fleet, but we kept it for situations like this when all the others were rented out. I grabbed the keys, a life jacket, and a rope, and headed out. With a big smile on my face, I untied the vehicle from the dock. I shouldn't have been happy someone was stuck or late, but it meant I got to be out on the lake for a little bit.

After I got past the five-mile-an-hour buoys, I cranked the gas and picked up speed. Water sprayed out on either side of the WaveRunner, creating a fine mist on my legs. The lake was choppy today and crowded with boats. The sequoia trees created a dark green band against the blue sky. There were spots of rust-colored trees as well—dying trees. Some were suffering from the drought, some from a beetle that had infested the area a few years back.

The cove was up ahead, hidden by a bend in the lake and an outcropping of rocks and trees. When I rounded the corner, the first thing I saw was a fancy speedboat, its engine off. Two guys were standing inside the boat; one, who looked to be about my age, manned the wheel, and the other guy, who looked to be in his twenties, stood beside him, talking. I should've instantly recognized the boat as belonging to the Youngs but I didn't until I recognized the driver: Frank.

I growled and applied more gas. When Frank heard the sound of my approach, he turned. Sitting, stalled, on the other side of his boat was our WaveRunner, empty of an occupant. I glanced around the lake to see if the driver was somewhere nearby. Then it occurred to me that our customer must've been the twentysomething guy Frank was talking to in his boat. I slowed and came up alongside the watercraft.

"Ah, they did eventually send someone out, Cody," Frank said to the other guy. Then Frank gave me a smug smile and added, "Looks like one of your vehicles is out of commission again."

I should've said, *Again? Our crafts are only ever out of commission due to operator error.* But I didn't. Not only because a customer was standing right there, but because my mom had told me never to give the Youngs a reason to come after us. If we were always taking the high road, she said, they'd never be able to put up roadblocks. Her analogy didn't quite work, though, because the Youngs always seemed to be able to throw roadblocks from whatever road they were on.

I grabbed the left handle of the stalled-out WaveRunner and cut my engine. That's when I noticed the rope that Frank had attached to our WaveRunner. He was going to tow it in himself.

"What happened?" I yelled over to the customer. Cody, Frank had called him.

"I don't know," Cody said. "It just stopped working."

I leaned over to look at the controls. The key was in the ignition, so I turned it one click. The indicator on the gas gauge didn't jump at all. "You ran out of gas." I tapped on the indicator. "You have to keep an eye on this and fill up when it gets close."

"What?" Frank called from his perch in the speedboat. "It's hard to hear you down there. Why don't you join us up here, Kat?"

I took a steadying breath and told myself not to snap at him. It would only make me look like the bad guy. I tied my craft to the back of the stalled WaveRunner. Then I walked across the two seats and jumped up onto the back deck of the Youngs' fancy speedboat. Frank held his hand out for me but I ignored it as I hopped down into the main section, joining the two guys there.

The boat was amazing—a backlit dual touch screen on the dash above the steering wheel, stainless-steel cup holders, long plush bench seats around the back and open bow, and two captain-style chairs in the middle. It even had a rear-facing bench on the deck in back. And was that a small bathroom compartment? If I didn't hate Frank, I would've asked him to take me on a tour of the boat.

But I did hate him, and he didn't need the ego boost.

"I said that you need to keep an eye on the gas gauge so it doesn't run out," I explained to Cody.

"Oh," Cody said. "Nobody told me."

I knew that wasn't true. It was one of the first things we told people who were renting.

"I won't have to pay for a late return, right?" Cody added. "I've been stuck out here for an hour. I would've been on time."

*If you'd been paying attention*, I wanted to say, *you wouldn't have been stuck at all.* But that was something else my parents would've frowned on. Customer service was top priority. "No. It's fine," I said. "If you'll just hop down onto the WaveRunner again, I can tow you back in."

Cody looked at Frank, like Frank had anything to do with this.

"I said I would tow him in," Frank said.

"No, that's okay. I have it."

I moved to jump over the back seats again but Frank stopped me. "We're already tied up and ready. It will be faster this way," he said.

I thought about my dad, and the new renter waiting back at the marina. Maybe if Frank saw the marina on this, our busiest weekend, he'd realize that we weren't going anywhere.

"Fine. I'll meet you back there." I started off the boat again.

"I'll ride you back, too," Frank said.

I checked over the side to verify that I had tied my WaveRunner off the back and not to the side where the two would smash into each other. Then I nodded. Frank turned on his boat and it roared to life, displaying its power.

Cody whooped appreciatively and sat on the bench. Frank took his place in the driver's seat and motioned for me to sit down in the other captain's chair. I did, but turned so I could keep an eye on the WaveRunners.

"Relax, Kat," Frank said. "Your toy boats will be fine."

"It's Kate," I said.

"I thought you'd changed your name. That you were redefining yourself."

Cody saved me from answering by saying, "My phone doesn't work out here."

"Cell coverage isn't very good," I said. "Maybe the Youngs should build a cell tower."

"Maybe we should," Frank said.

It wouldn't surprise me if they were already in the process of doing just that.

"You like to wakeboard?" Frank asked, and at first I thought he was asking Cody but then I realized he was talking to me.

"Yes." I loved to wakeboard. When one of our speedboats wasn't rented and the whole family was available, my parents would take me and Max out. It wasn't as often as I'd have liked.

Frank nodded up to his wakeboard that was nestled into a clip on the tower of his boat. "I'll take you out sometime."

"What?" Why was he being generous? I was so confused. This behavior was like a one-eighty from just last week. "No."

A flash of irritation shone in Frank's eyes, letting me know I was right to question his motives. But he didn't say anything else.

Frank pulled up to the gas pumps at the marina, proving that he'd heard me explaining the gas issue to Cody just fine. Susan, the employee working there, helped ease the boat up against the buoys, probably thinking Frank needed a fill.

"It's just the WaveRunner," I called out to her.

"Oh, okay, got it!"

Frank went to the back and untied the rope. He flung it to Susan, who pulled the WaveRunners in. Then Frank gave Cody a hand over the side and onto the dock.

"Thanks," Cody said, and went into the shop to collect his license and whatever other collateral he'd provided when he'd rented out the WaveRunner.

My dad stood on the far side of the dock, handing a paddle down to a woman who was renting a kayak. Dad kept glancing back toward me, probably wondering why Frank Young was docked at our marina.

I turned to Frank. "Thanks for your help," I said gruffly, then moved to disembark.

"Kate," Frank said.

I turned back to look at him.

"Truce?" he said.

I wasn't sure where this was coming from, but I *was* sure there was an ulterior motive.

I narrowed my eyes at him. "Why?"

"What do you mean 'why'? Does there need to be a reason for a truce?"

"Yeah, kind of."

"Maybe I'm tired of the grudge our parents hold against one another. Plus, we're in a class together this year."

"We've been in a class together before and it never resulted in a truce."

"But it's this tiny class and we have to interact more."

"Fine, whatever. Truce." I hopped over the side of the boat and walked straight into the shop. What had *that* been all about?

My dad stepped inside shortly after me. "What was that about?" Dad asked.

I smiled at our identical reactions. "Frank got to the customer first. Had already tied him up to tow him in."

"Oh, well, that was nice of him."

"Too nice?" I asked.

My dad tousled my hair. "Ah, don't be so cynical, kid. One can never be too nice."

I disagreed. Frank could be too nice, and there had to be a reason.

* * *

By Monday night, my skin felt hot from too much sun. I hadn't applied enough sunblock for the amount of time I'd spent outside over the weekend. This afternoon, it had taken me an entire hour to teach one tourist family how to use a paddle-boat. They kept turning it in circles.

I flipped on my ceiling fan and lay back on my bed, letting the air cool my skin. I reached over to my nightstand and retrieved my phone, then clicked on the icon that was like a portal straight into everyone's lives. I scrolled down the page of pictures to see how everyone else had spent their weekend. Most of the people I followed were acquaintances from school and yet I felt like I knew way more about them than I should. Maybe that's what kept me from posting more than I did: I liked to keep my life to myself.

I paused at a picture of Hunter. He was at some sort of a ranch with horses in the background. He wore a baseball cap but was surrounded by people in cowboy hats. Beneath the pic, he had written: *I guess I'm going to ride a horse for the first time. The things friends can talk me into.*

I clicked on the COMMENT button and typed: *Careful, or you might have to trade out your hat soon.*

My finger hovered over the ENTER button. I hadn't commented on one of his posts in weeks. I deleted the comment and quickly called Alana.

"Hey," she said. "Your child labor is done for the day?"

"They pay me."

"Yeah, yeah. All I know is that it sucks that you are busy on basically every major holiday from May through September."

"Love you, too."

She grumbled something under her breath.

"Guess who I saw on Saturday?" I said. The marina had kept me too busy to hang out or talk with her at all until now.

"Who?"

"Frank Young." I filled her in on what had happened with the WaveRunner and how Frank had asked for a truce.

"What does he want?" Alana asked when I had finished my story.

"Right? That's exactly what I wondered." I was glad Alana agreed with me that his intentions couldn't possibly be pure.

"Good thing I'm his partner in podcasting. I can keep an eye on him."

"Yes, please do. And report any suspicious activity."

She laughed. "I will infiltrate enemy lines to figure this out for you."

I opened the top drawer of my desk, pulled out a half full bottle of aloe, and began applying it to my shoulders. "How was *your* weekend?" I asked.

"Very productive. I completely randomly ran into Diego at the Oak Court grocery store."

"Completely randomly you just happened to be in a grocery store thirty minutes away from where you live at the same time Diego was there?"

"Okay, so I may have gotten some intel."

"From who?"

"Remember that guy I talked to who was hanging out with Diego at lunch? Bennett?"

"Yes."

"Sometimes I text him and ask him what he's doing. Then he tells me, and occasionally he's with Diego so then *voilà*, I find out where Diego is."

I shook my head with a laugh. "You seriously should consider being a detective when you grow up."

"No. Then I wouldn't get to be a chef . . . or a newscaster. Or maybe I could have my own cooking show, and it would be like the best of both worlds."

"That does sound like the perfect career path for you." I put the cap back on the bottle of aloe. "So? You ran into Diego at the grocery store and what happened?"

"We talked for like fifteen minutes. It was great."

"Only fifteen minutes?"

"I had convinced my mom we needed groceries and she was checking out, so I had to leave."

"Oh." I popped the aloe bottle back in my desk and sat down on my bed again. "And?"

"And what?" she asked.

"Were you able to listen to his voice and confirm he was the guy who called in to the podcast?"

"I was able to listen to his voice. But I'm still not sure he was the mystery caller."

I pursed my lips. *She* may not have been sure, but I was fairly certain. I'd have to talk to him myself.

# CHAPTER 13

I sat cross-legged on my bed, my Math textbook on one side of me, my History book on the other. In my ears, the *Movie Mashup* podcast was playing. My attempt at multitasking wasn't going well.

Jerry, the podcast host, was saying, "The problem: They made the monster talk. They turned him from a horrific monster à la *Alien* to the relatable, sympathetic monster of *E.T.* who just needed to be sent back to his motherland. It wasn't scary. I found myself rooting for the misunderstood monster. And when they blow his head off in the end, I was angry. Listeners? Agree or disagree?"

Jerry hosted the show by himself. He occasionally took a caller. He played sound bites of movies, did reviews, and rarely had anything good to say about them. I wondered why he watched them at all, when he hadn't liked a single one so far. Half the time he made me question whether *I* had really liked a movie I had seen, but he was funny, so I could forgive him.

My mom appeared in my doorway.

"Hey," she said with a smile. "Listening to a new podcast?"

I tugged my earbuds out and nodded. "I know it doesn't

technically count as homework," I said. But Wednesday was nearly here again, and I didn't feel like anything would be different than the week before without some extra preparing.

"It's okay," Mom said. "You seem to be having a good time in that class."

It had been more stressful than fun, but that wouldn't prove the point that I wanted to eventually make to my parents: that I could love something else and still choose the lake.

"Yeah, it's . . . different," I said.

Mom smiled. "I listened to your second podcast yesterday. It was good."

"I still have some work to do."

"I just hope you're not getting graded on the amount of words you say per episode." Mom winked at me, as if it was a joke, but it felt like her passive-aggressive way of telling me I needed to talk more. I didn't need her to tell me; I already knew.

"Well, I better get back to this." I held up an earbud.

"Good luck."

* * *

As I walked through the parking lot the next morning, I saw a guy holding a poster next to a car filled with balloons. Had someone driven that thing with all those balloons in it? That didn't seem safe. The poster read: *It took a lot of hot air to ask you to the Fall Festival. Please don't deflate me with a no.* A girl read the poster with both hands over her mouth. Then she squealed and threw her arms around the boy's neck.

"Isn't that sweet?" Alana said, coming up beside me with her bookbag on one shoulder.

"Nothing says sweet like using 'hot air' in a sentence."

"How did Hunter ask you last year? I forgot."

"He walked up to me while I was getting my Math book out of my locker and said, 'So . . . Fall Festival?' "

Alana snorted. "And you said yes to *that*?"

"We had this discussion a year ago."

"And was I outraged then, too? Please tell me I was."

"You were."

"Good, because that's ridiculous. But Victoria was right. Apparently you're not the type of girl who needs an elaborate ask."

"A sincere one would've been nice, though," I said, repeating what I'd said on the podcast.

"What?" Alana said. "A negative review of something Hunter did? It's a miracle!"

"Whatever. I just don't need to witness any more of these invitations today. They're depressing me."

* * *

I shouldn't have put a request out in the universe like that, because that school day I got to witness three more people being asked to the Fall Festival. I was relieved that I made it to my last period without permanently damaging my eyes with all the rolling they'd done.

Ms. Lyon stood at the front of the classroom and cleared her throat. "I need your attention and your brains for a minute, class."

Victoria, who had been telling me about the subtleties of voice inflection, stopped talking and turned toward Ms. Lyon.

"This year we've been assigned a booth at the Fall Festival carnival."

"We have to work a booth?" Victoria cried. "A lot of us will have dates!"

I refrained from rolling my eyes for the millionth time that day.

Ms. Lyon nodded. "Yes, that's why I wanted to discuss the best options for the night. We can definitely take turns at the booth. Maybe do thirty-minute shifts. But first we need to think of an idea for the booth itself. I'm told dart throw, rope ladder climb, and basketball are already taken."

"What about that carnival game where people throw quarters on plates?" Mallory suggested.

Ms. Lyon wrote *Quarter Toss* on the board. "More ideas?"

"Something with water guns?" Jamie called out.

"Frog racing," Alana offered.

"We're a podcasting class," Frank said. "We should do a podcast. Right there at the carnival. With everyone watching." He raised his eyebrows at me.

Alana, who was sitting beside Frank, elbowed him in the ribs. "A carnival isn't exactly the best place to record a podcast."

"No. Wait. It's a good idea!" Victoria said, brightening. "A live audience. There will be clapping and cheering and a fun energy. We should totally do it."

A couple of other classmates gave me sideways glances, like I was going to jump out of my chair and protest this idea. I wanted to—a live show sounded like my worst nightmare—but I didn't do anything. I'd learned Ms. Lyon's game. She liked to push people to stretch themselves. The more I protested, the more she'd dig in that we *had* to do a live show. Instead, I'd sit here and pretend like this idea sounded like the best thing in the world.

"Maybe we can gather questions that week during lunch," Mallory suggested. "If we have a big sealed box, then people can just drop their questions in a slot at the top."

Ms. Lyon was starting to slowly nod. Uh-oh. That wasn't a good sign.

"And we can take live questions the night of the carnival, too," Victoria said.

Alana was still trying to help me. "But the carnival is loud," she said. "Are we expecting everyone to stop what they're doing just to listen to our show?"

"We'll set the show up on the outskirts of the fair," Ms. Lyon said. "We'll rope off the area. And we'll use specific types of microphones that won't pick up so much surrounding noise." Her eyes sparkled behind her glasses. "This is a great idea, guys. We'll have some members of our class present it to the student council for approval. Okay, now back to work."

A live audience in less than four weeks? I wanted to groan. I wanted to run and hide.

But no. I sat up straighter. I needed to change my attitude. I *could* do a live show. It would be no different than the class watching me through the glass, right? Plus, I had a few more weeks of our not-live podcast to help me prepare. And I'd listen to more outside podcasts for practice. This would be another chance for me to prove to my parents that I was good at something besides the lake. I'd even invite them to the live show. They could see it for themselves.

After class, Alana and I walked down the hall together. "You okay?" Alana asked.

I nodded.

"Really? Maybe we can ask Ms. Lyon if other people can host that night, since it's a special night. It would give other people in the class a chance to practice."

Although part of me wanted to look for a way out, I knew I should try to stick with my plan. "I can handle it," I told Alana. Then I noticed Diego in the hallway up ahead. "Look," I whispered to Alana. "There's Diego. You should go say hi."

Alana grabbed my hand and squeezed. "I'm staying with you." She waved to him as we walked past, and he waved back.

"Is my confidence in the podcast scaring you this much?" I asked my friend.

She laughed. "Yes. You should be freaking out right now."

I didn't have time to freak out. I had a podcast to master.

# CHAPTER 14

"It's our favorite day of the week," Victoria said into the mic after we'd finished giving our opening lines.

"Speak for yourself," I said.

Victoria laughed. "Kat loves all of you, she just has a hard time showing it. But it looks like you guys love us, too, because I've been told four callers are waiting on the lines."

Mallory patched the first one through.

"You're on *Not My Problem*," Victoria said.

The caller came in fast. "My parents favor my younger sister, and I don't know what to do about it. They are constantly comparing me to her. Asking me why my grades aren't as good as hers, why I don't dress as nicely as her, why I don't want to wear the style of makeup she wears. It's frustrating and I don't know how to make them see me as my own person."

"Have you told them that it frustrates you when they do this stuff?" Victoria asked.

"They get defensive, say that's not what they're trying to do. That they are just pointing out things that I can improve on."

"By using your sister as the measuring stick?" I ask.

"Exactly."

"That *is* frustrating," I said.

"I think she wants real advice, Kat," Victoria said, "not just an agreement."

"Oh, right, I'd almost forgotten why people call in."

The girl laughed a little. "It's actually nice to hear someone agree with me. I'm so used to having to defend my side against people who don't."

"Your friends don't agree with you?" Victoria asked.

"I don't really talk to my friends about family drama."

"Well, there's your first piece of advice from me," Victoria said. "You need to vent more. It helps."

"I agree with Victoria. Venting is validating. Whoa, that was a lot of Vs." I was learning to just say whatever came into my head. It seemed to work well for the other podcast hosts I'd been listening to lately.

"And just keep trying," Victoria said. "Hopefully your parents will hear you."

*Advice. Advice. Come on, Kate, you can think of actual advice, not just snark.* "Write a letter," I blurted out. "Sometimes, when someone can read something, without being able to interrupt, they process it better. They don't get as defensive."

"I haven't tried that one yet," the caller replied. "I think I will."

"Good luck," Victoria said. When the caller hung up, Victoria gave me a little nod. I wasn't sure if that meant she approved of my input or what, but it seemed encouraging.

Mallory put the next caller through.

"Caller, you're on *Not My Problem.* How can we help?" Victoria asked.

"I'm a vegetarian," the caller said.

"Is that the problem?" I asked.

"Well, it's part of the problem. I get that people can't make special accommodations for me all the time. But whenever my friends and I go out, they want to go to Burger Palace. You know, the place that only sells burgers?"

"They sell fries, too," I said.

"I would know. That's all I ever get. And I don't mind tagging along with them week after week, but every once in a while, I'd love it if they wanted to go somewhere *I* want to go. Every time I suggest a new place, they turn their nose up at it and say that I can meet them at Burger Palace with my *special* food."

"Tina?" Victoria asked. "Is that you?"

"I want to be anonymous," the caller said.

"So you call my podcast?"

"It's not yours. It's Kat's, too."

"It's actually our whole class's—" I started to say but was cut off.

"Sometimes we go to your places," Victoria said into the microphone, looking much more flustered than usual. "We don't go to Burger Palace *every* time. But there's five of us and one of you!"

I bit my knuckle to keep from laughing, took a deep breath, and said, "Come on, Victoria, you really should go someplace that offers more veggie options. Burger Palace?"

Victoria rolled her eyes. "I know. The guys always pick it. I'm sorry, Tina. I didn't realize it was bothering you so much."

"Are you really going to use my name on air?" Tina asked.

"Do you think people won't know who you are? There are only like ten vegetarians at this school!" Victoria said.

Tina laughed. "I'm sure there's more than ten. But, fine, hi, everyone! Can we lay off Burger Palace?"

"Yes, Tina. Your dissent has been noted," Victoria said. Then she added, "My friends aren't allowed to call in anymore."

I laughed this time, the kind of laugh Victoria always gave, the ones I always thought she forced. Maybe they were real.

We were on a roll and three callers still waited, which meant another one had called in while we were talking.

Victoria answered the next one. "You're on *Not My Problem*, we're listening."

"Hello?" the caller said. "Am I allowed to call again?"

My heart jumped to my throat. It was him. The guy who had called last time. The one I'd thought was Diego. He was still using a husky voice to hide his identity.

"Yes, of course," Victoria said. "What can we help you with today? Did you talk to your parents about a schedule?"

"No, I'm still working on that. But I was thinking about something else you said."

"Which part?" Victoria asked.

"The last part, about how something else might be making me more aware of my time constraints lately."

The more he talked, the more I could hear his distinct inflections, the tone of his voice. It was Diego. It had to be. My tongue seemed tied to the roof of my mouth; I couldn't speak. I was glad Victoria never seemed to get tongue-tied.

"So is it the girl? The one you mentioned last week?" she asked. My eyes shot to Alana. She was sitting next to Frank on the couch, taking her job of infiltrating enemy lines seriously. They shared a laptop and were distracted by something on the screen, obviously not listening to the voice that was being broadcasted on their end through the speakers.

The guy who sounded like Diego answered, "Maybe. Is that lame? I can't let a girl make me resentful of my family."

Finally, Alana seemed to register the voice she was hearing. She looked up and her eyes shot over to me. *You think?* she mouthed.

I nodded.

"Maybe the feelings of resentment were always there. This new situation is just making them more apparent," Victoria suggested.

"That's probably true," he said.

"What do you like about this girl?" Victoria asked, shifting on her stool.

"She's nice and funny and just easy to be with."

I raised my eyebrows at Alana, who grinned.

"That's so sweet," Victoria said.

"It would be," he said. "But I don't think she feels the same way about me."

Alana's eyes went even wider with that statement.

"Why do you say that?" I was finally able to spit out.

"I don't know. I just sense it, I guess. When we're somewhere together, she doesn't stick around for long. And," he continued, "she seems altogether indifferent toward me."

"Indifferent?" I echoed. Alana was not indifferent toward anyone.

"Well, she treats me the same as she treats everyone else."

Oh, that made more sense. Alana did sort of treat everyone the same, with her fun and flirty ways.

"Ah," Victoria said. "Maybe she's trying to tell you something in a nice way without hurting your feelings. Maybe it's best to move on."

"No!" I let out in a loud burst. I cleared my throat. "I mean, no, I think maybe you're reading into it too much. Maybe she's just shy."

Alana bugged her eyes out, and I nearly laughed. *Shy* was not a word anyone used to describe Alana.

"If she's shy and you come on too strong, you might scare her away," Victoria said.

"Yeah," the caller said. "I guess my question is: How do I find out if she likes me without scaring her away? I enjoy hanging out with her. I don't want to ruin that by pushing my feelings into it if it's just going to make things weird between us."

It was hard to get the advice for this one right. He was asking as an anonymous caller, and unlike Victoria with her friend, I wasn't going to call him out. Plus, what if it really *wasn't* Diego? What if he wasn't talking about Alana at all? I knew I needed to treat this like I didn't have insider information here. Especially because maybe I didn't.

So I said, "Why is everyone in such a rush to jump into a relationship? What happened to good old-fashioned patience? If this girl is worth it, and like you said, you don't want to ruin the friendship, can't you just see how it naturally plays out?"

Alana crossed her arms over her chest and gave me a pout.

"I say just go in for the kiss," Victoria said with a laugh. "The sooner the better to see if this is going to work out."

Alana gave a thumbs-up to that advice.

"You have the opposite sides of the spectrum here," I said. "I guess you'll have to go with your gut. My gut is always wrong, so good luck with that."

He gave a polite chuckle.

"Yeah, I didn't think it was that funny, either," I said.

"No, it's not that. I'm just conflicted now."

"You are the sweetest," Victoria said. "Will you please call back next week and give us an update?"

"I'll try."

He hung up and it took everything in me not to whip off my headphones that moment and race out of the booth toward Alana. I was proud of myself for sitting through two more calls and Victoria's closing spiel. I even added a "Yes, thank you" at a point where I was almost certain it made sense.

When we shut down the equipment, before I could run out, Ms. Lyon came into the booth.

"A word," she said to me and Victoria.

We exchanged a look. Were we in trouble?

Ms. Lyon cleared her throat. "A caller wanted to be anonymous today, and you didn't allow that to happen. We've promised the callers anonymity."

"I know, I'm sorry," Victoria said. "I made sure I didn't say her name after just recognizing her voice. Only after she shared all those personal details. Everyone would have thought it was weird if I didn't recognize her after that. Tina's one of my best friends."

Ms. Lyon crossed her arms. "So I shouldn't have tomorrow's lab edit all of that out?"

"I can talk to her and make sure," Victoria replied, "but I think in the end she thought it was great."

"Okay," Ms. Lyon said solemnly. "Please let me know tomorrow in class."

Victoria nodded, then hooked her arm through my elbow. We walked out of the booth and through the otherwise empty outer room together. When we arrived outside in the hall, we both laughed.

"I thought she was firing us for a minute there," Victoria said.

"I did, too."

"And you didn't seem relieved about it."

"I would've been when it sunk in."

"Kate!" Alana called from where she was waiting at the end of the hall.

"See you tomorrow," I said to Victoria.

"Bye."

I walked as fast as I could until I collided with Alana.

"So?" I said as soon as I reached her. "It sounded like him, right?"

"Why is he changing his voice?" Alana asked.

"Maybe he doesn't trust us," I said, and laughed.

"He'd be right not to," she said.

"But if it is him, he's right, you *are* sending him mixed messages."

"I don't think I am. He's probably just not used to having to work to get a girl. He's going to have to try a little harder with me. I have faith in my ways."

I rolled my eyes.

"*Or* I could just tell him that I know he's been calling in to the podcast," Alana offered.

"No! You can't do that," I said.

"Why?"

"Ms. Lyon made a huge deal about the whole anonymity thing just now. We got a stern talking-to."

"About how Victoria outed her friend?"

"Yes. But Victoria smoothed it over because her friend had given lots of clues to her identity."

"True."

"Diego hasn't given any clues. He could literally be anyone. So be patient. If it's him, he obviously likes you. Just make yourself available. Hang out with him more. It's only a matter of time. He'll either kiss you, like Victoria told him to do, or wait for it to happen naturally, like I told him to."

"Why did you tell him that?" Alana asked.

"I wanted my advice to help others, too. Do you honestly want guys just walking around kissing all the girls they like if the girls aren't into them? I just saved all of girl-manity."

"Or at least the ones here at Sequoia High."

"Right."

"Well, if I can't tell him, then I'm shifting to DEFCON 1 on the flirting. Time to up my game." Alana gave a decisive nod. "I'm asking him out."

# CHAPTER 15

"Are you having Cousins' Night tomorrow?" Alana asked me. It was Thursday after school and we were walking down the hall toward the exit.

"Yep. It's the second weekend of the month and it's my family. We will have Cousins' Night until the end of days."

"You sound like this one is more of a cruel and unusual punishment than normal."

"No, it's the normal angst. You know I secretly love it."

"Yes, I do. And it's fun and weird and when I asked Diego if he wanted to do something tomorrow night and he said he was watching his niece and nephew, I may have invited them all to your Cousins' Night."

I stopped in the middle of the crowded hall and turned toward Alana. "You *what*!"

Someone bumped into me from behind and Alana tugged on my arm to move me forward again. "This is all part of my DEFCON 1 flirting phase," she explained calmly.

"Inviting him to *my* house?"

"I know. Are you mad?"

"Um . . . I'm trying to decide."

My family was . . . well, my family. Outsiders had a hard time understanding our living situation. Even Hunter had always thought it was a bit odd.

Alana and I pushed through the doors and walked outside into the parking lot. I let out a breath.

"You know, Samantha and Tami would make fun of you for this idea of a first date," I said at last.

"Who are Samantha and Tami?"

"From the podcast you recommended? *First Dates*."

"Oh. Right. Well, Diego thought it sounded like a lot of fun and that his niece and nephew would love it."

"So you've already prewarned him about the Bailey family situation?"

"I kind of had to."

"Okay." I stopped at my car, accepting the reality of the situation. "So I guess there will be guests at my Cousins' Night, then."

Alana gave me a kiss on the cheek. "Thank you, thank you!"

* * *

Cousins' Night was in full swing—popcorn everywhere, video games on the big screen, comic-book action scenes being acted out in the corner, and my energy nearly drained—when the doorbell rang. Levi, my seven-year-old cousin, who was closest to the door, answered it while I worked my way around the couch cushions dotting the floor.

"Kate, the carpet is lava!" Cora said.

"Oh, right." I jumped on a cushion and continued my journey to the door.

"Are you guys cousins?" I heard Levi asking when I hopped off the last cushion and onto the tile entryway.

Alana and Diego stood there, along with two kids.

"They are honorary cousins tonight, Levi," I said, pulling my young cousin aside. "You know Alana."

Levi shrugged and ran off.

"Hi, guys," I said, opening the door wider.

Alana had a big smile on her face. "This is Camilla, and that's Samuel." She pointed to the two dark-haired, brown-eyed kids standing with Diego. The little boy looked like a mini version of Diego. He was adorable. They both were. But they also both looked a bit apprehensive.

"Hi, I'm Kate. How old are you guys?"

Diego put his hand on Camilla's head and said, "Seven." Then he moved his hand to Samuel's. "And ten."

"Nice. Levi is seven, and my cousin Morgan is ten." I stepped aside. "Come in. There are snacks in the kitchen, comic-book acting in that corner, video games in that one, and board games in the dining room."

Liza, who'd been hanging out with Max in the comic-book acting corner, strolled over to see what was happening. "Diego?" she asked in surprise.

"Hey, Liza," he said. "Which comic book are you acting out?"

"One Max wrote. It's pretty awesome."

A beanbag flew past me and hit Diego in the shoulder. I winced, but he only leaned over, picked it up, and lobbed it toward Morgan on the other side of the room. Morgan shrieked and ducked behind a cushion before it hit her.

Camilla took this as a sign to join the beanbag war while Samuel wandered over to the video gamers. Levi promptly handed him a controller. Alana's smile had turned to a nervous *What have I done?* face, but Diego didn't seem fazed at all.

I gestured around the room. "What's your poison?"

"Observation?" Alana asked, pointing to the couch.

"If we're only going to observe, I want snacks first," Diego said.

This was the first time I'd talked to Diego since his second call in to the podcast, and I listened carefully to his voice to make sure I had been right.

"What?" he asked.

"What?" I echoed.

"Why are you staring at me like that? Do I have something on my face?" He ran a hand across his cheeks and forehead, pushing his wavy locks to the side.

"No. I just . . . I . . . what were you asking for?"

"Snacks," Alana said, giving me wide eyes.

"Oh, right. Follow me. But the carpet is lava so choose your path carefully." I led the way to the kitchen and turned once to see Diego and Alana actually using cushions and blankets along with me to avoid the carpet. Alana had a hold of

Diego's shoulder to help her on her journey and they were both laughing.

"The tile is safe?" Alana asked as we reached the kitchen.

"Very safe," I said. "Plates and bowls are over there. Help yourself."

"Gummy worms?" Diego asked. "I don't remember the last time I've been to a party with gummy worms."

"I wouldn't really consider this a party," I said. "More like family chaos."

Diego loaded up his plate with gummy worms and chips. Alana got a bowl of popcorn. I opted for a handful of M&M's since I'd already had at least a plateful earlier. We took our treats back to the other room. Alana stopped in front of the couch and was about to sit when she realized all the cushions were gone—they were being used as safe zones.

"Oh, give me a sec." I ran to the guest room and stole a pile of pillows. I spread them out on the couch and we all sat. Diego was in the middle with Alana and me on either side. I watched Samuel win a game of *Mario Kart* on the big screen. He lifted both hands in the air and gave a loud cheer.

"He's very gracious in victory," Diego said.

I smiled.

"What were you doing before we got here?" Diego asked, using a chip to point around the room.

"*Mario Kart* champion."

"She's a gracious winner, too," Alana said.

Diego laughed.

"Are you the youngest in your family?" I asked Diego, thinking about the fact that he already had a niece and nephew.

"Yes, and my sister is the oldest. There are two in between. The brother just above me is in college and the one above that lives across the country."

"Three boys and a girl," Alana said as if she'd already had this conversation with him.

"Alana is the youngest, too," I said. "Her two older sisters are in college."

Why I felt the need to give Alana's family dynamics, I wasn't sure, because once again, when Diego only nodded, I could tell they'd had this conversation.

"That's why Kate comes to my house when she wants quiet." She actually had to yell this sentence over the noise in the room.

"Where are all the parents?" Diego asked.

"So once a month, they have a grown-ups' dinner party next door and we do Cousins' Night."

He smirked at this. "They know how to work the system."

"Yes, they do." I didn't begrudge them for it, though. "But it's nice. It helps them stay close. It helps us all stay close."

"True," he said.

Alana had been quiet for a few minutes, and I looked over to see her typing furiously on her phone. Diego just shrugged when he observed the same thing.

Levi opened the back door before I could tell him no, and Uncle Tim's dog came barreling in. CD immediately went to

Diego and sniffed his elbow, then proceeded to lay his body across Diego's legs. Diego let out a surprised grunt but then he scratched the dog behind the ears.

"CD, no." I shoved him off, which was much harder than it looked. Max, seeing the commotion, came over and took the dog by the collar and led him back outside.

"Thanks, Max!" I called after him.

"CD?" Diego asked, brushing some fur off his pants. "Do you have an obsession with music storage?"

"It stands for Community Dog. We share him. Along with the trampoline and the gazebo."

Diego laughed. "That's new."

"It's okay to say weird."

"Weird is relative."

Before I could ask him to clarify, Cora, my four-year-old cousin, came running toward me, crying. She flung herself onto my lap, saying something I couldn't understand.

I patted her back. "What happened?"

"Levi stole it."

"What did he steal?" I asked.

"My candy."

Diego held out his plate, which still had a pile of gummy worms on it. "Do you want some of mine?"

Cora immediately stopped crying, proving it was a fake cry to begin with. She nodded. When she picked up one worm and brought it to her mouth, Diego said in a small voice, "Noooo, don't eat me."

Cora burst out laughing. "Candy doesn't talk."

Diego widened his eyes. "That sounded like talking to me. You might not want to eat it."

Cora shoved the candy in her mouth and ran off. I smiled.

Alana slammed her phone down on her leg. "Ugh."

"What is it?" I asked.

"Guess who has to keep the same partner in podcasting with the new jobs? Guess who is the only one in the whole class who does?"

"Me?" I asked.

"Aside from you," she said.

"Umm . . . Mallory?" I guessed again.

"Funny. No, me. Even after my speech about how changing partners challenges us."

"Maybe that's why you had to keep the same partner. Because Ms. Lyon knew you wanted to change. That seems to be what she does."

"You're probably right. Ugh," Alana said again. "And now Frank's texting me about bringing me the partner contract that's due on Monday because he's going out of town."

I had forgotten about partner contracts. They were in the binders that day we'd been assigned our roles. The contracts basically said we had to put equal work and support into the project.

"I told him to drop it off here," Alana added.

"What? Why?" Diego at my house was one thing; Frank was a whole different story.

"Because he's leaving tomorrow."

"Oh." I looked around the living room at the craziness.

"Don't worry about it," Diego said. "It's called having a family."

"All right," I said with a sigh, and Alana texted Frank back.

Why did I let her talk me into things?

A beanbag zipped by my head at the same moment that my phone buzzed in my pocket. I pulled my phone out and saw that I had a new text.

How have you been?

It was from Hunter.

# CHAPTER 16

My heart seemed to stop in my chest. A text from Hunter. After all these weeks.

"I . . ." I held up my phone. "I'll be right back."

Alana gave me a questioning look and Diego just nodded. I didn't pause to explain anything to Alana, I just went to my room. I stared at the text some more, biting my lip so hard I almost bled. I released my lip from my teeth and startled when Alana appeared in my doorway.

"What's wrong?" she asked. Then, without waiting for my answer, she marched forward and held out her hand for my phone.

I placed the phone in her upturned palm, knowing I needed some of her classic advice right then.

She read the text and her face went from curious to angry. "Kathryn Bailey, you better not be thinking about responding to this."

"I haven't decided yet."

"Don't. It's time to officially let go. And look, now it will be *your* decision, not his."

I sat down on the edge of my bed, my heartbeat slowing. "I don't even remember what his voice sounds like. Is that weird?"

"Why are you trying to remember what his voice sounds like? Stop it." Alana walked over and sat down beside me. "And no, it's not weird, because you haven't talked to him in months. Months! That's what happens when he never calls or texts or responds to you."

"Okay, I get it," I said.

"And . . ."

"And I'm not going to respond." And I wasn't. She was right, of course. Why should I?

The doorbell rang, and Alana handed me back the phone. "That would be Frank," she said. "I better go collect the contract so he can be on his way."

I followed her out of my room. Despite what I'd said seconds ago, I actually wasn't convinced that my willpower would hold up if I was alone. A quick scan of the living room revealed that Diego was now sitting over by Liza and Max, reading through some papers, probably Max's comic.

Alana opened the door and instead of just collecting the contract and sending Frank on his way, she invited him inside. Guess I should've answered the door with her.

I went to intercept them before Frank made it any farther into the living room.

"Kitty Kat," Frank said when I reached the two of them.

"Don't call her that," Alana said. "She hates it. You are purposefully trying to annoy her."

"I didn't know she hated it," he said. "That's the name she uses on the podcast. That's the name you used when you called in from the hall that first day," he added to Alana with a grin.

"Shh," Alana said. "Where's the contract?"

Frank was wearing his backpack and he slung it off his shoulder. He knelt down to rifle through it. Diego walked over to join our group of three.

"Hey, Frank," Diego said. "You're ditching school Monday?"

"Soccer tournament with my traveling team."

"You two know each other?" Alana asked.

"We go to the same school," Frank said.

Alana looked at me. "That means nothing."

"It's true," I said. "I know nobody."

"Now everyone knows you, though," Diego pointed out.

I gave a single laugh. "I try not to think about that."

Frank freed the contract from his bookbag. "Here it is." He handed the stapled papers to Alana. "I already signed my part. Even the part about how we're supposed to get along and look out for each other."

"Are you saying I don't do that?" Alana asked, sharing a frustrated look with me.

"I said nothing," he said.

"No, you said something in that supercondescending voice you like to use." Wow. I was used to being more hostile toward Frank than Alana was. What had changed? Did she find out he really was exactly who I thought he was, despite our supposed truce? I'd have to ask her for more details later.

"I have no idea what voice you're talking about," Frank was saying.

"That voice," Alana snapped. "You just used it again."

"That's my voice. I can't do anything about it."

Diego started walking slowly backward. He grabbed hold of my sleeve and pulled me along with him as Alana and Frank kept fighting. We made it to the kitchen before we both started laughing.

"What's going on with those two?" he asked.

"Frank is not our favorite person," I explained.

"Why?" he asked.

"Longstanding family feud."

"Over what?"

"Land, basically."

"What is this, the Wild West?"

"No, more like the Roman Empire," I said.

"There's two sides to every story," Frank said as he walked into my kitchen. Why was Frank in my kitchen?

My eyes went to Alana, who said, "Keep your enemies closer?"

"Are you staying?" I asked Frank, appalled.

"You see, Diego," Frank said, ignoring my question. "My family and Kate's family are like the Montagues and Capulets. Our grandparents were sworn enemies and the hate has been passed down from generation to generation."

"Did you just compare us to Romeo and Juliet?" I asked.

Frank picked up a gummy worm and popped it in his mouth. "I did."

"Not sure that has the ending you want," Diego said.

Frank contorted his lips into a frown, seeming to consider whether or not Diego's statement was true.

Diego threw an M&M at him.

Frank laughed. "Hey. Did I see you out fishing the other day in a crappy boat?" he asked Diego.

"Yep," Diego said.

"Next time, text me. Then you can fish in the lap of luxury," Frank offered.

"Are you referring to *your* lap?" Alana asked him.

"Ha ha," Frank said.

"Well, nobody talks like that," Alana said.

"Obviously, somebody does because I just said it."

"You shouldn't have," she retorted. "That's my point. It's gross. I'm trying to help you out here so we can let you be around real people."

This time Frank picked up an M&M and threw it at Alana with a smirk on his face. Maybe Alana knew how to play him after all.

A loud bang and laughter sounded from the other room.

Alana jumped, then took a deep breath. "We should calm all the kids down," she said. "Maybe we should put on one of those boring documentaries you love, Kate."

I grinned at my friend. "I sense that was meant to be an insult, but I wholeheartedly agree."

* * *

It only took thirty minutes for the soothing voice of Morgan Freeman on the penguin documentary to quiet down the cousins and lull Cora to sleep. She had snuggled up between me and Diego on the couch and was now leaning against Diego's arm, eyes closed.

"That's so adorable," Alana said. She was right, it really was.

I looked around but realized Frank wasn't on the far side of Alana where I had last seen him. "Where is Frank?" I asked.

"He went to the bathroom."

"I'll make sure he didn't get lost." I didn't trust Frank Young wandering my house alone. And I was right not to. When I made it to the hall, he was coming out of my dad's office. He looked alarmed when he saw me.

"What are you doing?" I demanded.

"I was looking for the bathroom."

"And that took walking all the way into my dad's office?"

"I didn't walk all the way in. I was just shutting the door when you saw me."

That wasn't true. I knew what I'd seen.

"You have trust issues, Kat," Frank whispered, then walked to the next door, the actual bathroom, and shut himself inside.

I did not have trust issues. I had Frank issues. I walked into my dad's office and straight to his desk to see what Frank might have been able to find. In the top middle drawer, I knew, was a ledger that recorded outgoing and incoming money. I'd never looked at it myself. I opened the drawer and rubbed my hand over the cover. What could seeing our financial information do for Frank or his family? Not much. That was between my parents and their lenders. My hand stopped at the edge of the cover. But what if our business was in trouble? Was that why my parents were pushing me to do something else besides the marina? To try other things?

I flipped open the book and stared at the numbers on the page. These numbers would have to carry us through the off-season, but I was surprised by how good they were. My parents were doing great, actually. So what was their problem? Were they trying to subtly tell me that I might not be good at running the marina? I shut the drawer and came out of the office just as Frank came out of the bathroom.

"The bathroom is right here, Kate," he said. "Might not want to go nosing around."

I shoved his arm, feeling a little guilty. My parents' finances really weren't *my* business, either. "You aren't funny."

Frank and I walked back into the living room together. Both Alana and Diego looked our way.

"Found him," I said, by way of explanation.

Frank glanced at the TV screen. "I like penguins as much as the next guy, but I'm going to go now." He headed toward the door, and Alana stood and followed him, probably wanting to interrogate him about what he'd been doing wandering around my house. I hoped she could find out more than I had.

Cora was still leaned up against Diego's arm. I looked at my phone. It was already eleven o'clock. Although I had been doing a good job of not thinking about Hunter's text, I couldn't help myself now. I pulled it up and stared at it. I should've deleted it. I didn't, though. I just tucked my phone away.

"Here, let me take Cora to bed," I said, finishing the walk to the couch.

"I got her. Can I carry her somewhere?" Diego shifted her into his arms and stood.

"Her bed is in the house next door."

"Lead the way," he said.

"Right." We walked outside and turned right. The grown-ups were having dinner at my aunt Marinn's house, so Uncle Tim's still sat empty. I led Diego around to the back glass door. Our back doors were all generally left unlocked, so I wasn't surprised when it slid open easily. Diego followed close behind.

We both walked inside the dark living room, and I shut the door behind us. "Light," I whispered. "Let me find a light." I moved toward the wall and tripped on his foot, catching myself on Diego's arm before I fell. Thankfully, I didn't clip Cora's head in the process.

"Sorry," he whispered.

"No, it's my fault. I can't see."

He gave a breathy laugh. I ran my hand along the closest wall and finally found a light switch that turned on a few lights above us.

"Her room is upstairs, follow me."

I switched on lights as we moved through the house until we got to Cora's room. That light I left off so that she wouldn't wake up when we laid her down. I arranged the comforter on her bed, put her pillow in place, then moved aside for Diego. He gently lowered her onto her bed and pulled the blankets up around her. "*Dulces sueños*," he whispered.

We left the room, shutting the door. "What did you say to her?" I asked.

"Have you not taken any Spanish in school? I'm offended," he said, even though it was obvious by his smile that he wasn't.

"I actually did. But I don't remember anything."

"Language is slippery when not practiced."

"For sure." I paused for a minute. "Or when not learned very well to begin with."

We headed down the stairs and he asked, "Are you going to leave her here alone?"

"I'll text her mom and wait here. Will you tell Alana bye for me?"

"Of course." He paused by the back door, his hand on the handle. "*Dulces sueños*. It means 'sweet dreams.' "

"Do you speak Spanish at home?"

"When I was little and my grandparents were around more, I did. Now, not as much."

This probably wasn't a conversation to be having with his hand on a door handle, ready to leave, but I couldn't stop myself from asking, "Where are your grandparents now?"

"My grandmother passed a couple of years ago and my grandfather lives in a home now because he has Alzheimer's."

"I'm sorry," I said.

"It's okay. It's life, right?" He slid open the door. "Bye, Kate."

"Bye, Diego."

He let himself out. I texted my aunt, then stared at the text from Hunter again. After a few minutes, I heard laughter outside. I walked to the living room. It was dark, barely lit by one of the lights I had turned on in another room. I parted the front curtains and watched as Diego, his niece and nephew, and Alana headed along the front walk from my house toward his car. Alana grabbed hold of Diego's hand, pressed it between both of hers, and said something to him. He laughed. Then she picked up Camilla and spun her around before placing her on the ground again. I let the curtains fall back in place.

# CHAPTER 17

"Kathryn!"

My lights flipped on, and I winced against the sudden brightness.

I held my hand up to block the light and sat up, disoriented from sleep. It was Saturday morning and the sun wasn't even up yet. A quick glance at my cell phone showed it was five a.m. "What?" I asked in confusion. "Is everything okay?"

My mom stood over me. "We had a break-in last night."

Now I was fully awake. "Someone broke into our house?"

"No, the marina. They released all the WaveRunners." Mom's face was drawn and worried.

"Released them?" I had no idea what that meant. At night we kept the WaveRunners on the south side of the dock, locked behind chain link.

"They're scattered all over the lake."

I climbed out of bed and opened my dresser to grab one of my swimsuits. "They just let them loose on the lake? They didn't steal them?"

"No, they didn't steal them. We can see them on the GPS, scattered everywhere."

"That's so weird. Did they take the keys, too?" I asked.

"No, they must've had a boat or their own WaveRunner and dragged them around that way," Mom said, turning to go.

"And Patrol didn't catch them? Nobody reported noise on the lake last night?" Powered vehicles on an otherwise quiet night were loud.

"Nothing makes sense. We're still trying to get answers. I'll meet you down there."

She was right. Nothing made sense. I changed into my suit, pulled on a windbreaker, and slipped into a pair of flip-flops. In the hall I met up with Max, who had bedhead and was mumbling about sleep. Together we went out the front door, around the corner, and across the street to the marina. As I passed through the gate and onto the dock, I paused to look at the padlock. It was cut and hanging lopsided on the latch.

Inside the shop, my dad stood talking to my aunt and uncle. CD came over and nudged my leg with his snout until I petted his head. Then he moved on to Max.

"Hey, kids. Any idea how this happened?" Dad asked.

I looked at Max, who shrugged. Why would *we* have any idea?

"Friends playing a prank?" Max offered.

"Friends playing a . . ." I closed my eyes. "Frank?"

"You think the Young boy did this?" Dad asked.

"I don't know; he's the only one I can think of," I answered, my suspicions growing the more I thought about it. "He was here at the marina the other day, saw how we kept things."

Plus, he'd been nosing around our house the night before; maybe he'd seen the inventory list dad kept with the ledger. "He has a boat and a WaveRunner. He could've easily done this. And you know his family has an in with the Patrol and a problem with us."

"I hope you're wrong," my dad said.

Suddenly, I was sure I wasn't. "Where's Mom?" I asked, glancing around the store.

"She went to make a report. Uncle Tim is going to take a boat out to the first WaveRunner and drop you off. You'll drive Max to the next WaveRunner. Take walkie-talkies. I'll direct you both from there. Don't tow more than two at a time, please." He looked at his watch on his wrist. "Hopefully, we can get this done before we open."

On Saturdays, we opened at six a.m. Mainly for our fishing boats and supplies, but also for the hardcore skiers who liked their water like glass, unaffected by the choppiness that more boats on the lake produced.

Uncle Tim patted his leg and CD ran over to him, his tail knocking against some swimsuits, sending the hangers swinging.

Aunt Marinn stilled the hangers. "I'll drive," she said, shoving my uncle so she could get out in front of him. He chased after her.

My dad handed me two sets of keys, for the first two WaveRunners he was directing us to. We could tow in the rest without powering them on. Max retrieved the life jackets and ropes, and we all, including CD, boarded one of our three powerboats, which were nowhere near as nice as Frank's. Uncle Tim shoved us off from the dock, and we were on our way.

The sun would rise over the mountains any minute now, which I was glad for. I may have loved the lake, but the thought of riding alone on it in the dark wasn't an appealing one.

"Looks like we'll avoid the lake monster," I said, poking Max in the ribs. He wasn't a morning person so I knew that was about all the teasing he could probably handle.

"Now we'll just have to deal with the forest one," he said, surprising me. I should've known he'd jump on the family stories. He was a storyteller, after all, with his comics. "She stays out until at least seven."

"Yes, she steals as many fish as she can."

"You two are scaring CD," Uncle Tim said, covering the dog's ears.

"You're right, CD is kind of a wimp." He hid during Fourth of July fireworks, and every time there was a thunderstorm.

"There's one!" my aunt called, pointing out the windshield into the distance. "That's good to see."

My uncle nodded at the sight of the WaveRunner up ahead. "I know. I thought maybe they'd taken the GPS trackers out and thrown them in the lake."

I hadn't even considered that possibility. So we weren't dealing with real thieves, just pranksters. Which made me even more certain it was Frank.

Aunt Marinn pulled up alongside the WaveRunner, and I peered over the side.

"Can you get me any closer?" I asked. End of season water was warmer than beginning of season water, but still, it was too early to get wet this morning.

"Who's a wimp now?" Uncle Tim said.

Aunt Marinn circled one more time, and my uncle was able to reach over and grab hold of the handlebar. I climbed on and Max followed behind me.

The next test was seeing if the runner actually turned on. I stuck the key in the ignition and it powered to life. I breathed a sigh of relief. My uncle handed me the walkie-talkies and ropes I had left on the seat in the boat. Then he and my aunt drove away the boat, waving to me and Max.

I radioed in to my dad to find out the location of the next closest vehicle. It was in the cove.

As Max and I took off, the water was still black, the sky barely a light gray. I thought it would be brighter, but the sun hadn't quite made it yet.

"This is how you wanted to spend your Saturday morning, right?" I called back to Max over the wind.

"You really think Frank did this?"

"Yes," I said. "You don't?"

"I don't know."

"Who else would?"

Max didn't answer, probably because he knew I was right.

For the second time in a week, when I rounded the outcropping of trees and rocks to get to the cove, I saw a boat floating beside our WaveRunner. This time, it was a small fishing boat. No lines were cast and the occupant—a dark-haired guy my age—was sitting on our WaveRunner. He was studying the metal placard we had on all our power vehicles, the one that bore the name of our marina and our phone number. The guy had his phone in the air as if that would help him get a better signal.

He turned at the noise of our arrival. To my surprise, it was Diego.

"Hey!" he called out, obviously recognizing me.

"Hi," I said.

"I was just trying to call the marina."

"There's no signal here in the cove."

"I was learning that." He looked at my brother behind me. "Hey, Max, nice to see you again." Diego stepped off our WaveRunner and back into his boat.

"Hey." Max climbed off the back of one WaveRunner and onto the other.

"You're out early," I said to Diego.

"I have to beat the forest monster to the fish," he said.

Max's eyes shot to Diego. That was a family story. I was surprised, too.

"Where did you hear that?" I asked.

"It must've been your mom who told it to me a couple summers ago when I was buying bait at the marina," Diego said. "I didn't know it was your mom at the time, but she looks a lot like you."

"Yes. She does."

Max used the key I handed him and the engine turned over.

"What happened with the WaveRunner?" Diego asked, nodding toward the one Max was on.

"We're not sure. How long have you been out here?" I asked.

"About an hour or so."

"Did you see anyone out on the lake this morning?"

"I saw a big fancy boat first thing, but I think it was heading in."

I tried to keep my grumble to myself but it was hard.

Max had his own walkie-talkie and he gave me a questioning look.

"Yes, you're good to go," I told him.

"See you around," Diego said, and Max waved at us before taking off.

"You've been out here for a couple hours? By yourself in the dark?" I asked Diego.

"Yes."

"It doesn't scare you out here?"

A slow smile spread across his face. "Does the lake scare you at night?"

"Not the lake. Just the water."

He laughed. "Isn't that the same thing?"

I ran my hand over the handlebar of the WaveRunner and shrugged. It was hard for me to admit there was any aspect of the lake that I didn't love.

"What's wrong?" he asked.

"Nothing. I just . . ." I always said too much around him. He was too easy to talk to. "Nothing. Have you caught anything yet?" I asked, noting the red ice chest in his boat.

His dark eyes danced. "That is a question you are never supposed to ask a fisherman."

"So, no."

"No." He sighed.

"Is this *your* boat?"

"I saved up six months for this piece of garbage and yes, it's all mine."

"I'm impressed, piece of garbage or not. That's a lot of time saving for something. I should save money. Instead I spend it all on gas."

"Gas?"

I patted the WaveRunner. "Yes, I have a problem. Maybe now that fall is coming and I won't go out on the lake as much, I can save up. But I mostly work during the summer. It's ironic. The only time I would have extra money is the time I don't work."

"You don't do snow sports?" Diego asked. "Skiing or snowmobiling or . . . I don't know, what is that sport where you tie baskets to your shoes?"

"That's not a thing, but I don't do any of the above. I need to find some winter hobbies, I guess." I gave his boat a once-over. She actually wasn't as bad as he claimed. She was silver and well maintained. I could tell he took pride in owning her. "What's her name?" I asked.

"I haven't named her yet. I need to."

"Yes, you do. Every boat deserves a name. Might I suggest Forest Monster? Then she might actually catch some fish. She's out early enough."

"Funny."

"I try."

He looked past me to the lake. "I'm surprised Alana isn't with you this morning. You two are always together." He wished Alana were here. That was cute.

"She's sleeping, which is what I'd rather be doing. Only fishermen and moon worshippers are up at this hour. And we know we can't trust either of them."

"For sure."

I powered on my WaveRunner. "I guess I better get back to work."

"Good luck," he said.

It was nice to see Diego out on the lake, like he actually belonged there. Like it wasn't foreign to him. Like it was a destination only thirty minutes away, and not an eternity away like so many people in Oak Court seemed to think. Diego would fit in well with the lake stock. I'd let Alana know.

# CHAPTER 18

"Have you seen Frank?" I came to a breathless stop at Alana's locker Monday morning. I'd run from my car to Frank's locker and now to hers in less than five minutes.

"What?" Alana asked, turning around with books in her arms.

"Frank. Do you know where he'd be right now?"

"He's not here today. Remember? Soccer tournament."

"Oh. Right." I let my anger melt away now that I knew I couldn't confront him.

"Why are you looking for Frank?"

"I want to talk to him about the marina incident." I'd told Alana in hurried texts about what had happened over the weekend but didn't tell her who I thought was responsible. Maybe because I wasn't willing to commit to it until I confronted him. "When did he leave for the tournament?"

"Today. But wait, you think *Frank* did that?"

"Yes."

"It doesn't sound like him."

"He's upping his game."

"Huh. If it was him, I'll find out."

"Me too."

She shut her locker. She was wearing an oversize gray hoodie I'd never seen on her before.

"Is that new?"

She smiled. "It's Diego's."

"Really?"

"He let me wear it Friday night after we left your house."

"And you incorporated it into your wardrobe?" I didn't know why this seemed to bother me.

"I'll give it back to him. But this is Flirting 101: Let a boy see you wearing his clothes."

"Because then he associates you with his possessions?"

She shook her head and shoved my arm. "No. Because he thinks you look cute with his stuff draped around you." She motioned her thumb to the side. "Come on. Let's get to class."

I'd come early to confront Frank, so we still had some time before the bell rang. "I'll meet you there. I need to go to my locker."

"I'll come with you."

We navigated the halls and came to a stop at my locker. I dug below a stack of papers and grabbed my history book.

"Who even needs books for class?" a voice behind me said.

I let out a small yelp and my history book fell to the floor with a slap.

Diego smiled but then bit his lip, looking apologetic. "Sorry, I didn't think talking in a loud hallway could scare someone."

"She can be jumpy," Alana said.

"Noted."

Alana pulled at the sleeves of the hoodie she wore—Diego's hoodie—as if to draw attention to it. "What's up with the golf club?" she asked him.

I hadn't even noticed he was holding a golf club until she'd pointed it out. He moved it up onto his shoulder like a baseball bat.

"Do you golf?" Alana asked.

He took it off his shoulder and held it out as if evaluating it. "Yes and no."

"How is that a real answer?" I asked.

"Well, I don't golf, but I like to go to driving ranges sometimes. And Garrett Wilson bet me that I couldn't hit a golf ball through the goalposts from that big hill behind the stadium, so I did what had to be done."

"What had to be done?" I asked, straight-faced.

Alana laughed. "He had to hit a golf ball through the goalposts. How far do you think that is, anyway?"

"Probably like two hundred yards . . . give or take," he said.

"I'm guessing more take than give," I said.

He chuckled.

"So did you?" I asked.

"Wow," he said, gripping his chest. "You have no faith in me."

"Geez, Kate," Alana said.

"Do I have to prove it to you, too?" he asked.

"I just know that wouldn't be easy."

Diego narrowed his eyes, a smirk on his lips.

Alana squeezed my arm. "There's Bennett. I have to give him some notes from Math. I'll see you in class." She waved to Diego and then was gone. I couldn't tell if this was part of her strategy again. Now that she'd gone on an official date with him (even if it was only to my house) and was wearing his hoodie, was she trying to show him that she had other options?

Diego stared after her, an unreadable expression on his face. Sometimes I wasn't so sure about Alana's strategies.

I turned back to my locker to get my history book but couldn't find it anywhere.

"It fell," Diego said.

"Oh, right." I had forgotten I'd dropped it when he first arrived. I reached down to grab it off the floor. When I stood, my temple whacked into the corner of my locker.

Pain instantly radiated from the point of contact. I threw a hand over it and winced.

"Are you okay?" Diego asked, stepping closer.

"Yes, I'm fine."

"How bad is it?"

"Not bad. Just a little bumped."

"Can I see it?"

I kept my hand at my temple, wondering if it was bleeding. I couldn't feel any moisture. Diego reached up and lightly grabbed my wrist, moving my hand away from my face.

After inspecting it for a moment, he said, "Looks like you'll live."

"Thanks, doctor."

He met my eyes, ignoring my joke. "I'm sorry."

I shrugged it off, embarrassed at the attention.

Still holding loosely on to my wrist, he used his free hand to draw a *V* on my temple with his finger. "Valor. Do you know that word?"

"Yes . . . why?"

"We have that word in Spanish, too. When I used to get hurt, my mom would trace that word on my arm or my head or my back. It's pronounced a little different but it means the same thing in Spanish as it does in English. 'Valor. Courage.' "

I laughed a little. "Are you saying I'm courageous after my near death experience with the locker?"

"Well, it's a noun, not an adjective. So it's more like courage is being given to you."

"Oh, so you're saying I'm not brave and need some."

He smiled and finished spelling out the word on my temple.

My skin seemed to heat up with each letter.

He shrugged. "It works better on seven-year-olds."

"It worked on you?" I asked.

"Always."

I could've sworn it was working on me, too. My head felt perfect. The bell rang.

He released my wrist. "I'll see you around, Kate."

"Yes, see you around," I said.

He left and it took me a minute to remember what I was doing. I looked down at the history book I still held, shook my head, and shoved the texbook in my backpack.

"Kate!" I heard my name being called, and for one second, I thought it was Alana. Had she seen that whole exchange? Why had Diego done that? Because I'd just whacked my head on a locker. Diego was just being nice. He was nice.

I looked around but didn't catch sight of Alana. Seconds later, Liza was pulling on my backpack. She was breathless and dragging a red-haired girl behind her by the arm.

"Kate. Wait up."

I slowed down. "Hi, my cousin, do you not get enough of me at home?" I said.

"This is Chloe," Liza panted. "She wanted to meet you."

Liza's friend had a huge smile on her face and was looking at me like I'd just handed her a hundred dollars. "Hi," she said.

"Um . . . hi?" I gave Liza a questioning look.

"She's a fan of yours," Liza said to clarify, but that didn't help at all.

"What?" I asked.

"The podcast," Liza said, drawing out the words.

"You're a fan of the podcast?" I asked Chloe.

"You, in particular," Liza said. "She thinks you're funny."

"If I'm funny without trying to be, does that still make me funny?"

Chloe laughed. "I really liked your advice about Mrs. Pomroy. Someone asked for study guides in class and it helped."

"Mrs. Pomroy? Oh! That wasn't about her, it was about Mr. . . ." I stopped myself, realizing the offending teacher's name had been edited out.

"Well, either way," Chloe said, "it helped our class, too."

Liza looked like a proud mother when she said, "See, your advice helps people."

"That's great," I said. "Nice to meet you, Chloe."

Chloe beamed at me, as if I were a real celebrity. Then the girls scurried off together. I watched them go, then turned to head to History class. This morning had been weird.

# CHAPTER 19

Are you coming to Liza's tutoring session today? I texted Alana after school, once I was home.

Alana: I'll meet you over there.

Before I left to go to Liza's house, I stopped at Max's bedroom door and knocked twice.

There was a mumbled reply that I interpreted as "Come in," so I opened the door. Max sat at his desk, drawing in a sketchpad.

"Hey, I'm leaving," I said.

"Okay," he answered without looking up.

"Do you want to come with me?"

"Nope."

"You have a lot to say today," I said. He'd been quiet on the ride home, too.

"Yep."

I picked up the nearest article of clothing on his floor, a green Harry Potter shirt, wadded it up, and threw it at the back of his head. Max threw it back. It landed on the floor in front of me, and I noticed it was ripped at the collar.

"What happened to your shirt?" I asked.

"It caught on a fence."

"What fence?"

"The one around the baseball field."

"Fences are just jumping out and grabbing you these days?"

"I took a shortcut through the baseball field after school and the gate was locked. I had to climb it."

"Wow. Look at you being all athletic."

He flexed his biceps, and then shooed me away.

I pulled the door closed and walked next door to my aunt's house. I found Liza in her bedroom sliding her feet into a pair of ballet flats. The first thing she said to me was, "You're totally famous now."

"Because one of your friends thinks I'm cool?"

"It's more people than thought you were cool yesterday."

"You're a brat." I looked her up and down, realizing she'd changed her outfit since getting home from school. "Are you dressed up for Tommy?" I teased.

"This isn't dressed up. I was just gross from school." She picked up her backpack. "You ready to take me?" She was looking at my outfit now, like she thought I should go change.

I glanced down at my jeans, two-toned T-shirt, and Chucks. "What?"

"Nothing," she said. "Let's go."

* * *

When we walked through the front door of the tutoring center, Diego was at the front desk.

"Do you work here every day?" I asked him.

"Mondays, Tuesdays, and Thursdays."

Liza knew the routine now and walked past Diego to meet Tommy at the back tables.

The phone rang and Diego answered it, so I sat down in the waiting area. This time I'd brought my backpack and homework, but it didn't stop me from checking out the magazines. There was another new one: *Hobbies*, it was called. I don't know why I felt the need to note the magazines every time I came in now, but because I'd studied them so closely the first time, the new ones were easy to recognize.

Diego must've noticed me looking, too, because when he hung up the phone he said, "Do you read that one?"

"*Hobbies*? No. But it looks interesting." I dug into my backpack and retrieved my Math homework for the day. "Alana would like it."

Speaking of Alana, I looked over my shoulder. Where was she?

"Oh yeah?" he asked. "Why?"

"Because she's good at everything. Introduce the girl to a new hobby and she masters it." I picked up the magazine, set it on top of my Math book, and flipped it open to a random page. "Knitting. See, I bet she'd be great at that." The article in front of me reported on the projects an eighty-year-old woman had knitted over her lifetime. The list was over five hundred projects long. "She once knitted a sweater for a baby penguin at a zoo."

"Alana did?"

"Oh. No, sorry. There's an article about this woman and her lifetime of knitting. She did a sweater for a baby penguin. How awesome is that?" I flipped through more pages, then shut the magazine and put it back on the pile.

"She likes to cook, right?" Diego asked, leaning his elbows on the counter.

"I'm not sure; the article only highlighted her knitting. There's also a story of a man who knows over a hundred bird calls."

"I mean Alana."

He was asking about Alana again. That was a good sign.

"Yes! She does. She has all these Hawaiian recipes because, as you probably know, she grew up in Hawaii."

"I'd heard. When did she move here?"

"In the seventh grade. That's when we met. You'd think I would have been the one to take her in, show her around because she was the new one. But it's always been the opposite."

"Really?" Diego asked.

The door to the center opened with a ring of the bell. I looked over my shoulder, ready to welcome Alana, but it wasn't her. It was a lady who looked to be in her late twenties, followed by two kids I recognized—Camilla and Samuel. Diego's niece and nephew.

"Monica, I can't. I'm at work," Diego said by way of greeting.

"I know. Believe me, I know," the woman said, "but when you're at home, Mom and Dad won't let you help. It's all about your perfect schedule."

He clenched his jaw. I wasn't sure if he was annoyed by her request or by what she had said about his parents.

"I wouldn't ask if I weren't desperate," Monica continued. "I can't very well take them to an interview. Two hours. Tops. Please, Diego." She clasped her hands together and placed them on the counter in a plea.

"Are you trying to get me fired?"

"If your boss comes in, you can say they're clients."

"But my boss knows they're my niece and nephew. Remember? She's met them before. Last time you did this."

"Your boss won't come in. Two hours." Monica didn't give Diego a chance to say no again. She kissed her kids on the cheeks, then left quickly.

"My sister, ladies and gentlemen," Diego said as if the room were full of people. His frustrated expression quickly turned to a smile when the kids looked up at him. "Hey, guys," he said. "Did you bring homework?"

They nodded.

"Samuel, Camilla, you remember Kate," Diego said.

I waved, then he ushered them toward the back, pausing where he was for a moment while they ran ahead.

"You're a good uncle . . . and brother," I said.

"Did you mean to say pushover?"

"No. I didn't."

"Thanks, Kate." He went to join Samuel and Camilla and that's when Alana walked in. She looked over at me, then at the empty counter with a questioning shrug. I nodded toward the seat next to me and she sat.

"His sister came in with his niece and nephew and he's supposed to watch them for two hours at the expense of his job," I whispered.

"So I'm just in time. Alana to the rescue. Would it be weird if I offered to take them to the park?" she said.

"Probably, since they barely know you."

"Next door for some cookies from the grocery store?"

"Better," I said.

She cracked her knuckles and walked to the counter. It didn't take long before I heard Diego say from the back, "Alana?"

"Oh, hey. You work today? I just swung by to keep Kate company."

"That's nice of you," he said.

"You know me."

I gave a scoff, and she shot me a look over her shoulder.

"Are these your tutoring subjects for the day?" Alana asked, gesturing to the kids.

"My sister just dropped them off."

"Oh, you run a babysitting service here, too?" she asked. She was good.

He moved back up to the front, probably so he could speak more quietly. "Not technically. They're really not supposed to be here."

"Do you know who's amazing with kids?" Alana asked.

Diego's eyes shifted to me, still sitting there like some third wheel.

"No," Alana said, obviously noticing, too. "Well, I mean, she is because she has like a thousand cousins, but I was speaking about myself."

He smiled at her.

"I can take them next door to get a cookie or something?" Alana offered. "I think they have one of those quarter-operated rides as well."

I coughed instead of pointing out that the children were probably way too big for one of those.

"They might've outgrown that three years ago," Diego said.

"You never outgrow a quarter-operated horse ride." Alana recovered gracefully, as usual.

"I couldn't ask you to do that," Diego told her.

"Why not? We're friends, right?"

"Yes."

"Friends do stuff like this for each other all the time. Right, Kate?"

"Yep. I rode a quarter-operated horse for her just the other day."

Liza walked around the counter with Tommy, and I stood.

"You done?" I asked my cousin.

She nodded. "Thanks, Tommy," she said.

When Tommy saw me, he held out his fist. I assumed that meant I was supposed to bump it with mine. I complied.

"Your podcast is awesome," he said. "You are very funny."

"Thanks."

"I should call in and ask about something."

"Do you have a problem?" I asked.

"No, but I want to hear how my voice sounds through that voice disguiser thing you have on the phones. You wouldn't even know it was me. I could make up some really good problem."

Liza giggled.

I wasn't about to tell him that I'd definitely know it was him. That the "disguise" was added in after the fact. "Yes, you should call in. It would be fun."

He bit his lip as if trying to think of a problem he would call in with right then.

I inched for the door and glanced toward Alana to make sure she didn't need her wingwoman any longer. She and Diego were still talking.

"See you later," I said. "Bye, Alana, Diego."

They both looked over. "Bye, Kate," Alana said. She was glowing.

"Bye, guys," Diego said. "See you next Monday, Liza."

"Or at school," she called to him. "You know I'm in high school."

"Oh, right. Of course," he said.

I tried not to laugh. She'd obviously said that for Tommy's sake. We walked outside, and Liza looked over at me. "Alana and Diego, huh?"

"Yes."

"They're cute together."

"I agree."

She linked her arm through mine. "Thanks for being such a good cousin and taking me to tutoring, but I think I'm good now."

"You're done with tutoring?"

"No, I think I can handle it on my own from here on out. My mom can drop me off."

"Oh."

She smiled, then skipped to the car. I didn't know why I was so disappointed by this pronouncement.

# CHAPTER 20

Wednesday, after school, I saw Frank heading for the recording studio. I weaved my way through the crush of bodies in the hallway, trying to reach him before he got into the room. He hadn't been in podcasting class today but he was obviously showing up for lab. He had just reached the door when I finally caught up with him.

"That's what you call a truce?" I asked. The words had been stewing in my chest for too long now. Maybe I should've just confronted him after lab. I had this notion that this would be more private. It didn't feel private, as my outburst made several heads turn.

"What do you mean?" he said calmly, reaching for the knob on the door.

I took him by the arm and dragged him around the first corner and beneath the stairs.

"If you wanted to be alone with me, Kitty Kat, all you had to do was ask."

"Don't be stupid." I lowered my voice. "Why did you do it?"

"I have no idea what you're talking about."

"I think you know exactly what I'm talking about."

"I'm too tired for this. I literally just got back from a five-hour bus ride," he said. "What? What is it that I'm supposed to know?"

Even if he wasn't involved in the actual "prank" on my marina, his family would've heard about the report we filed. The fact that he was playing innocent just irritated me more. "Did you think it was funny? Was it supposed to be some *truce* joke?"

"Oh, is this about the pictures? Talk to Alana about those."

"The pictures?" I asked, my anger making way for confusion.

"On the website. Of you and Victoria."

"There are pictures on the website of me and Victoria?"

"Like I said, talk to Alana." He crossed his arms over his chest. "Are we done here?"

"What? No, no, we are not done here. I'm talking about the stunt you pulled at the marina Saturday morning."

His expression was utterly clueless. He was either the world's best actor or telling the truth. Was he telling the truth?

"Look, here's Alana now. Take up the picture issue with her," he said as if this was still about the pictures. He reached out and pulled Alana in to join us.

"Ooh, a secret rendezvous under the stairs," she said. "What are we talking about?"

"Tell Kate the pictures were your idea," Frank said.

"You *told* her?" Alana asked.

"She already knew," he said.

"I did not know!" I cried. "I still don't know."

"Don't kill me," Alana said. She linked one arm through mine and one through Frank's and led us back toward the recording studio.

"I'm not done with him." We walked a few more steps, then I said, "Wait, *what* pictures?"

"We put your picture and Victoria's picture on the website. We thought it added a personal touch."

"Which pictures?"

"Your school picture," Alana said.

"The world's worst picture of me?"

"We also added a candid Frank took while you guys were recording the podcast last week."

"Consider it our gift to you," Frank said smugly.

"I'm kind of tired of your gifts," I mumbled as we walked through the door.

The recording studio looked different. It took me a minute to understand why. We had all new equipment. I hadn't realized podcasting class had the budget for that. Maybe one of the other classes had upgraded it.

Ms. Lyon clapped her hands. "Everyone, have a seat before we begin."

We sat around the room where we could. There were only eight of us, so between the couch and the rolling chairs there were just enough seats.

"You'll notice the upgrade to the equipment. This was donated thanks to our new sponsor."

"Sponsor?" Victoria asked.

"Yes," Ms. Lyon said. "Kat, I have a little ad that you will read along with your disclaimer from now on."

"Okay, cool."

"It's on the iPad." Ms. Lyon couldn't have looked more pleased. "This just proves that our show is a hit and that businesses are recognizing that."

That *was* pretty cool. Victoria and I walked through the door and shut ourselves behind it.

Victoria started off as normal. "Welcome, listeners, to another episode of *Not My Problem*. Another week, another set of problems. And we want to hear them. Don't we, Kat?"

"I have nowhere else to be," I said.

She laughed and handed me the iPad.

I took the iPad and gave the intro I knew from memory. "As I always say, we are not professionals. If you have a real problem, call 911 or refer to any of our emergency numbers listed on our website." Then I glanced down at the words I was supposed to read. " 'We'd also like to thank the sponsor of our podcast, Young Industries.' " I coughed on the surprise of that announcement, then tried to recover so Frank didn't gloat any more than he probably already was. " 'The number one leader in development and services in Lakesprings, Young Industries has been serving the community for over fifty years and thanks you for your continued support.' "

I refused to meet Frank's eyes through the glass. Had he requested that I be the one to say that? Was I going to have to say that every week? Ms. Lyon had acted like some random business had recognized the quality of our podcast and come forward. But Frank's dad wasn't some random person. His son was in the podcasting class. This had nothing to do with our show *being a hit*.

"Yes, thank you, Young Industries," Victoria said as I handed her back the iPad.

"Lots of email love for the show," Jamie said from the other room. "Do we want to read any praise on air?"

Ms. Lyon nodded and pointed to the iPad. Victoria pulled up a waiting email. The subject line read "Love."

"We're going to read a few emails from our listeners now," Victoria said. " 'Hello, Victoria and Kat. I love your show. I especially loved the guy who called in about the conflict he had between school responsibilities and love. He was so sweet and sincere. Where can I find a guy like that?' "

"Good question," I said.

"I think it was a rhetorical question," Victoria said.

"Was it, though?"

Victoria read through several other emails that all basically said the same thing before saying, "We completely agree with all of you. We adore Mr. Looking for Love as well."

"Is that the name we're going with for him?" I asked.

"I thought it was catchy," she shot back. "Alliteration and all that."

"Let this be a warning to you, listeners: If you don't name yourself on our show, we get to name you . . . with alliteration."

Victoria giggled. "It's true."

"Looks like we have some callers waiting," I said.

Victoria nodded toward Mallory, and she clicked the first call through.

"You're on *Not My Problem*, we're listening," Victoria said.

"I want to wear whatever I want to school," the caller said. "Why do we even have dress codes?"

"What specifically do you want to wear that you can't?" Victoria asked.

"Pajamas."

"We can't wear pajamas to school?" I asked. I'd never really read through the dress code in the student manual so that detail was a surprise to me.

"We can't," the caller said. "I got dress-coded for it yesterday."

"How did they know they were pajamas?" Victoria asked.

"Because it was plaid flannel pants and a tank top."

"All I can say is that if you don't want a dress code anymore, you have to take that up with the PTA and the school board," Victoria said. "Showing up to school in your pajamas, unfortunately, isn't going to change anything."

"What do you think, Kat?" the caller asked.

What *did* I think? I was feeling more comfortable on air, getting braver and doing better. But I still rarely voiced my opinion. Being a good podcast host would require doing that from time to time. So I took a deep breath and said what I thought. "I agree. I know they have council meetings. Go to one of those in your pajamas, do some math problems, show them that wearing your pajamas doesn't impede your learning. Then hope for the best."

The caller sighed like this was the last thing she wanted to do, but she didn't argue our logic.

"Thanks for listening," she said, and was gone.

I smiled over at Alana, thinking if anyone would agree with dress code issues, it would be her, but she wasn't paying attention. She was writing something in a notebook that was on the table between her and Frank. I hoped it said something like, *Did our show really need a sponsor or did you do that just so you could hear Kate praise your company? Oh, and by the way, tell the truth about breaking into Kate's marina.*

Victoria looked at me. "Listeners, I think I see a smile on Kat's face. She might actually be enjoying herself. Remember during the first episode how she said she was going to be bad at this? I personally think she's very good at it."

A feeling of warmth at the unexpected compliment bloomed in my chest. "Thanks, Victoria. You taking the lead makes it much easier for me."

"Thanks, cohost. We better move on before this love fest takes over," Victoria said. "Next caller." She paused to let the call come through. "You're on *Not My Problem*," Victoria said. "What can we help you with today?"

"You told me to call back and give you an update." My pulse picked up speed. Diego. Alana was at full attention now.

"Mr. Looking for Love," Victoria said. "We were just talking about you."

"Wait, is that my moniker?"

"You don't like it?" Victoria pouted.

"Um . . . I can deal with it."

"We're so happy you called," Victoria said. "Listeners love you. So tell us, any progress with your girl?"

"Yes and no."

"That's not a real answer," I said.

"So I've heard." He cleared his throat, almost like he thought he'd given himself away with that bit of info. And he had, by repeating something he had said at the lockers just the other day. It was the first thing the caller had done that let me know without a doubt that it was Diego. "Here is a real answer. Yes, I was able to spend some more time with her. We had fun. She's everything I described before—funny, easy to be with, sweet. I'm trying to be patient like Ka—Kat suggested." He'd almost called me Kate but stopped himself in time.

"And it's not working?" I asked.

"I think it is."

"But . . ." Victoria prompted.

"But there's another guy."

Victoria gasped and my eyes shot straight to Alana. Her brows went down.

"You think she likes someone else?" Victoria asked.

"I'm almost sure of it," Diego replied.

"Maybe you're reading too much into it," I said. "Have you asked her?"

"No, I haven't. I'm exercising patience, Kat, like you suggested. You basically implied chivalry was dead."

"Look at you reading into things again. I said nothing of the sort. I said *patience* was dead. It's been beaten to death with an instant-gratification stick."

"Ouch," Diego said.

"Do you disagree?" I wasn't normally this confrontational, but it was Diego and our exchanges always brought something out in me.

"Yes and no."

"Ha," I said.

"I'm still a fan of just kissing her," Victoria said.

I nodded. "My point exactly."

"I can have patience," he said. "I just wonder if my patience will result in anything."

"Isn't that one of the definitions of patience?" I asked. "Waiting without being certain of the result?"

He chuckled. "Okay, I get it. Thank you, once again, for listening."

"Thanks for the update," Victoria said. "We can't wait to hear about the results of this." Diego ended the call, and Victoria spoke into the mic. "And to all you listeners out there, I sense love in the air. The Fall Festival is still a few weeks away, plenty of time to ask a date. There will be games and food and rides and music and lots of fun!"

"I think there might be football in there, too, somewhere," I said.

Victoria laughed. "Football? Who goes to the Fall Festival for football? Before I get angry emails, that's a joke, people. I love football. I can't wait to cheer the team on and then afterward celebrate at a carnival."

After a couple more calls, we closed out the show and I walked out of the booth to meet Alana in the outer room.

Frank smiled at me. "That was some excellent reading, Kat."

"Why did you donate all this stuff?" I snapped. "Feeling guilty?"

He put his hand on his chest. "I can't win with you, can I? You accuse me of pranking your marina and here I am supporting the podcast and you think it's because I feel guilty?"

"Yes."

"It was nice," Alana said.

"Yes, so big of you to spend your dad's money," I said.

Alana took my arm and pulled me away. "Not worth it," she said to me quietly.

When we were outside of the room, I asked, "How do you stand him?"

"I have him under control," she said.

"What does that mean?"

"It means, he thinks he's playing me, but I'm playing him."

"I still don't know what that means."

She laughed. "You'll see. The more important question is, why does Diego think I like someone else?"

"So you agree that it's Diego?"

"Yes, I think you're right. It's him."

I nodded toward where we'd just left Frank. "That's why he thinks you like someone else."

She gasped. "Why would he think I like *that*?"

"Maybe because you invited Frank over to my house and he basically crashed your date? Diego asked me what was up between the two of you that night."

"Why didn't you tell me this before?" Alana asked, wide-eyed.

"I'd forgotten he had asked it until now. He thinks you like Frank. Or maybe it's Bennett. You know, the guy you've been texting to find out where Diego is at all times."

She threw her head back and groaned. "I need to fix this."

"Maybe you should stop strategizing and just be yourself. I think yourself is pretty great. And he obviously does, too."

She brought the sleeve of his hoodie that she was wearing again today up to her mouth to hide her smile. "You're right. I think it's time."

"Time for what?"

"What says *me* more than a cook-off?"

"You're finally going to make it happen?"

"Yes. Once he tastes my cooking, he will pledge allegiance to me forever."

# CHAPTER 21

My dad stood on the dock, talking to the police officer. I held a rope attached to the front of the kayak and dragged it alongside the dock toward its slip. I had paused the podcast I'd been listening to, trying my hardest to eavesdrop, but they were talking too quietly. They had to be talking about our WaveRunners being scattered. Had Frank been questioned? Were there other suspects?

I moored the kayak to the dock. It was hard to look busy when I'd already done the entire closing routine. I untied and retied a couple boats. My phone buzzed in my pocket, and I sat back on my knees and pulled it out.

I deserve to be ignored.

I stared at the new text from Hunter, shocked for two reasons. One, because I didn't think he'd text me again after being ignored. Two, I had ignored him. No, I had more than ignored him. I had forgotten about his first text. Life had been so busy, and I hadn't thought about Hunter in days. I hadn't even checked his social media.

My finger, which had tapped on the screen to check the message, now dropped, accidentally typing an *L* into the blank bar. Crap. The stupid dots would appear on his phone, like I was typing back. I had to say something now.

My first thought was to say, *Yes, you do deserve to be ignored.* I even typed that out. But then I deleted it. That seemed too bitter. Too invested. I was neither. So I typed, Been super busy. How have you been?

I hit SEND.

Why had I asked him a question? I didn't want to start a conversation here. But as the flashing dots appeared in the text box on my screen, I knew that's exactly what I'd done.

Hunter: Texas is a lot different than Lakesprings. I miss it.

Me: Nothing compares to Lakesprings.

Hunter: How did I know you'd say that?

My brows went down. It had been more than three months since we'd talked, and he wanted to act like it was yesterday? Like he still knew me so well?

Me: Guess I'm predictable.

From the other side of the dock I heard my dad saying good-bye to the policeman.

I quickly stood, tucked my phone away, and brushed off my knees. "Dad!" I called.

He stopped to wait for me before exiting the gate.

"What happened?" I asked.

"Nothing. He came by to say they don't have any leads."

"Did he question Frank?"

He held the gate open for me. "No. He said he doesn't have enough evidence to question anyone."

"Evidence is the thing they have to have to *arrest* someone. Questioning someone doesn't require evidence."

He shut the gate behind us and locked the heavy replacement lock he'd bought after the break-in. "I'm just repeating what he said. He doesn't have evidence to question anyone."

"Anyone? Or Frank? I'm sure if Frank's last name wasn't Young that he'd be just fine questioning him. When you own over half the town, I guess you own the cops that go along with it."

"I don't know what to say, Kate. We got all our WaveRunners back. I think it's time to let it go."

I sighed. "Yep. Letting it go." I was so not letting it go.

Speaking of letting things go, once I was in my room, I pulled out my phone to see if Hunter had responded. He had.

That's not what I meant. You're not predictable. Far from it these days. Hosting the school's podcast? I never would've guessed that. Nice pic, btw.

He knew I was hosting the school podcast? Did this mean he'd listened to it? Was that why he'd reached out after all those weeks? And what pic? I suddenly remembered the website and the pictures that Alana and Frank had supposedly uploaded there. I slid into my desk chair and opened my laptop.

Like Alana had said, it was my school picture, taken after the lady had said, "Smile," and I started to say, "Hold on." She didn't hold on. The candid shot that Frank had taken of me and Victoria was no better. I looked like I wanted to kiss the microphone. Ugh. Alana was right, this did inspire thoughts of killing her.

I shot her off a text: You approved of these pictures? I thought we were friends!

She quickly responded: You look adorable! Seriously, you're super photogenic.

I reminded myself that murder was still illegal in all fifty states and texted: You're lucky awkward is a good look on me.

Alana: Oh, btw, keep next Friday open. I did it. I challenged Diego to a cook-off and he said yes.

Me: What does that have to do with me?

Alana: We're doing it at your house.

Me: Why?

Alana: Because you have a better kitchen. And we need a judge. He's bringing someone, too.

Me: Okay. We must talk tomorrow.

Alana: About the cook-off?

Me: About Hunter.

My phone rang one second later and I answered.

"You think I can wait until tomorrow with a setup like that?" Alana asked.

"He texted again."

"And you didn't answer again."

"Well . . ."

"Ugh! Kate. Tell me everything you said."

I relayed the exchange to her, and she was silent for several long minutes before she said, "Huh. You haven't screwed everything up. Your replies sounded almost distant." She seemed impressed by this. "Maybe you're not as hung up on him as I thought."

"Touching the hook!" Maybe it was less than that actually. Because I realized that, aside from irritation, I'd felt almost nothing when reading her the texts.

She laughed. "There's hope for you yet."

We hung up, and I stared at Hunter's texts again. I waited. I waited for my heart to pound or for the butterflies to take flight. There was nothing. I closed my eyes and I ripped that hook, the one I'd only been touching, off the wall and flung it into the toilet. Because in my mind it had been a bathroom hook, of course. Then I flushed. And since it was all in my head, it easily went down the drain. When I opened my eyes, I deleted the messages and Hunter's name from my phone. I unfollowed all his social media accounts. I'd never felt so light.

# CHAPTER 22

"Kat!" a voice called to me from across the lunchtime commons.

Anytime someone used that name at school now, I knew they only knew me from the podcast. And they only recognized me from those awkward pictures on the website.

The floppy-haired boy caught up to me. "Kat!" he repeated.

"Hi, thanks for listening." That was my go-to phrase. Most of the time it was enough. This time it wasn't. The floppy-haired boy wanted to talk.

"Hi," he said. "I need advice."

"Can you call in on Wednesday?" I asked. "We like callers on the show."

"I tried to call in last Wednesday and never got through."

"You didn't?" I asked. "Like you got a busy signal?"

"Yes."

"Wow." I hadn't considered that was possible. "Okay, I'll try to give you advice, but honestly, asking a friend would probably be just as effective."

"No, you don't hold back. I like that."

I scoffed.

It didn't faze him. "I want to try out for football."

"Okay," I said, not understanding what part of that required my opinion.

"But look at me," he said.

I did. He was a small guy. I'd initially thought he was a freshman, but maybe he wasn't. "That's what pads and helmets are for, right? You obviously won't be on defense. Maybe you can be the catcher person."

He scrunched up his face.

"See, you should ask your friends," I said, backing up. "Or ask Victoria, she's sporty. I know nothing about football."

That didn't deter him. "I would try out, even being as small as I am, but it's my parents. They won't let me."

I stopped in my retreat. "Oh."

"Yeah, my mom's afraid I'll break every bone in my body and my dad doesn't even like football. He told me I'm more suited for golf."

"Golf is cool." I thought of Diego. "One of my friends hit a golf ball through the goalposts from the hill behind the stadium." I paused for a minute. "Off topic?"

"Slightly." The boy yanked on his backpack straps. "And by the way, your friend is exaggerating. I've seen guys try to do that and fail miserably."

I stepped out of the way to let a group of kids pass us. "Right?" I said. "That's what I told him. He swore, though. I really should have him prove it to me."

"Back to me, here."

I laughed. "Okay, let's see. I'm kind of stumped on this one. I can see where your mom is coming from."

"Thanks a lot. This is why I should've called in. You wouldn't have been able to see me and be influenced."

"You're right. So if I couldn't look at your totally breakable bones, what would I say?"

He bit his lip as if his life depended on my answer. I gave it some more thought, then spoke again.

"I'd say, compromise?" I suggested. "Tell your parents that if they let you try out for the football team and you don't make it, then you'll try golf."

His eyes lit up. It was the part about giving advice that I didn't get on the podcast, the part where I could see that the solution presented made sense to them.

"That's . . . a good idea," he said.

"Don't act too surprised." Although I was. I had given advice . . . good advice . . . without Victoria there to back me up or elaborate.

I started to look around again, in search of Alana. She hadn't answered any of my texts and she wasn't in our normal place—our lunch bench—but she wasn't in any of our not-so-normal places, either. I sighed and noticed my advice-asker was still standing in front of me.

"This is obviously advice for next year, right?" I asked. "Since football season started weeks ago."

"Yes."

"So you have a whole year to put on some weight. Do that Michael Phelps diet thing." I may or may not have watched a documentary about Michael Phelps.

"What diet is that?"

"The one where he basically eats all day and works out in between eating. Or at least he did when he was training for the Olympics."

"Sounds painful," he said.

"I agree." I gave him a small wave. "I better go. Thanks for listening to our show."

I took a step to my right when I heard another voice say, "Wait."

I turned around and saw that a petite girl with long black hair had been standing behind the football boy, as if there was a line forming.

"Hi?" I said to the girl.

"I wanted advice, too."

I shot the football guy a look, and he left with a shrug.

"Okay, what can I help you with?" Maybe I needed to set up a booth and start charging. Thankfully, the girl asked an easy question, about which way I thought would be better to ask her girlfriend to Fall Festival. I answered her, she nodded happily, and I took off at a fast walk toward the library.

Once inside, I stepped behind the nearest shelf of books. I let out a breath, and freed my phone from my pocket to see that Alana had texted me back.

Alana: I'm making a presentation.

Me: What does that mean? I'm in the library.

Alana: I'll explain later. The library? Why?

Me: I'll explain later.

Alana: Lunch is almost over. I'll see you in podcasting.

I tucked my phone away. Lunch *was* almost over, and I hadn't eaten anything. My hunger did not outweigh the thought of facing the commons again, though. I peeked out from behind the shelf and scanned the library, wondering if there was a vending machine in here. I obviously did not frequent the library enough.

Then I saw Max sitting at one of the long oak tables in the center. I smiled and made my way to him. He was sketching in a notebook like he often did these days, more dedicated than I'd ever seen him to his comics.

"Brother," I said. "Tell me you have food." I sank into a chair across from him.

"We can't eat in here. It's against the rules."

"Really? So where do you eat?"

"I eat on my walk over here."

"That's some fast eating. That cannot be good for your digestion."

He gave me a Max look, one that said he didn't think I was as funny as I thought I was.

"It wasn't meant to be a joke," I said.

He gave me a half smile this time.

"That's better." I took in all the empty chairs around us. "Where are your friends?"

"They like to eat at lunch," he said.

"Jerks."

That one got a chuckle.

A moment later, Liza walked in and sat down next to Max. "Are we having a family meeting?" she asked. "Nobody told me about a family meeting. I thought I was going to help you on the girl voice in your comic. Did you ask Kate to help you, too?"

"Don't worry, he didn't ask me," I said. "I'm not sure if I should be offended or not. I'll let you both know in a minute."

"Don't be offended," Liza said. "I've read more of his comic than you have, so I know what he's looking for."

"Now I'm pretty sure I'm doubly offended."

She rolled her eyes. Max didn't grace me with a response. I kicked his foot under the table but then turned my attention to Liza.

"How was tutoring yesterday?" I asked her. This was the first week she'd gone without me.

Liza's eyes went to the tabletop, and a small smile played at her lips. "It was good."

"I'm proud of you for going on your own."

"Are you making fun of me?" she asked, snapping her head up.

"What? No. Did it sound like I was making fun of you?" Apparently I needed to work on my tone.

"A little. But thanks."

"Is Aunt Marinn going to make you keep going after the first quarter?"

"I don't know. But you were right. It's not bad having a time where I'm forced to do my homework and someone on hand ready to help."

"Did I tell you that? I think Alana told you that."

"Hmm. Maybe. I feel like it was you, though, and that's what matters."

"Ha." I looked at Max. He'd been so quiet through this whole exchange. He was generally quiet, but it seemed more so than normal. "I want to read your comic sometime."

"Okay," he said.

"It's a Bailey family meeting!" Alana said, plopping down in the seat beside me and pulling a taco out of the bag she held. It smelled amazing.

"I thought I wasn't going to see you until podcasting class," I said.

"The taco line was shorter than I anticipated."

"You can't eat in here," Max said.

"I can. It's a special rule, just for me. It's called the Alana Does What She Wants rule. It's a hard rule to explain, lots of nuances and sublaws, but I'm sure you get the gist of it."

"So, the presentation?" I asked.

"Frank and I were presenting the 'recording a podcast at the carnival' idea to the student council," Alana explained, taking a big bite of her taco.

"Oh. And what did they say?"

She chewed and swallowed. "Sorry. They approved it. They were even excited about it."

The live show was happening.

"Why are you sorry?" I asked, trying to act casual. "I'm fine about it. Cool with it."

"Do you hear your sister, Max?" Alana asked my brother. "She is so not cool with it."

Max smiled.

Alana turned back to me, holding her taco. "Maybe it would help if you admitted your fear."

"So you and Frank made the presentation?" I asked, changing the subject.

"I know, I know, I'm fraternizing with the enemy. But you told me to spy and I am. I'm learning lots of good stuff. Like the fact that I think he might be sincere about wanting to let go of grudges his parents have held."

I glanced at Max and Liza. They both looked as skeptical as I felt.

"I don't think Frank knows what sincere is," I said. Because *sincere* definitely wasn't snooping through my house and sabotaging our business.

"Don't worry, I'm still being wary," Alana said. "I think a mending with the Youngs can only be good for your family, though. Maybe it will start at the bottom." She took another bite of her taco. "This is delicious."

The smell of her taco had my stomach growling with hunger. And thinking of Frank only made me grumpy.

"Presenting the podcast reminded me how awesome this festival is going to be," Alana went on through her mouthful. "Which reminded me that Diego still hasn't asked me. So when he calls in to the podcast this week, tell him to ask me already, okay? I'm hoping he'll ask at our cook-off date this Friday, but I think a little encouragement will go a long way."

I froze. Then I widened my eyes at her and nodded toward Max and Liza.

"Oops." A piece of stray lettuce clung to her lip and she used her finger to swipe it into her mouth. "Do they not know he calls in?" She pointed at them. "You guys are sworn to secrecy."

Liza made an *X* over her heart with a finger.

Alana smiled at me. "There. All fixed."

"Seriously, guys," I told my brother and cousin sternly. "You can't breathe a word."

"We won't," Liza swore, and Max nodded solemnly.

I wanted to be comforted by that assurance, but uneasiness settled into my chest. Diego couldn't find out.

# CHAPTER 23

The podcast that Wednesday felt off. On the surface, everything seemed normal. Victoria was doling out lots of advice, I was adding my fair share of sarcastic quips mixed with useful suggestions. Our classmates and Ms. Lyon sat on the other side of the glass making sure everything ran smoothly. But something wasn't quite right. For one, Diego hadn't called in yet. He'd called three weeks in a row; I assumed he'd call again. People liked him.

But he wasn't calling, and it was getting later.

Second, it was freezing in the studio. Victoria and I sat in our chairs, shivering. The weather was cooler than normal for the end of September, but the school's air-conditioning was still programed like it was mid-July.

And third, Alana wasn't in the production lab anymore. The newest round of job changes switched her and Frank to Thursdays.

It all seemed like little changes, but it took me back to my first week behind the microphone, my nerves as raw as if I had never done this before. And with these feelings churning in my gut, Sarah, our new email person, spoke into our headphones.

"We have an email for you to read."

Victoria handed me the iPad. "We have an email, listeners. And since Kat's an excellent reader, she gets the honor."

I scrunched my nose at her but opened up the email. " 'Dear hosts who probably have no idea what they're talking about but are my only option right now.' " I laughed. "I like this kid."

"We at least *think* we know what we're talking about," Victoria said. "But thanks for the confidence."

I continued reading the email. " 'I have a problem. I am being bullied. Every day, I dread going to school. I am picked on relentlessly. I don't know what to do. When I stand my ground, it gets worse. When I try to ignore it, nothing changes. I'm out of options obviously, since I'm writing you. Sincerely, Bully Magnet.' "

My laughter stuck in my throat. The dread that had been brewing in my stomach doubled. How had I never considered that people would present us serious problems like this? Problems beyond crushes and teacher drama . . . and cheese. Problems we were more than unqualified to answer.

"You're right," I said. "We are not experts on this. You should talk to a teacher, or parent."

"Bullies feed off of your fear," Victoria said as though she'd suddenly become a leading expert on the teen psyche. "You need to work on projecting confidence. Try to surround yourself with friends and support. People like the ones you're describing are cowards. They won't pick on groups of people. They want you to be alone and vulnerable."

I scanned the students on the other side of the glass. Nobody seemed as alarmed as I was. "Can we get some fact-checks on what we're saying, or at least add a professional quote to the mix? I feel weird about going into this one with just our opinions," I said, knowing this would be edited out.

Everyone's eyes went to Ms. Lyon. "You two are doing great," she said.

I swallowed another protest, and said into the mic, "But really. You should tell an adult you trust. We don't want to see you get hurt."

The email correspondence was harder than a caller. I wanted to ask questions, to get clarifications. But an email couldn't talk back or answer any of my concerns. How come nobody else seemed as worried about this as me?

The rest of the show went on as if that email was just like any other one we'd received.

Then we were ending the show and the equipment was turned off and Victoria stood.

"You okay?" she asked me.

"What?"

"You were kind of off today," she said.

"It was cold in here."

"Right? I hope it warms up more for the festival."

"Me too."

She smiled. "See you tomorrow."

She headed for the door.

"Victoria?" I called.

"Yeah?" She turned back.

"Thanks for carrying us on the show."

She shrugged one shoulder. "I like it."

I left the room and made my way outside to my car. I was surprised to see Diego leaning against it. I wanted to ask him why he didn't call in. Why he had to throw me off like that. But I couldn't very well say that when he still thought he was anonymous. And even if I could, it made no sense that him not calling in would throw me off. It shouldn't have.

He looked past me, like he was hoping someone else was with me. Of course he was. He was hoping for Alana.

"Hey," he said when I reached him.

"Alana changed jobs on the podcast," I said. "She comes on Thursdays now."

"She did?" he asked. "What does she do now?"

"Um . . ." I didn't remember. "I'm not sure. You'll have to ask her." So would I, apparently.

"I'll ask her Friday."

"What's Friday?"

He bit his lip. "The cook-off? Right? Aren't you judging it?"

"Oh yeah. I mean yes. I am."

"Are you okay? You seem down."

"I'm fine."

"Did it not go well in there?" He nodded toward the building behind me.

"Not my best showing."

"How so?"

I didn't need to tell him this, but maybe it would help to get it off my chest. Maybe he'd ease my mind about the advice we gave. "We got an email today about a kid who's being bullied."

"Oh, wow. That's heavy."

"I know. I had no idea what to say so I repeated the same thing twice. And then Victoria became Super Psychologist, and I'm just worried we gave bad advice."

"What did you repeat twice?"

"That he . . . or she, I guess, the email didn't specify . . . should talk to a trusted adult."

"That's good advice. What did Victoria say?"

"Something about projecting confidence and being surrounded by friends at all times."

"That's probably good advice, too."

"It's the *probably* part that worries me. Should I do something else?"

"Like what?" he asked.

There was a parking curb to my right and I sat down on it, suddenly feeling really tired. "I don't know. Is there some way we can find out where the email originated? Find out who sent it? Send the person help? Maybe a teacher can talk to whoever wrote it."

Diego lowered himself onto the curb next to me. "Did the email mention they wanted to hurt themselves?"

"No."

"Then you should probably respect their privacy. But maybe you can say something at the beginning of next week's show if that makes you feel better. Encourage the emailer to call in and ask more questions? Or even just give some more advice."

I nodded. "That's a good idea."

He bumped his shoulder into mine. "It's a call-in advice show, Kate. Whoever wrote that email knows this. They couldn't have expected too much."

"Yeah, that's what they said in the email."

"See."

"Just when I think I'm getting the hang of this, I'm reminded that I'm not."

"You make the show, Kate."

My heart thrummed in my chest and I met his eyes. Why was he always so good at making me feel better? That was his talent. Making people feel better. No wonder Alana liked to be around him. I broke eye contact and for the first time noticed he was holding a magazine rolled up in his hand.

"What's that?" I asked.

"You didn't come to tutoring with Liza on Monday."

"Oh, right. I was dismissed."

He smiled. "Liza is funny."

"Yep, she's always had a big personality."

He tapped my leg with the rolled-up magazine. "We got a new magazine at the center I thought you should know about."

"Well, I guess I *am* the magazine inspector." How embarrassing that he'd noticed.

He unfurled the magazine and I immediately recognized it as my favorite water sports one, *Lake Life*. "Do you read this one?" he asked.

"I do!" I held out my hands for it, and he placed it in them. I studied the cover. "This one isn't three years old, though." The date on it was this month.

"I know. Someone left it. Have you read this month's yet?"

"No. We have them at the marina, but I haven't had a chance."

"You can keep that one."

"I don't need to steal it from the counseling center. I can get my own."

He laughed. "You've seen how many magazines we have there. It's like we're starting a magazine museum."

"Okay. Thanks."

He waited expectantly, almost like he thought I'd open it right there and begin reading. But I'd already embarrassed myself enough with my apparent magazine fascination.

I stood and brushed off the back of my jeans. "I better get home."

Diego casually stood as well. "Happy reading."

I smiled. "Yeah. You too." I took one step back toward my car. "No, I mean, not you too, you're not reading. I mean, you might be, but I mean . . . yeah. Bye." What was wrong with me?

A smile spread across his face. "Bye, Kate."

# CHAPTER 24

Friday, after the podcast aired, we started getting the most outraged emails we'd ever seen. Mr. Looking for Love hadn't called in, and people weren't happy with us. As if the podcast was staged, and we arranged who did and didn't call in.

Alana read the emails to me as we were getting ready for the cook-off at my house. Apparently part of Alana's new job in postproduction was responding to emails we didn't have a chance to read on air, and deciding which ones we should read on future episodes.

"This girl says that she feels you guys strung her along and forced her to listen until the end with your fake promises," Alana said, looking at her phone as we stood in my kitchen.

I let out a single laugh. "That's probably because at the beginning of the show Victoria said *I wonder if Looking for Love will call in today.* Do you think people will stop listening because of this?" I asked, suddenly worried.

"No," Alana said decisively, putting her phone down on the counter. "People are obviously emotionally invested if they are this angry. And besides, people don't listen just for Diego."

"These emails sure are making it seem like it."

Alana turned to her grocery bag and pulled out a pineapple. We had gone to the store right after school for Alana's supplies. Diego was bringing his own.

"How are you going to respond?" I asked, nodding toward Alana's phone.

"How about: Get a life?" Alana offered with a mischievous grin.

"Not sure Ms. Lyon would approve of that."

She walked back over to her phone and checked the screen. "Here's a good email."

"Yeah?" I put the chicken in the fridge.

" 'Dear Kat.' " She paused and wiggled her eyebrows. "It doesn't include Victoria."

"I'm scared."

" 'I love you on the show. What advice would you give to someone who wants to ask you out?' "

"Ugh," I said.

Alana glanced up. "Why is that an *ugh*? I thought it was nice."

"He doesn't know me at all!"

"What do you mean? He listens to you every week and he's smitten."

"Okay, fine, then I don't know *him* at all."

"He obviously wants to change that. I think it's cute."

"No. Not cute." I pulled a box of chicken broth from the grocery bag. "What are you making tonight, anyway?"

"Hulihuli chicken."

"Mmm. I love that stuff."

"I know. It will transform Diego's heart into putty."

"Is that a weird way of saying it will give him a heart attack?"

"No! It's an amazing way of saying he will finish falling in love with me."

"Oh. Got it." Our bags were unloaded and in an hour Diego would arrive.

"He's bringing a friend, by the way," Alana said. "Someone else to judge, because he thought you'd be biased."

"Who's he bringing?"

"He didn't say."

"Should we go change?" I asked. We were still both in our school clothes, and I felt sweaty and grimy.

"Definitely," Alana said. She picked up her phone and followed me to my room. " 'Dear Kat and Victoria,' " she read aloud while she walked. " 'We want less homework advice and more love advice.' "

I rolled my eyes. "Because let's not forget what's really important right now in our lives."

"My unromantic friend," Alana declared, "love makes the world go 'round. It will always be important."

"Well, I don't dictate who calls in."

"I am not the one writing these emails. No need to get mad at me," Alana said as we walked into my room.

"But you're the one reading them!" I pointed out, closing my door. "Why are you still reading them?"

"You're right." Alana put her phone in her pocket and smiled. "Let's concentrate on the cook-off."

⁂

An hour later, I answered my door to find Diego and Frank standing on my front porch.

I was confused. "*This* is who you brought to judge?" I demanded of Diego.

"Yes," Diego said. "I needed someone biased in the complete opposite way. Plus, I've been told there's some sort of truce?" He cringed as he said the last sentence, like he just now realized he'd been given the wrong intel.

I glanced at Frank, who, for once, had the decency to look penitent. He really did seem to be adamant about this truce thing. I'd give him that.

"Fine. Come in." And for the second time ever, Frank Young walked into my house.

My dad came down the stairs right at that moment. "Hey, there are people in my house!" he said in his joking way.

"Yes, Dad. This is Diego, a friend from school, and you know Frank."

"Frank Young," Dad said.

"Yes, sir," Frank said. "Nice to see you again."

"They came over to cook," I explained, seeing the surprise on my dad's face.

"I only came to eat," Frank said.

Diego shifted the grocery bag he held in his right hand to his left and shook my dad's outstretched hand. "I came to cook. I've been told you have an amazing kitchen."

My dad smiled. "Oh. Thanks. I haven't gotten that one before. My top three compliments are: I have an amazing golf swing, I have an amazing ability to sand docks, and I have an amazing head of hair." He rubbed his hand over his bald head. "But thank you. I'll add kitchen to the list."

"It's really my mom's kitchen," I said. Not that she used it much. But she had designed it.

"And look at that. My daughter snatched it right back off the list." Dad grinned.

"Speaking of golf swings, Dad, Diego claims he can hit a golf ball through the goalposts from that hill behind the stadium?"

"What?" Diego said, indignant. "This again? You still don't believe me?"

"Your credibility was called into question recently and reminded me that no, I don't."

My dad held up his hands like this wasn't his fight. "It *would* be impressive."

"Exactly. Thanks, Dad."

"He didn't agree with you," Diego said.

I laughed, then said to my dad, "I think Mom went next door to Aunt Marinn's."

"And that's my daughter's subtle way of dismissing me," Dad said.

"Was it subtle?" I asked.

He laughed and I hugged him. Because occasionally he needed a sign that I loved him. He left the house still chuckling.

"Alana is already in the kitchen," I told Frank and Diego, leading them there.

"Has she started?" Diego asked.

"I think . . ."

I didn't get the chance to finish that sentence because Diego rushed by me, calling out, "Do we not have rules? We get the same amount of time."

"What is this, *Chopped*?" she asked back.

Frank and I were left standing together. I met his eyes. "I just need to go lock an office door, I'll join you in the kitchen in a minute."

"Hilarious," he said, but didn't give a jab back, like he normally did, so I was left feeling like a jerk.

I took a deep breath. "Let's go."

In the kitchen, Alana had taken over half the island and two burners on the stove.

Diego began practically flinging his ingredients onto the island beside her stuff.

"No cross-contamination," she said, playfully swatting at his arm.

Frank pulled a barstool out and sat down.

"Does anyone want anything to drink?" I asked. "We have soda or water."

"I'll take a Coke." Frank was the only one who answered. Both Diego and Alana were too busy with their food.

I retrieved a can from the fridge and handed it to Frank.

"Thanks," he said.

"You're welcome." Were we in some alternate universe where Frank and I could be civil to each other?

Diego put a pan on the stove and poured oil into it. He unwrapped a fish fillet from some brown paper.

"Did you catch that?" I asked.

He looked up at me through his long lashes with a smirk on his face. He had very long lashes and a very cute smirk. "No, I did not."

He put the fish in the pan and it sizzled.

Alana was running around the kitchen like she really was on *Chopped* and the announcer had just declared there were five minutes left. She pulled open the oven door and slid a pan of chicken onto the middle rack.

"I usually marinate the chicken overnight," she said. "So it won't be as amazing as it normally is, but it'll come close."

"Are you making excuses, Alana?" Diego asked.

"I won't need excuses when I win."

Diego drizzled some herbs over the fish in the pan and then covered it with the lid. A pot of white rice was also cooking on the stove. I assumed Alana had that going. She wiped her hands on a towel and sat on the stool, apparently having some downtime now that the chicken was in the oven.

"Have you been reading the emails?" Frank asked me and Alana.

In that moment, I realized that Frank might know the secret of Diego's caller identity, too. He obviously had talked to him, knew his voice. And he had listened to that voice in the recording studio. Had he put two and two together?

But even if he had, I reminded myself, he'd gotten the same speech from Ms. Lyon about keeping identities secret. He wouldn't say anything. At least, I hoped he wouldn't.

I gave Alana panicked eyes, and she gave the slightest shake of her head. Did that mean Frank didn't know?

"Yes, we have," Alana said. "They're pretty brutal."

"What emails?" Diego asked from where he stood at the stove.

"For the podcast. They're boring," I said, trying to downplay them so Frank didn't feel the need to elaborate. It didn't work.

"I think they're super entertaining," Frank said.

"Of course you would," Alana retorted.

"What's that supposed to mean?" he asked her.

"Well, obviously they're upsetting to Kate! You're over there devouring them as your Friday night entertainment," she said huffily, even though she had been reading them one after another to me only an hour ago.

"Why are they upsetting to Kate?" Diego asked.

"I'm wondering the same thing," Frank said.

I opened my mouth to answer when Alana said, "Because they're making her stressed about the future of the podcast."

"Not that stressed," I said.

"Can someone fill me in here?" Diego asked.

"Oh, when Looking for Love didn't call in this week, listeners weren't happy," Alana said.

Diego occupied himself with chopping tomatoes. "Why is that Kate's fault?"

"It's not," Alana said. "But listeners like to take it out on someone and she's one of the faces of the podcast, so she gets the privilege of being yelled at."

I shifted uncomfortably on my stool.

"You were yelled at?" Diego asked.

"Well, yelling through emails," I said.

"They were in all caps?" he asked.

I laughed.

Alana rolled her eyes. "Okay, Mr. Literal, they weren't in all caps but . . ."

"Here," Frank said, taking out his phone. "I'll read you one and you can see for yourself."

"No need to read one," I said, but Frank was already speaking.

" 'Kat and Victoria. Why didn't Looking for Love call in? You need more phone lines so people can get through. It's always busy. You can't run a good show if the interesting people can't get through.' " Frank put a finger in the air. "I actually heard that's true. That people are getting busy signals. Maybe he did try to call in."

"He probably didn't," Diego said, tasting a spoonful of his sauce. "I mean, maybe the caller didn't have an update last week. Maybe nothing happened."

For the first time since Diego called in, I felt guilty for the secret I held. In the beginning, I wasn't quite sure it was him.

Once I was surer, I thought of it as a moral obligation to keep his identity private. But now, as his friend, I felt like he should know that *we* knew. Why hadn't I thought to tell him before?

But then again . . . it wasn't like he was being forthcoming with us. He knew we worked on the podcast, obviously. He wasn't offering up the fact that he was the caller in question. If he wanted us to know, he'd tell us. But we *did* know. Gah. I felt torn.

I looked at Alana to see if she was having the same internal battle as I was, but she was standing up and checking on her chicken.

"You're probably right," Frank said, putting his phone facedown on the counter. "Let people complain. It creates buzz."

Diego opened up a package of corn tortillas. Then he put both hands on the counter and met my eyes. "I'm sorry people are complaining."

I almost said, *it's not your fault*, but stopped myself. In this case, it was, and I couldn't bring myself to say that lie. "It's okay," I said instead. "Don't worry about it."

"The podcast gets lots of fan mail, too," Alana said, closing the oven door. "Nothing to worry about. Kat had a guy ask her out through email today."

I sucked in an indignant breath.

"You *did*?" Frank asked. He snatched his phone back up and started scrolling through it.

"Please, let's not talk about this." I could feel my face getting hot.

Alana laughed as Frank read the email out loud. Diego had a huge smile on his face, too.

"I'm going to kill all of you," I said, but was actually glad for the lightened mood.

Diego began assembling his tacos with cabbage, cheese, salsa, and the fish that was now blackened to perfection. Alana pulled her chicken out of the oven and plated it as well. As they worked side by side in the kitchen, they kept bumping elbows and shoulders. It was so obvious they were doing it on purpose, too. I found myself staring too often, a nervous feeling forming in my stomach. I was just nervous for Alana, I told myself. Worried that she was going to be disappointed if he didn't ask her to the festival. He'd ask her. I needed to stop worrying about it. That thought did nothing to calm me.

After they arranged the food, the plates were set in front of us. Frank and I sampled each of their dishes.

"And the winner is?" Alana asked.

Diego's tacos were amazing. The best I'd ever had. But he was right, I was biased. I pointed to Alana. And in a surprise move, so did Frank. Alana cheered.

Diego growled. "Do you think your dad will let me borrow his golf clubs, Kate?"

"No need to take out your anger on the kitchen," Alana joked.

Diego smiled her way. "If I can't win the cook-off, I have something else to prove."

# CHAPTER 25

We sat on the hill behind the school, the goalposts of the football stadium barely visible in the dark. Alana was next to me, clinging to my arm because she was cold. Frank was on the other side, leaning back on one hand, holding a flashlight with the other. Diego stood, a golf ball on a tee, my dad's golf club in his hands. He surveyed the distance, then turned our way.

He pointed the end of the golf club at me and winked. "This one's for you."

My heart gave a happy flutter. And that's when I realized it—what all my unexpected reactions around him had been about lately—I had a crush on my best friend's crush.

No.

This couldn't happen. It wasn't happening. I cleared my throat. "I'll believe it when I see it," I said, but my voice came out funny. I tried not to look at Alana next to me.

Diego wound up and swung. The thud of the metal connecting with the ball echoed, and I watched as the ball flew into the air, highlighted by the beam of Frank's flashlight. Then it disappeared into the night.

Alana laughed so hard that she snorted. "It's too dark," she said between her laughter. "You can't prove anything."

"He can if we turn on the stadium lights," Frank said.

"We're not turning on the stadium lights," I responded. "We can just do this after school Monday."

"The football team will be practicing Monday," Frank said. "I'm going to go turn on the lights." He stood.

Alana did, too. "I'll go with you."

"No, this is a stupid idea," I said.

"It sounds fun to me," Alana said.

I stood. "We should all go, then."

"No, because when we turn on the lights, Diego has to be up here to hit the ball," Frank said. And with that he, his flashlight, and Alana went back down the hill, leaving me and Diego in the dark.

"Wait!" I called out, but they didn't stop.

Why would they do that? Alana knew I hated Frank, but why hadn't she sent me down the hill with him so she could be alone with Diego? Considering she was the master flirter, she was doing this all wrong. Even I knew that. Was this another one of her games? Was she trying to make herself look more appealing? What was Alana thinking? Probably not that I had feelings for the guy she just left me alone with. Why would she think *that*? Only a horrible friend would like the guy her best friend liked.

I rubbed my arms and turned slowly away from Alana's disappearing back and toward Diego.

He stood there, with his golf club, watching them disappear down the hill as well. He seemed just as disappointed by this turn of events as I did.

Okay, I could do this. I'd *been* doing this. Nobody needed to know about my feelings, including him. I sank back down to the dirt and looked up at the sky. The stars were so numerous that they seemed to be close to bursting through the blackness.

"It's amazing up here," I said.

Diego looked up, too. "I agree. But I wish I could see this sky over a million different cities."

"Really?"

He propped the golf club on the ground and leaned on the end of it. "You don't?"

"I don't know. This is my home. It's my comfort zone."

"I would argue that you can feel that way anywhere," Diego said thoughtfully, "if you are comfortable in your own skin."

Maybe that was part of my problem. I wasn't all the time. I was only truly comfortable when right in the middle of the lake. It's when I felt the most like me.

"And that is what is called confidence, Diego. I've always known you had it."

"I'm not confident about everything," he mumbled. "So I get it."

"Get what?"

"I get how you might feel out of your element sometimes."

My eyes had adjusted to the dark, and I could see much

better now. I picked up a stick that was on the ground next to my leg and began drawing in the dirt. "Who taught you how to cook?" I asked.

"My grandmother. She was amazing at it. To her, food meant love, and there was never a shortage of it growing up."

"And your grandpa?"

"He was a field worker. Back-breaking labor for pretty much no pay. But it's what brought them here from Mexico, and my dad got to go to college and live the dream. He's a pharmacist."

"And your parents want you to go to college?"

"Of course."

"And you don't want to go?" I don't know why I assumed that but his talk of seeing the stars from under a million different cities gave me that impression.

"I want to go to culinary school. But first I want to go and travel around the world and visit small villages and learn from little old women or men steeped in tradition. I just know those are things I'd never learn in any school." His gaze was distant, like he was imagining this now.

His passion was contagious. "That does sound exciting."

He straightened up, his dreamy gaze disappearing. "But not practical."

"Is that you talking or your parents?"

"A little bit of both, I think." He paused for a minute. "It was nearly impossible to even come *here* tonight. And this is only thirty minutes away."

"What do you mean?"

"It's always a battle to get out of the house. In my parents' dream world I would only do school stuff, work, and sleep." Our eyes met, and I wondered if he was going to tell me he had been calling in to the podcast. This complaint was similar to what he had said the first time he called. I held my breath in anticipation, trying to decide what I'd say if he admitted it. I'd tell the truth. That I knew it was him. But he didn't admit anything. He just went quiet.

"So they don't know about *your* dream world," I finally said. "Your desire to travel?"

"No. This is actually the first time I've said it out loud. It mostly lives in my head."

He'd shared it with me first? *That means nothing*, I told myself.

"Any expert advice for me?" he asked.

Right. I was the advice giver. He wasn't sharing this with me. He was sharing it with Kat. "I need my cohost here to give proper advice," I joked.

He lifted one side of his mouth into a half smile.

"Let's see. Advice." I tried to think, even though my heart was beating faster than normal. "Isn't part of being young being able to do impractical things? When else will you be able to travel the world without responsibilities?"

"Yeah . . ." He looked down the hill. "They should've found the lights by now."

Diego was private, I was learning. Just when I thought I'd broken through and he'd revealed something about himself, he seemed to back off. I understood. I liked to keep things inside, too.

I followed his gaze down the hill. "Maybe they don't know how to turn the lights on. Or more likely, the control box is locked."

"Probably true. Should we head down and try to find them?"

"Sure."

We stumbled over twigs and roots and around trees with only our phone flashlights to guide the way. Diego dropped the golf club off in his car, which was parked at the bottom of the hill. Then we had to walk through a parking lot and around the outside of the stadium to the entrance, which was locked.

"Do you think they found a way in?" he asked.

"If it was up to Alana, then yes. She really is adventurous," I said. After hearing what it was he wanted to do after high school, I realized even more how much of a good fit he and Alana were.

We kept walking, skirting around the baseball field, which had chain link instead of cement walls. We found the gate but it was chained shut.

"My brother climbed this once and he's not athletic at all. I'm sure we could," I said, but then I remembered Max's ripped shirt. I really didn't want to rip my clothing tonight.

Diego tugged on the gate, and the chain was loose enough for a body to squeeze through. I wondered why Max had to climb the fence at all. Maybe he climbed it at a different section or the chain was tighter that day. I slid through, and Diego followed after me. The baseball field connected to the football field at one end zone, separated by another gate that wasn't locked. And then we were in.

Alana and Frank hadn't found the lights yet, but we walked the length of the field toward the goalpost at the opposite end. Diego had his eyes on the ground and it wasn't until he said, "See!" that I realized why. The light from his phone highlighted the single golf ball, which had come to a stop at about the ten-yard line right in the middle of the field.

He picked it up with a smile and held it out for me.

"You think this proves something?" I asked.

"It absolutely proves something. Look where it was." He took me by the shoulders and guided me to the exact location of the ball's landing and turned me to face the goal. "Look."

I looked. I stood in almost the exact center. To land here, the ball would've had to come through those posts.

"Admit it," he said as if he knew I had come to the conclusion I had.

"It could've bounced off the—"

"No it couldn't have."

I laughed. "You're right."

He was still behind me, holding my shoulders. "What's that?" he asked.

"You're right!" I yelled.

He pulled me back against his chest with a laugh. "Yes, I am."

That's when the stadium lights went on and a loud "Woo-hoo!" sounded from the top row of seats. Diego dropped his hands from my shoulders, and I took two quick steps forward. We both looked toward the noise to see Alana standing there with her hands in the air. Frank joined her a minute later.

He pointed to us on the field. "You can't hit golf balls from there, Martinez!"

"I already proved my point!" he yelled back.

"Don't you have to prove it to them?" I asked.

"You were the one who didn't believe me."

"I believe you now," I said.

"Hey!" a deep voice called from beyond the stadium seats. "You kids are trespassing!"

"Run!" Alana yelled.

Diego didn't hesitate. He grabbed hold of my hand and pulled me back the way we'd come. The stadium lights went out, and we were plunged into darkness. I wondered if Frank had done that to make it harder to find us.

My heart was pounding a thousand beats per minute as we sprinted toward the unlocked gate that separated the football and baseball fields. When we crossed from one field into another, the beam of a flashlight swept back and forth over our heads. At first I thought it was Frank, but then there was another light. Diego pulled me behind the metal bleachers to the left and we smashed ourselves between the chain-link fence and the seats.

My temple pressed against the side of his neck where I could feel his pulse racing.

"My parents are going to kill me," I whispered. It was always so important to them that I kept an upstanding reputation at all times. It always felt like our livelihood somehow depended on it.

"We won't get caught. It'll be fine," Diego said just as quietly back.

Shouts rang out from behind us and I closed my eyes, as if that would make us more invisible. I tried to calm my breathing, take in one breath at a time as evenly as possible. In through my nose and out through my mouth. Diego smelled good—a sporty scent mixed with mint. He was chewing gum, I realized. My heart slowed its pace, and I came back to my senses, making me fully aware of the fact that I was smashed up against Diego, seemingly every inch from my ankles to my head touching a part of him.

"Did you get a chance to read any of that magazine?" he asked softly.

Magazine? What was he talking about? Oh, right. He'd given me the latest *Lake Life* magazine that was now in my car somewhere. I actually *had* read an article from one of the copies in the marina. He was trying to get my mind off of our situation, I was sure. I was acting like a huge wimp right now.

It was nice of him to distract me. What was that article about? "Wakesurfing. I read an article about wakesurfing."

"Oh yeah?" he asked. "Was it good?"

"I haven't tried it yet. It made me want to."

"Is that all?"

"So far. I'll read more . . . later."

"Okay." He took a step back the way we'd come, and I nearly stumbled without his support. "I don't hear them anymore," he said. "Want to make a break for the car?"

"Do you think security saw the car?"

"No, it's parked over by the hill. They wouldn't have checked there. It's not even on campus."

"Okay, let's go."

* * *

Alana and Frank were already at the car when we arrived. They were laughing and retelling the story to themselves loudly.

When Alana saw us, she flung her arms around Diego's neck. "You made it!"

"Barely," I said when she gave me a hug as well. "That was close."

"Close?" Frank asked. "As if you were getting hauled off to jail?"

"Obviously not jail but there would've been some consequence."

He scoffed. "Were you seriously scared?"

A burst of anger flamed in my chest looking at his mocking face. "You weren't scared because you get away with crap like that all the time. Even when everyone knows you did something, nothing happens to you. You're Frank Young."

"Then why wasn't Alana scared? Or Diego?"

I looked at the other two, waited for them both to tell me they were, but they didn't.

"Guess your theory about the spoiled rich kid didn't work this time," Frank said.

I swallowed back embarrassment, my pride tasting bitter in my mouth. "Let's just go before security decides to check the city block." I climbed into the back seat of the car, having to move the golf club to do so.

"For the record," Alana said loudly as she and the others joined me, "I was a little scared of getting caught, too. I think Kate is right. You have never experienced real consequences, Frank." She squeezed my hand, letting me know she'd said that just for me. I appreciated it.

"Whatever," Frank said. "Don't pin this on me this time."

We drove home, more silent than we'd been on the way there. When the boys had left and Alana stood in my kitchen gathering her things, she said, "Diego didn't ask me to the Fall Festival tonight."

"Well, half the night you were with Frank. I think maybe you were sending him the wrong idea," I said.

"Maybe he's not into football . . . or carnival rides. Maybe he doesn't want to go at all."

“That could be.”

She nodded like she’d just solved a mystery and felt much better. She picked up the grocery bag she’d loaded full of left-over supplies and said, “You know I love you and always have your back.”

“I know,” I said, seeing where this was going before she even continued.

“And most of the time I agree with you about Frank.”

“I know. I was wrong this time.”

“You were.”

“Thanks for sticking up for me anyway,” I said.

“Always.” She gave me a hug and headed for the door. “But maybe you should apologize to him,” she dropped on the way out.

I didn’t want to apologize to Frank. But I knew Alana was right. He had been decent. Nice even, and I had thrown unfair accusations at him. So I’d apologize. I wasn’t going to search him out and beg his forgiveness. But when the opportunity presented itself, I’d do it.

# CHAPTER 26

"Humility. It goes a long way," Samantha said. I turned the volume up on my phone one notch because my dad was dropping blow-up tubes into a box, and it was loud. I was across the store, boxing the swimsuits. Our season wasn't quite over but it was getting close. Come October, the only people who came to the marina were fishermen. "I like a confident guy as much as the next girl," Samantha continued, "but a guy who doesn't relate every course at dinner back to one of his accomplishments would be better."

"How did he relate the salad course to his accomplishments?" Tami asked.

"Apparently he grew a winter garden. He has quite the green thumb. Plants love him, as do cows."

"Did you have steak?"

"We did."

I smiled. The *First Dates* podcast was quickly becoming my favorite of all the ones I'd been listening to lately.

There was a tap on my shoulder. I turned to see my mom, her mouth moving.

"What?" I asked. I pulled out my earbuds. "Sorry. Can you start over?"

"I was just saying, you seem to live in those earbuds lately." Mom held out the packing tape to me. "I found this in the stockroom. Thought you might need it."

"Thanks." I took the tape and set it down next to the box. "So . . ."

My dad walked over and held out his hand. "Can I borrow that tape for a second? This box is full."

I threw the tape to him.

"So?" Dad asked, obviously realizing I had been about to say something.

"We're recording a podcast at the Fall Festival this year."

"Oh yeah?" Mom said.

I nodded. "There will be an audience and everything. I don't think it's going to be as long as our normal podcasts. Kind of a special edition. But if you guys want to come . . ."

"Of course we do," Mom said.

"Wouldn't miss it," Dad added.

"Okay. Good."

Mom smiled. "Good."

I held up my earbuds. "Guess I have more studying to do, then."

★ ★ ★

"Hello, lovely listeners. It's Victoria and Kat here, once again ready to tackle your problems. Tackle. Do you like what I did there, Kat?"

"Yes, I do."

"Because the big Fall Festival game is this weekend."

"I got it. Very clever."

"I thought so. Anyway, after you *hit* our listeners with our disclaimer, we'll *intercept* our first call."

"Are you going to do that the entire episode?" I asked.

"Of course I am."

I chuckled. "Okay, we may be full of bad puns today but we are still not professionals."

"Do you mean bad punts?" Victoria joked.

"I walked right into that one."

"You really did."

"But, remember, if you have a real problem, please call 911 or any of the emergency numbers listed on our website. And thank you, Young Industries, for your sponsorship. They have been serving Lakesprings for decades." I tried not to make a face when I said this.

"Okay, first caller, what can we help you with today?" Victoria asked once the call was patched through.

"Hi, this is Tamara Sorres."

It was so rare to hear someone say their name on the show that I almost told her that we'd edit it out.

"Tamara Sorres, our student body president here at Sequoia High?" Victoria asked.

"Yes," Tamara said.

"What can we do for you?"

"I'm inviting you and Kat to participate in one of our Fall Festival Week activities tomorrow. You have been requested by popular vote."

"Really?" Victoria asked. "Which activity?"

"Dunk tank."

I laughed. "People are requesting to dunk us?"

"Yes, actually. In large quantities."

"Sounds fun," Victoria said.

"I'll pass," I said.

Victoria clicked her tongue in disapproval. "No, she won't. We will both be there. So bring on the baseballs, Sequoia. We don't go down easily!"

"You realize by the time our listeners hear this, we will probably have been dunked many times over," I said.

"I maintain my declaration," Victoria said.

"Lunchtime," Tamara said. "See you then."

"Wait!" Victoria said, before Tamara could hang up. "You did call in to an advice show. Any advice we can give you today?"

"Uh . . ." Tamara was clearly caught off guard but seriously considering the question. "How do you get people you carpool with to chip in for gas?"

"I think you just did," I said.

"I agree," Victoria said. "Ask. And now you have. Good luck with that. And, people, come on, if someone is giving you a ride every day, don't be a cheapskate."

Tamara hung up and Victoria looked over at me. "You ready to get wet tomorrow?"

"Not particularly."

"It'll be fun." The phone board was lighting up. "Hello, caller, you're on the air."

"Hi. It's me . . . I don't remember what you named me," Diego said.

I smiled.

"Looking for Love," Victoria said. So she was able to recognize his voice now, too.

"Oh yeah. Still not a huge fan of that."

"We can change it out for your real name, if you'd rather," Victoria said in a voice I hadn't heard her use before. Was that her flirting voice?

"I'll stick with the love one."

I laughed.

"How have you been?" Victoria asked. "The listeners missed you last week."

"Yes, I didn't really have an update so I didn't call in." Was he trying to make it clear for our audience that he hadn't reached a busy signal?

"Our theme this week is the Fall Festival," Victoria said, even though it really wasn't, she had just made it into that. "Have you asked your lucky girl to be your date?"

"I don't think my . . . she, I don't think she's into football."

I wouldn't say Alana was into football but she also wasn't

*not* into it. She'd been to her fair share of games, if not for the football, at least for the social aspect.

"Are *you*?" I asked, curious. Alana thought that answer was no, but maybe she was wrong.

"I don't play, if that's what you're asking."

"But are you a fan?"

"I can cheer with the best of them."

"The festival's not only about football, anyway," Victoria jumped in. "Don't forget about the carnival after. If your crush isn't into football, maybe she's into fun."

"Maybe," he said, with a smile in his voice.

"But you haven't asked her?" I pressed. I'd told him to have patience, but this was getting ridiculous. I needed him to ask her. To squash my silly crush permanently.

"Actually, I sort of did," he said.

"You did?"

"How can you *sort of* ask someone?" Victoria shook her head.

"I was trying to be clever and thoughtful, do something that meant something to her, but I think she said no in a really polite way."

"Did you ask in code or something?" I asked. Alana would not have said no unless she didn't realize she was being asked.

"In a way, I guess."

"You need to just ask her straight-out at this point," I said.

"But I think I got my answer."

"If your girl is saying no," Victoria said, her flirt-voice still in place, "you have a backup right here."

I coughed.

"Who?" he asked.

"Me, of course," Victoria said.

"Oh. Well . . . uh . . . thanks."

"I thought Brian asked you in rose petals," I said to Victoria.

Victoria giggled. "He did, it was cute. Good luck to you, Looking for Love. We're all rooting for you."

"Thanks."

"Don't forget, listeners," Victoria said after Diego had ended the call. "We have a bonus show this week. We'll be recording live at the Fall Festival, Friday night after the football game. So even if you have to go solo to the carnival, come for us. You can ask your question live or leave an anonymous question in the box you'll see in the cafeteria this week. We can't wait!"

When the show ended, Victoria shook out her hands and took off the headphones. I'd never seen her do that before.

"You okay?" I asked. "You did good today."

"We have to be in a dunk tank tomorrow."

I sighed. "You readily agreed to that dunk tank. And said it would be fun. Twice."

"You're right. I'll be great." She stood up and moved toward the door.

"Victoria, you don't have to be in the dunk tank tomorrow if you don't want to be."

"Of course I do. I'm changing the world, right?" She forced out a laugh.

Hmm. For all her bravado, Victoria wasn't as fearless as I once thought. Did everyone put up a front at all times? Was confidence a front for fear? Did true friendship mean being able to see through that? Or being willing to drop the front?

"If anyone can, it's you," I said.

She flashed me her podcast smile and left.

I unplugged both of our headphones and returned them to the sound room. Then I sent a text to Alana. Unwittingly, she'd turned Diego down for the Fall Festival. We needed to analyze every conversation they'd had recently. And we needed a new plan.

# CHAPTER 27

"I cannot think of any way, coded or not, that Diego asked me to the Fall Festival," Alana said at her house that afternoon.

Alana had the best house ever. It was quiet and big and always full of food. We sat at her kitchen island, stuffing our faces with cookies her dad had made. They had coconut and chocolate and some sort of delicious crunchy rice in them. I had already eaten three.

"Are you sure that's what he said on the podcast?" she asked me.

"I'm positive," I said through my mouthful. "Did he spell out the invite in the food the other day or something?"

She smiled. "That would've been funny and awesome, but I don't think so. I guess I just assumed he wasn't asking because he wasn't into football."

"I know. Okay. It's time to pull out the big guns."

"What guns are those?"

"You have to ask him yourself," I said.

"Done," she said.

I ignored the tight feeling of jealousy in my chest. I wasn't allowed to be jealous. "That wasn't hard to talk you into."

"Did you think it would be?" She raised her eyebrows.

"No." I looked at the tray of cookies on the island. "If I have another one, will I get the world's worst stomachache or just the second worst?"

"Have another one."

"Okay." I plucked a cookie from the tray. "Now, how are you going to ask him?"

"I have an idea."

* * *

It was bad enough to sit on the metal seat in the dunk tank, behind the glass, in my swimsuit, like I was on display. But it got even worse when Diego and Frank appeared at the front of the line with Alana. I had no doubt Alana had texted them about an opportunity they couldn't pass up.

Diego picked up two baseballs. "I wonder if this will be as easy as driving a golf ball through the goalpost," I heard him say.

"Ha ha!" I shouted.

He winked at me and my stomach flipped. My best friend's crush or not, Diego was pretty flirty himself. He needed to stop that. He wasn't allowed to flirt with *everybody* when he was asking advice about Alana on air. I saw him smile over at Alana and felt a burst of annoyance.

So far I had managed to avoid getting dunked. Victoria hadn't been so lucky. The baseball team had shown up for her stint, and she was plunged six times. Now she sat at a nearby table, wrapped in a towel, talking to one of the team members. The water had turned her hair into tousled beach waves. And she was smiling. She'd conquered something today, and I was proud of her. I wondered if life was about facing fears. Sometimes we overcame them and sometimes they overcame us. On the days we won, we had every right to celebrate.

Victoria held up a white box and shook it. "Don't forget to submit anonymous questions for our carnival live podcast!" she yelled to the people waiting in the line.

"Are you ready?" Diego called out, bringing my attention back to him.

"If ready involves sitting here, then yes, so ready!" I called back.

He twisted the baseball once in his hand then threw. I cringed. The ball whizzed by the glass, right above the target. *Whew.* The line behind him stretched twenty deep so I knew he really would get only the two chances. He tried again and the baseball bounced off the glass.

"Nice try!" I taunted. Diego frowned.

Alana stepped up. I was most worried about her. Alana was good at everything she tried. But both of her attempts missed their mark. I let out a relieved breath.

And then it was Frank's turn. He tossed and caught the ball in one hand several times as he stood there.

"Hello, Kitty Kat," he said with a sly smirk.

It occurred to me that I still hadn't apologized to him. I sensed karma was about to bite me for that. Alana was saying something to him that I couldn't hear. Then Alana shouted to me, "You're going down!"

I almost believed that she knew something about Frank's history with a baseball that I didn't. But when he missed on his first try, I relaxed on my cold seat. I thought he'd toss the next ball a couple times in the air like he had the last, but the moment he had it in his right hand, he threw.

There was a second of delay between the ball hitting its target and it triggering the release mechanism on my seat. When I realized what had happened, I let out a scream and then down I went.

The water was cold. Colder than the lake. My chest tightened with the change in temperature and at first my feet couldn't find the bottom to launch myself back up. Finally I found the floor and pushed off. And then my head whacked into the bottom of the seat so hard that I saw stars.

A collective intake of breath sounded from the line of people still waiting. Then I went back under the water. I hadn't meant to. But I'd had plenty of hard falls in water before so I knew not to panic. I relaxed for a moment, letting my head clear. Then I stood.

I coughed several times before I realized someone was above me, leaning on the seat and reaching a hand out to help me.

"I'm sorry," Frank said.

"For what?" I coughed out. "Playing the game, right?"

"I didn't mean for you to get hurt."

"I know."

I moved toward the metal stairs to let myself out. That was when I heard someone pushing the release button for the seat. And then Frank, clothes and all, fell into the tank. I tried my hardest not to laugh. I knew it was Alana's doing even before I heard her laughing.

Frank came up sputtering. "I had my phone in my pocket, Alana!" He'd obviously heard her laughter, too.

"Oops," she said.

The waiting line thought this was the funniest thing they'd seen. There was an excited buzz of talking and laughter.

Frank splashed water out the open door and all over Alana. He seemed mad at first but when I sent a splash his way, his face melted into a smile. He returned his own splash. Then he climbed out of the tank fast and chased Alana down. When he finally caught her, he smashed her into a big, wet hug, while Alana shrieked.

I wasn't sure if my time was up in the booth, but my head hurt so I climbed out. Diego waited with a towel open for me. I stepped into it, and he wrapped it around my shoulders.

"You okay?" he asked. "You kind of have a bad habit of hitting your head on metal objects."

"Only when you're around, it seems."

He chuckled. "Does it hurt?"

"Maybe."

"You need some of my magic, right?"

I knew he was kidding but I leaned forward anyway and he drew a *V* on the top of my head.

"All better," I said, stepping back and trying not to blush. "By the way, I used that on Cora the other day and it totally worked."

"You did?" he asked as if this surprised him.

"Yes, I think your mom's tradition is cute."

"She'd be happy to hear that."

What was I doing? He was so easy to be around. Too easy. I took another step away from him.

"Kate!" Alana called. "Save me!"

Frank still had her in a bear hug and was now shaking his wet hair all over her. She pushed out of his hold and ran to hide behind Diego. She grabbed hold of the sides of his T-shirt and I averted my gaze.

"Saved by the only one here who doesn't deserve to get wet," Frank said.

"I need to go change before the bell rings," I said.

I headed toward the locker room and they all followed me. Alana had linked her arm through Diego's, for protection or closeness I wasn't sure. Probably a little of both.

Frank was walking on Alana's other side. I met his eyes. I cleared my throat, then cleared my throat again.

"Just spit it out," Alana said.

"I'm sorry," I said.

"What?" Frank asked. "Was that for me?"

"Yes. I'm sorry for making it seem like you didn't care if we all got in trouble last Friday."

"Oh. Right." We walked a few more steps toward the gym and he said, "It's hard to break our habit of saying whatever jerky things we want to each other."

I laughed a little. "It is."

"I'm glad we're trying."

"Me too." And I meant it.

# CHAPTER 28

In the parking lot after school, Alana handed me a grocery bag full of Post-it notes. "Are you *sure* Diego works at the tutoring center today?" she asked me.

"Yes."

"Okay, after lab, Frank and I will meet you over there. Will Diego see you?"

"No, I think they make employees park in back to save the spots out front for customers."

She nodded.

"Which color am I using to spell out the words?" I asked, putting the bag in my car.

"The blue is to spell *festival* and the question mark. The orange is to cover the rest of the car."

"This is going to be cool," I said.

"Let's pray for no wind." Alana grinned at me. "Anyway, I think he'll be so surprised he'll have to say yes."

* * *

An hour later, Alana and Frank met me behind the tutoring center, where I still hadn't finished covering Diego's car.

Alana snatched a packet of Post-its out of the bag by my feet and threw the packet to Frank. "Start coating, baby."

The three of us got to work. A few minutes passed, and Alana said, "Post-its always remind me of Hawaii."

"They have a lot of Post-its in Hawaii?" Frank asked.

"No, but they have these open-air markets where locals sell trinkets and jewelry," Alana explained. "Mainly to tourists. My mom used to help set up. There was this one lady who loved Post-its and she'd use them to price all her stuff. One day I was bored and I switched all the price tags around. Every time that lady saw me after that, she shooed me away while mumbling something in Pidgin."

"So you've always been a brat," Frank said.

Alana backhanded him across the chest but then said, "Yes."

I laughed.

It took us nearly another hour to finish Diego's car. Then we moved to the back fence and sat down on the curb to wait for Diego to come out.

"Are you nervous?" I asked Alana.

"Of course not," she said, and I completely believed her. *I* would've been nervous. Who was I kidding. I *was* nervous. In the darkest reaches of my obviously horrible heart, I wanted Diego to turn her down. This made me an awful friend.

No. I wanted him to say yes. Then my horrible heart would get the hint. Then I would know, beyond a doubt, that Diego had been talking about her on the podcast all this time.

Frank had been pretty quiet during the whole car decorating and I wondered why.

When he spoke, he seemed to answer my unspoken question.

"And after weeks of calling in to the show, he finally gets his girl."

I widened my eyes and looked at Alana.

"Seriously?" Frank said. "You thought I didn't know it was him? I do *know* the guy. And us podcasters do not, in fact, manipulate the voices until after the fact."

"We don't?" Alana asked in mock surprise.

"You're not going to tell him, are you?" I asked Frank.

"She still thinks I have no integrity," he said to no one in particular.

"No, it's not that. I just think . . . I don't know." I was rambling. "I don't want him to find out that we've all known all this time." I couldn't imagine he'd feel good about that. Why hadn't we told him again?

"He won't find out from me," Frank said.

I squeezed his arm. "Thank you."

"How's your phone, Frank?" Alana asked with a smile.

He bumped his leg into hers. "Totally dead, courtesy of the dunking booth incident, thank you very much."

We all heard the back door open, and we all jumped up simultaneously.

Diego saw the car first. How could he not? His whole face lit up with a smile. Then he searched the surrounding area until his eyes locked on to the three of us, standing against the fence.

"So?" Alana asked when he didn't say anything at first.

"Oh! Yes!" he said.

Alana ran forward and threw her arms around his neck in a hug.

My heart seemed to fall to my feet.

At least it got the hint.

"Wait here," Frank said to me. Before I could ask him what he was doing, he ran the ten feet to his car and started rooting around in the trunk. Meanwhile, Alana and Diego walked over to me. She held Diego's hand in hers and she was beaming.

Okay. Alana and Diego. It was about time this thing between them started moving forward again. It felt stalled for a while there, which was odd for Alana. She always got her man, and usually fast. This one had been a little more work. But, by the look on her face, it had obviously been worth it.

"I hope you guys are sticking around to help me clean this up," Diego said, meeting my eyes.

"Of course," Alana said.

Frank headed back toward us, one of his hands behind his back.

"Kat," he said, breathless.

"Kate," both Diego and I said at the same time.

I gave him a playful nudge with my elbow. "Jinx."

"Kate. Right, sorry. I just listen to a lot of podcast talk." Frank had a weird smile plastered on his face, and I couldn't figure out why. Alana seemed to be confused by this interaction, too, because she dropped Diego's hand and crossed her arms.

"What?" I asked Frank. "Do I have something on my face?"

Diego chuckled. "That's my line," he said.

"No." Frank removed his hand from behind his back, revealing a long-stem red rose. "Will you go to the Fall Festival with me?"

My stomach tightened. *What?*

"Oh. I . . ."

Frank bit his lip. "I know I should've asked in a more elaborate way. I had something planned but it didn't work out last minute. The phones were busy."

"You were going to call in to the podcast?" I asked.

He shrugged and a cute, shy smirk took over his face. I was glad the phones had been busy. That would've been so embarrassing. I didn't need the whole high school and town listening to someone ask me out.

I couldn't help but glance at Alana. Her expression was unreadable. I refused to glance at Diego. Then I looked back at Frank.

"Um . . . yes," I finally said. Why not? My heart was already on the floor. Maybe going to the festival with Frank would help matters. And we seemed to be getting along better lately.

"Yes, you'll go with me?" he asked in surprise.

I nodded.

He grabbed my hand, kissed my knuckles, then said, "I'll pick you up at five thirty for dinner before the game." He turned toward Alana and Diego. "Should we all go together?"

Alana nodded. "That would be fun."

"Okay," I said.

Frank flashed one last smile at me, then backed toward his car. "I'm going to leave before you change your mind." He nodded toward Alana. "You can get a ride home with Kate?"

"Of course."

With that, he got into his car and drove away.

I took a small breath and stared at the rose in my hand. The bud flopped over a bit. "That was weird."

"Good weird?" Alana asked.

"Well, it's Frank Young . . . but I guess we called a truce, right?" I said.

Alana shrugged. The fact that she seemed as unsure as I was about this whole thing made me question myself. Maybe I shouldn't have said yes.

I set the rose down by the fence, picked up the empty grocery bag, and began undoing our hard work. Alana and Diego joined me. As we cleaned, Alana would wad up notes and throw them at either Diego or me, which for a while started a bit of a war. When I realized this was creating more work for us, I stopped.

I got to the back bumper and Diego sidled up beside me. "Did you get to take care of the bully thing you were worried about on the podcast yesterday?" he asked.

I brought my hand to my forehead. "I completely forgot. I usually just let Victoria lead, so I'm not used to introducing a topic. I'll have to think about how to do that for next week." How could I have forgotten something so important? This kid was getting bullied, and it completely slipped my mind.

"I'm sure you'll figure it out." He took off another row of orange Post-its and added them to his growing stack. "You and Frank, huh?"

"Let's not get ahead of ourselves."

"Everything starts somewhere." He looked over at me through his long lashes, his soft brown eyes lit with a smile.

He was right. Everything did start somewhere. And as I stood there beside my best friend's crush, removing sticky notes from his old Corolla, I knew exactly when I had started liking him. It was when he drew a *V* on my temple standing in that empty school hallway. It was when those same brown eyes had met mine that day, all sweet and caring.

*We know where we stand*, I reminded my heart. Firmly in friend territory.

# CHAPTER 29

"I'm going to kiss Diego tonight."

I dropped the mascara wand I'd been holding.

Alana and I had gone straight from school to her house and were now sitting in front of the mirror in her bedroom, getting ready for the Fall Festival. Alana's room was various shades of pink. I wasn't sure if it was the lighting or the background color, but my skin always seemed to have a healthy glow there. Maybe I needed to change the paint in my room.

I now had a large black streak across my bare leg from the mascara. I picked the wand up from where it had landed on the ground. "Um . . . okay."

Alana took the cap off her eyeliner. "Where would be the most romantic place to do that?"

Did I really have to give her advice on this? "Probably anywhere it happens will be romantic."

She gave a dreamy sigh. "So true." She leaned forward and applied her eyeliner. "What about you?"

"What about me?" I retrieved a makeup wipe and scrubbed at my leg.

"Are you going to kiss Frank tonight?"

"No!"

"That horrific of a thought, huh?"

"Yes. I mean . . . no, not really, it's just, give me a minute here. I hated the guy like a week ago."

"Why did you say yes, then?"

"Should I have said no?"

"Well, no. But if he likes you, you're kind of leading him on."

"I don't think he likes me. I think he asked me because there was no one left to ask."

* * *

The football game was loud. It had been a while since I'd been to one and I'd forgotten. But here I was at a football game with the guy I used to hate, the guy I needed to start hating for my own sanity, and my best friend.

Frank pointed up ahead and yelled over the noise of the crowd. "Look, they lit up the Ferris wheel."

Alana clapped. "Oh! That looks fun! That's so awesome of your dad to pay for the rides."

I leaned forward so I could yell to Alana, past Frank, who stood between us. "You and me on the roller coaster later?"

"For sure."

"What?" Diego yelled. He was on the far side of Alana and probably hadn't heard a word we'd said.

"Ferris wheel!" Alana said. "Let's ride it later."

"Sure," he responded.

I wondered if that's where the kissing would happen. At the top of the Ferris wheel. I wasn't going to think about that.

"I'm going to get a soda!" I yelled.

"Okay," Alana called back. Frank moved like he was going to come with me, but she grabbed his wrist and said something I couldn't hear.

He laughed and stayed.

Why had she done that? Was she worried about Frank's feelings? That I was leading him on? Maybe it was *me* she was worried about. I did have a horrified reaction to the kissing question earlier. Maybe she was trying to save me. I took the stairs up the bleachers, then down the back side. I drew in a deep breath.

"Kat! Hi!" someone called as I walked by. "I loved your carpool advice!"

"Oh. Thanks!" I said.

"That's Kat from the podcast!" I heard someone else call.

Then I heard another voice.

"Kate! Wait up."

I turned to see Diego following after me. My heart liked this development. I tried to talk it down. Diego wanting a soda did not equal a declaration of any kind.

"It's so loud in there," he said. "I needed to give my eardrums a break."

Where we now stood, in the back of the stadium, it was still loud but not deafening. "I know," I said.

"You too?"

"I came to get a drink."

"Let's get in line, then."

We joined the back of a long line at the snack hut and proceeded to not say anything at all. I usually had no problem talking to Diego. I was making it weird because I liked him. I needed to make it un-weird.

I thought about the last time we'd really talked, on that hill behind the stadium. How he got so guarded. Why was he so guarded? "Tell me about your last relationship," I said because that was apparently the most un-weird thing I could think of. I cringed. "Or don't. I'm sorry."

He smiled. "Don't be sorry. It's a valid question. When I'm done talking about mine, I will return the same question."

Hunter. He wanted to know about Hunter? "Okay. It's pretty boring, but that's fair."

"Ditto. I dated Pam Argyle last year for a couple months. Do you know her?"

"Not really. What happened?"

He looked up at the sky, pursed his lips, and then met my eyes. "Good question. I'm not really sure. I don't have a lot of spare time."

"The schedule thing with your parents?"

"Yes. I think that bothered her. Plus, she complained that I never told her anything."

We inched forward in the line. "You're private."

"That or I just have nothing going on in my head."

I laughed. "Right. That's probably it."

Diego ran a hand through his hair. "Sometimes I hesitate to share important things because . . . I don't think people will care about them as much as I do. And then when I do share, the things are out there to be judged, or never thought about again. And I can't decide which outcome is worse."

"That's understandable. I pretty much judge everything you say."

"I figured."

I gave him a gentle elbow to his ribs. "You know I'm kidding, right?"

"Yes, Kate. I know when you're kidding. It's kind of your defense."

I started to argue but then nodded. It was very unfair that he seemed to know me so well. "Yes. It is."

The girl in front of us in line turned around. "I thought I recognized your voice," she said to me. "Hi, Kat. I love the show."

"Hi, thanks."

"Did you give the football players any advice before the big game tonight?"

"Um . . . no. Their coach didn't think to ask me. Go figure."

She laughed. "I'm going to come to your live show later."

"Thanks."

She turned back around.

"I'm sorry for what I said a minute ago," Diego said, his voice softer. "Was that rude?"

"No. It's true. Humor is my defense. It makes things easier sometimes."

"What things?"

I thought about it. "Pretty much everything."

He smiled. "So, your turn. Tell me about your most recent relationship."

I looked at the girl in front of me, wondering if she was listening in, waiting to share this with everyone. Thankfully, she was talking to someone in front of her now.

"Hunter Eller. Last year. We dated for a while. It was good. We got each other. And then he moved away and stopped texting or calling."

"And you aren't over him."

"What?"

He lowered his voice more, even though the girl wasn't listening. "Alana called in to the podcast that first episode."

"How did you know that?"

"One, because I recognized her voice. She was trying to disguise it but she slipped toward the end. And two, because of the way you were responding to her."

"I guess I was pretty obvious for those who know me." I couldn't remember the exact exchange on the podcast but I knew I gave advice like, *maybe you should let your friend get over him.* And I vaguely remembered saying something about eating new fish when I was ready. "But no. I am over him. I mean, I wasn't, or I thought I wasn't, but then he texted me a couple weeks ago and I realized there was nothing left but the idea of him. I wasn't over the *idea* of him but I was completely over *him*. It took him texting me to realize that."

"So then why . . ." Diego stopped himself, shook his head, and said, "Never mind."

"No, what were you going to say?"

It was our turn at the window and we stepped up.

"Are you getting something for Frank, too?" Diego asked.

Right. Frank. I was here with Frank, even if it was just a formality. "Yes. Two Cokes, please."

Diego ordered the same and we headed back with our hands full.

"What were you going to say a minute ago?" I asked.

"I was going to ask you why you hadn't moved on, but then I remembered you were here with Frank."

I let a sharp breath out. "I don't think I'm going to move on with Frank. We just barely started tolerating each other."

"Kat!" A boy who couldn't have been more than twelve came running up to me. "Can I take a selfie with you?"

"Fair warning, I take really awkward pictures."

"I know! I saw your pictures online. They're awesome."

I laughed and let him snap a picture of us and the two sodas I held.

"Thanks!" he said, running off.

"You've gotten a lot more comfortable with your role," Diego said. "I remember that first week, how you came into tutoring and were so hard on yourself and talked about how you would've given back the job if you could've."

"That has not changed."

"But you've embraced it."

"I guess I sort of have." I wanted to get good at hosting the podcast, and I had. And I'd still choose the lake . . . right?

"It's a good look on you," Diego said.

My traitorous brain said, *Maybe he'd like you if you told him how you felt*. I took a drink and swallowed that thought right down.

# CHAPTER 30

Our team won and that put everyone in an even better mood. The carnival was almost as loud as the football game had been. As promised, three big rides took up half the parking lot, along with booth after booth of carnival games—dart balloon pop, ring toss, water gun horse race, bounce house, and on and on down the line. There were also food booths everywhere, mostly candy, but some fried food on sticks as well.

And then there was the podcast stage. It was set up on the far end, with a big clearing for an audience. In one hour, I was supposed to go up there and talk, live, in front of a bunch of people. I waited for my nerves to kick up a notch but they didn't. Maybe I *had* embraced this new role.

Alana and Diego were walking side by side, taking in the sights. Frank and I trailed behind them.

"Do you want to go on the Ferris wheel?" Frank asked me.

"Sure."

"I have front of the line privileges for all the rides."

I rolled my eyes. "I'm okay waiting in line."

"Well, I'm not." He said it with a smile but I knew he was

serious. He took my hand. "We're going on a ride," he announced.

Alana and Diego turned around. My hand in Frank's did not escape Alana's notice. She wiggled her eyebrows at me. I took my hand back and walked toward the Ferris wheel.

Frank was indeed serious about cutting. And to my surprise, nobody cared. They all called out their thanks to him for providing the rides. Great. That would just encourage him.

Frank and I stepped forward and were strapped into the seat. Frank's arm immediately went around my shoulder as the ride jerked into motion. The motion stopped after ten feet, letting the next people on below us.

"Do you ever think that these parking lot rides are one loose bolt away from falling apart?" he asked, patting a metal support beam.

"Yes, actually. That is my first thought, followed by fear the rest of the ride."

He swung his feet as we moved forward again.

When we stopped at the very top, he leaned forward and looked around. I watched him locate Alana and Diego, who were throwing darts at balloons.

"How much will you give me if I can hit Diego with my gum from up here?"

"Gross," I said. "Don't throw your gum."

"I wasn't going to throw it. I was going to spit it."

I made a face. "Nice."

"Alana would've laughed at that," he said.

"And?"

"You don't find me funny."

"Sometimes you are funny."

Frank's arm was still around me, and with one of his fingers, he began drawing patterns on my arm.

I thought about telling him to stop. Oh no. Maybe he did like me. Maybe I *was* leading him on. But as I watched Alana and Diego down below, seeing how much fun they were having, I kept my mouth shut.

After several more rotations on the Ferris wheel, we reached solid ground again. "The bolt hung on for us," I said as Frank and I walked away from the ride.

"We are survivors for sure," he said.

"My turn!" Alana said, running over to us. "I don't want to wait in line either, so I'm stealing Frank for a second." She grabbed his hand and dragged him back the way we'd come.

"You didn't want to ride the Ferris wheel?" I asked Diego when he and I were left standing there.

"I do not have front of the line privileges."

"The front of the line is overrated."

"It's really not," he said, and I laughed. He gestured to the row of games behind us. "Can I challenge you to a carnival game?"

I checked my phone. "Yes, I have time." I pointed to the booth that was called Gone Fishing. Plastic fish went around a track, and the goal was to cast a magnet attached to a fishing line and catch a fish with its mouth open. "I believe you promised to take me fishing once."

"Did I?" he asked as we walked over.

"No, but you should've."

He chuckled. "Yes, I should've."

We were each handed a pole when we arrived.

"Okay, master, show me the ways," I said.

"You do realize this is nothing like—"

"Shhhh. Let me live in my delusion."

"Okay. It's all in the wrist." He stepped back from the counter and demonstrated how to cast. I followed his example. "Now, I will catch a fish," he said.

He did not catch a fish. His magnet bounced off a closed mouth and shot back toward the counter.

"Wow. That was impressive. I'm beginning to see a pattern here with you and fishing."

He narrowed his eyes at me, and I laughed and pushed him aside. "Let me show you how it's done." I watched the fish along the track and timed their movements. Then I cast my line and much to my own surprise, because I hadn't actually figured out a pattern, my magnet sailed directly into the mouth of a green fish. I threw my hands in the air with a cheer.

"You did not just do that," Diego said.

"I totally did. I beat the fisher!"

He laughed. "You *are* humble in victory, aren't you?"

The operator handed me a small stuffed fish, and we handed back our poles.

"Turns out there are plenty of fish in the sea," I said, showing Diego my toy. "Who knew I just had to literally catch one?"

He bumped my shoulder with his. "You're a dork."

"Maybe I should teach you some techniques for next time you go out fishing. If you come by the marina, I'll give you a lesson. I *have* actually fished before, you know. When I was a kid. Apparently it's all stored up in my muscle memory."

He shook his head but his lips were curved up into a smile he couldn't contain. Then he stopped at a food cart and bought a stick of pink cotton candy. I snagged a piece of the puffy sugar and let it melt in my mouth.

"Now here's something I need to learn to make," I said as we kept walking. "You think there is some cotton candy chef out there somewhere who can teach me?"

"I'm sure."

"Maybe when you go on your world food travels, you can send me a postcard from wherever you are when you find this person."

Diego tilted his head to one side. "You know, I was thinking about my impractical dream the other day."

"You can leave out the word *impractical* when you're with me if you want."

He paused for a moment, met my eyes, then nodded. "Thank you."

"What about the dream?" I asked.

We had reached the end of the line of games and were now at the fence at the edge of the parking lot that surrounded the baseball field. He leaned up against it. "Before my grandma died, she'd want to spend time with me in the kitchen and I'd be too busy or just had no desire. I mean, I obviously spent some time there, learning, but not nearly enough. I thought I had all the time in the world."

"Until you didn't."

"Exactly. And now, I feel . . ."

"Guilty?"

"Yes. Like I should've done more, learned more, soaked it all up while I had the chance. Maybe this is where this dream of mine comes from. This need to somehow replace the knowledge she would've given me."

"Guilt isn't necessarily a great reason to do something."

"Look at you with your expert advice again."

He'd just needed someone to listen, and I'd felt the need to put my opinion into it. "I'm sorry."

"What? No, don't be. I appreciate it."

"But guilt isn't the only reason, right? I mean, you do love it, too."

"Absolutely."

We started walking back the other way, slowly. "It's not like you have to decide your entire future right now. What's the rush?" I said.

"I've been told before I need to have patience."

My eyes shot to the ground, unable to meet his. *I'd* told him that on the podcast. Did he know that I knew? Was he trying to give me a hint that he was the caller?

"Right . . ." I said. I needed to tell him. What kind of friend was I if I couldn't tell him that I knew he'd been calling in? "About that . . ."

I glanced up at the Ferris wheel but couldn't see Frank or Alana. Maybe they were at the very top, which I couldn't see . . . Oh, wait, it was coming around now and, yes, those were Alana's green Vans and blue tank top and . . . I gasped. As the Ferris wheel rounded the bend, I could see that Alana's lips were very much attached to Frank's. Not just a small peck but a full-on make-out session.

My head whipped back around to Diego, but he was looking at me, his brows furrowed, probably wondering why I gasped. It felt like everything had turned into slow motion because I could see Diego's eyes shift, moving to look at what had caused my reaction. I grabbed his hand and tugged him around, pulling him in the opposite direction.

"Let's play another game!"

Why had I done that? I should've let him see. Alana was the one who just kissed Frank. She kissed Frank! What was she thinking? Maybe that should've made me happy, but it only made me angry. This was going to hurt Diego. He liked her and she was going to hurt him.

Before we made it another step, Victoria appeared in front of us, a big smile on her face. "You ready to do this?"

I checked the time on my phone. "I thought we weren't starting for another thirty minutes."

"Ms. Lyon just wants to go over a few things with us. Talk about the ways this live recording will be different and give us some tips."

My blood was still boiling and I knew I needed to get over this Alana thing quick so I could do the podcast. Live. "I don't know why she'd think we need tips," I said, trying to be sarcastic. But my voice sounded tight with anger.

Diego must've heard my tone because he said, "You'll do great."

"Thanks."

"Come on," Victoria said. "Bring your boy if you want. Brian is already over there."

"Oh, he's not my . . . He came with . . . This is Diego."

"Hi, Diego. You're very pretty," Victoria said with a wink.

Diego reached out and grabbed my hand. He gave it a squeeze. "I'll see you from the audience. Good luck."

I started to walk away but then turned back and stepped in front of him. "Diego . . ."

"Yes?"

"After the podcast, I need to tell you something."

I still needed to tell Diego that I knew he'd been calling in. I just hoped he wouldn't be too angry.

# CHAPTER 31

I saw my parents standing toward the back of the already-full audience. They'd come. My nerves, which had finally kicked in as more and more people filled up the roped-off area in front of us, ramped up another degree. My mom waved. Victoria and I would start in ten minutes. I took a deep breath and waved back.

Victoria and I were sitting side by side on the makeshift stage, behind a long table set up with microphones and headphones. Ms. Lyon and a couple of kids from the production crew stood off to the side, preparing the equipment.

Alana rushed around the stage and to the backside of the table to join me, her eyes wide. I bit the insides of my cheeks. Now wasn't the time to say anything. But Alana apparently thought now was the perfect time because she leaned close to my ear and whispered, "I need to talk to you."

"After" was all I could say.

"Please. I need my best friend."

I sighed and stood, walking off the back of the stage with her. She dragged me behind the row of carnival games forty feet away. It was darker and quieter. I was about to open my mouth to tell her I saw what had happened when she said, "Frank kissed me."

I wasn't sure what to say back. The kiss had looked very much mutual to me.

"I'm sorry," she added.

"What? Why are you apologizing to *me*?" I asked. Diego was the person she needed to be talking to right now.

Her face was flushed. "Because Frank was your date tonight and I thought you liked him and I'm sorry. I didn't mean for that to happen."

"You know I don't like him."

"I thought he liked *you* and that he was going to charm his way into your heart."

"So you don't like Frank?" I asked.

"I like Diego. You know that."

"I *saw* you and Frank kissing. On the Ferris wheel. You were into it, Alana."

Her mouth dropped open. "I was *not* into it. I was surprised! Did Diego see?"

I wished he had. "No," I said softly. "I need to go. We can talk more about this later."

Alana grabbed my arm before I could turn away. "Are you mad at me?"

Yes. "I don't know."

"So you *do* like Frank?"

"This has nothing to do with Frank."

Her brow wrinkled in confusion. "It has everything to do with Frank."

"Later, Alana." I walked away and back to my seat.

Victoria took one look at my face and said, "You better get past whatever drama is happening in your life right now and get your head into this." She nodded toward the crowd.

She was right. I had to try and forget about everything right now. I needed to focus.

"Kate! Kate!"

I turned at the sound of my name. My cousin Liza was weaving her way through the standing crowd, dragging a girl and boy behind her.

"Hi," I said with a smile.

"You remember my friend Chloe." Liza raised her left hand, which held Chloe's hand.

I nodded. "Yes, hi again."

"We're excited to listen tonight. It's fun to see this live," Chloe said.

Liza raised her right hand, which held the boy's hand, and said, "And this is my friend from school, Kurt."

"Hello," Kurt said shyly.

"We just wanted to say hi and wish you luck," Liza said.

"Thanks, cousin."

"Okay, bye." She turned. I watched as she and her friends found a spot to stand toward the center.

Victoria leaned over. "Ready?" she asked me under her breath.

"Yep."

"Hello, Sequoia High!" she said into her microphone, and the audience cheered. "Okay, so this is how this will work. Kat and I have a podcast to record. You are our live audience." She picked up the box full of questions that had been collected. "These are the anonymously submitted questions we've been gathering this week. But first dibs goes to people willing to out themselves. So if you are in the audience tonight and want to ask a question, please come up to the front and speak into the microphone right there." She pointed to a separate microphone that had been set up for audience questions. "Are you ready to get started?" The crowd cheered again and Victoria turned to me. "What about you, Kat? Are you ready to get started?"

I swallowed all my nerves and anger and whatever else was lodged in my chest, leaned toward the mic, and said with a straight face, "Am I ever ready to start?"

The audience laughed.

"No," Victoria said.

"But you're going to push that record button anyway," I said.

My cohost shot me a smile, raised her finger in the air, and lowered it dramatically down to the RECORD button.

"Hello, Oak Court, and welcome to our one—"

"And only," I inserted.

"Recording with a live audience. We're here at Sequoia High's Fall Festival. Say hello, everyone." At her prompt, the audience let out cheers and applause.

I scanned the crowd to see if Alana had joined it. It was hard to find anyone in the mass of people but off to the right, there stood Diego. He gave me a smile and a nod when I met his eyes. Alana and Frank weren't with him.

"The format of tonight will be similar to our studio-recorded podcasts," Victoria was saying. "We'll take questions and I'll do my best to answer them while Kat does her best to stay awake."

"Funny," I said.

"We won't have time for a lot of questions but we'll get to as many as we can. So who's going to kick this off?" Victoria asked the crowd, which suddenly became very quiet.

Uh-oh.

"Just because we're live doesn't mean we don't have editing powers. All this silence will be edited out on Monday so it will seem like we are the most engaging hosts ever," Victoria said. People laughed at that.

We waited for another couple beats, scanning the group.

"Okay, guess everyone is chicken tonight," Victoria said. "Let's go with our anons." She dug her hand into the box and pulled out a folded index card. She handed it to me. "Kat is a much better reader than I am."

"This is true," I said, and unfolded the card. " 'Victoria and Kat, I broke up with my boyfriend last month. We had just grown apart. I thought it was a nice breakup. There was no name-calling or nastiness. But then he started spreading lies about me all over school and even on social media. What am I supposed to do?' "

"Ouch," Victoria said. "Not cool."

"Have you tried talking to him?" I asked the crowd, putting the card down.

"Kat thinks nearly every problem can be solved by just talking."

"I think ninety-nine percent of misunderstandings are caused by miscommunication," I said, which made me think of Alana and Frank and Diego.

"Well," Victoria said. "Yes, you should confront your ex about this. But for the sake of argument, let's assume he's doing this to be vindictive, Kat. What then?"

"Yeah, then: Ouch."

Victoria laughed. "I would dispute whatever claims he's making on my own social media and then move along. If you obsess about it, it will just draw more attention to it. People have short attention spans. They'll forget."

I glanced over at my parents. My mom was smiling and my dad had his intense I'm-really-paying-attention look on. That seemed good.

I reached to grab another index card from the box when Victoria said, "Looks like we have a question from the audience."

"Oh, nice."

Liza's friend Chloe was making her way to the microphone. When she got there, she said, "I have a fear. A big one.

I can't seem to get past it. Kat, when you first started the podcast, you were afraid to do it. How did you overcome the fear?"

"I'm still afraid," I said.

Victoria gave me a playful push. "She practiced, she faced it. That's how. What's your fear?"

"I'd rather not say," Chloe said.

"You're never going to get over it if you can't own it," Victoria said.

Just then, my eyes found Diego's. He had a small smile on his face and he gave me an encouraging nod. One that said, *You're playing your role well but you're not actually saying anything*. Okay, I was reading into that nod. I was projecting. But I knew I'd reverted to my early podcast habits. I turned back to Chloe and cleared my throat.

"Have you ever heard the saying that courage isn't the absence of fear but the ability to move forward *despite* the fear?" I asked.

She nodded.

"You don't necessarily get over fear," I went on, "but you can succeed even if it's trying to hold you back. And Victoria's right, things do get easier the more you face them."

Chloe wrung her hands together and then said, "Thank you."

A lanky boy was waiting behind Chloe at the mic. When she stepped away, he came forward and said, "Kat, I hear you live in Lakesprings. What's the best thing to do at the lake?"

I laughed. I'd wanted to do a whole podcast on that question alone. "Um . . . everything?" I said.

"Kat is biased," Victoria said. "She would never leave the lake if she didn't have to."

I almost agreed, but then I stopped. "Actually, even though I love the lake and it's my favorite place ever, I wouldn't mind testing that preference by traveling a bit." This time I couldn't meet Diego's eyes. He'd know I said that because of him. I did say that because of him. He was making me see that maybe there were other things to explore before making permanent decisions.

"I'm with you on that," Victoria said.

"No, but really, there's lots to do at the lake," I said, focusing on the boy. "You can't go wrong. I'm into motorized toys, but if you can't swing those, then grab a couple inner tubes and an ice chest. There's picnic areas all over and an afternoon of floating is the best."

"Thanks."

The audience microphone was empty again, so Victoria fished out another card from the box and handed it to me.

" 'Katoria,' " I read aloud.

"They mashed up our names?" Victoria asked.

"Yes, they did."

"I love this person already."

I continued reading. " 'I want to ask a guy out but my best friend likes him. I don't think he likes her back. In fact, there have been several hints that he actually likes me. I don't want to lose my friendship over this, but I really, really like him. What should I do?' " My heart seemed to leap to my throat, making it hard to breathe. Thankfully, Victoria jumped in.

"If you know the feelings aren't reciprocated, I say, why should two people suffer? Your friend should be happy to see you happy. The key is honesty. Talking, right, Kat? Tell your best friend how you feel. Get her blessing."

"I don't know," I said, my throat tight. "This situation is a little trickier."

"How so? You mean your talking advice wouldn't work here?"

I shifted in my seat. "Maybe. It just depends how willing you are to risk a friendship. Because something like this can be a friendship-ender. I have a cousin who's way too young for a certain guy that she has a crush on. And he's cute. But even so, as far as I'm concerned, he is off-limits for me. I won't go after a loved one's guy no matter how cute he is. Friendship and family are more important."

There was a loud noise—a gasp—in the audience and my eyes found Liza's. Her mouth was open in indignation, and it took me two beats to realize what I'd just done. What I'd just said.

Crap. I'd just outed Liza in front of half the school.

# CHAPTER 32

"I'm sorry," I said, my palms sweating, looking at Liza. "We'll edit that out. I didn't mean to say that."

"What happened?" Victoria asked.

The audience seemed to sense I had made a grave error and had become deathly silent. So silent that when Liza shouted out, her words rang out crystal clear over the crowd.

"Why didn't you use your own life as an example, Kat?" My cousin's face was splotchy with emotion. "Your best friend likes the guy you like and so you're not pursuing it. You could've just said that."

My heart seized up. How did Liza *know*? Was I that transparent? Had she guessed? Had Diego guessed? Had Alana guessed? I scanned the crowd again for Alana but I couldn't see her anywhere. I purposefully avoided looking anywhere near Diego.

Liza continued, "Instead you have to throw your *cousin* under the bus with a story that's not even true?"

"It's not?" I asked, and then wanted to slap myself. That wasn't the point. "I'm sorry," I said again. "It just slipped out. I shouldn't have said that."

"It's just second nature at this point, right?" Liza snapped. "You exploit the people in your life for the benefit of the podcast. Just ask Mr. Looking for Love."

Liza whipped her head over to Diego and so did I. I shouldn't have looked at him. But it was too late. His gaze went between Liza and me. Then he turned quickly and walked away, sidestepping people and then the outer rope before he disappeared into the carnival.

I closed my eyes and took a calming breath because otherwise I was going to cry. When I opened my eyes, I saw that Liza, who I was sure had done that to get even with me, looked like she regretted the choice. But she huffed, turned on her heel, and stomped away, too.

"Well, that was dramatic," Victoria said.

There was rustling and whispering in the audience. I stayed in my seat because we were in the middle of a podcast and if I went running after Liza or Diego, that would just add to the drama. I didn't need the whole school in on this any more than they already were.

"Is there something you'd like to share, Kat?" Victoria asked me.

"Not really," I said. That's when I remembered my parents were in the audience. My mom looked worried. My dad was confused. Great.

Victoria answered one more question from the box. I didn't even hear what she said because my ears were ringing and my eyes hurt. Then, thankfully, Victoria said, "That's all the time we have for tonight, folks. We'll talk to you all again at our regularly scheduled time. Good night, Oak Court!" She depressed the RECORD button.

I immediately jumped to my feet. "I have to—"

"Go," Victoria said, holding her hand out for my headphones. I handed them to her and took off.

Diego and Liza were standing together when I found them just outside the carnival in the parking lot. I had no idea what she was saying to him but it couldn't be good. I skidded to a halt as I reached them.

"I'm sorry," I said again. To both of them this time.

"My friends are going to think I'm delusional," Liza told me, her cheeks bright red. "Tommy is in college! I'm a freshman in high school. I'm not an idiot. Sure, I think he's cute, but I do not, in fact, like him. I like someone else, actually, and if you weren't so wrapped up in your own life and fame then maybe you'd know that."

My face burned, too. "Tommy won't know. I'll edit it out."

She let out one single, ironic laugh. "People will talk. The whole school was there."

"They won't realize I was talking about you!" I protested.

"Even if I hadn't reacted, which I obviously did, everyone knows we're cousins. You used the word *cousin*. He will find out. Thanks a lot."

A loud shout sounded in a darker corner of the parking lot. I squinted to see a group of guys standing there surrounding one in the middle. Was there about to be a fight?

Liza let out a long sigh and said, "I can't do this right now." She marched away, leaving Diego and me alone.

We stood there for several long moments. I wasn't sure what to say. I'd screwed up. He was obviously mad.

"You knew Looking for Love was me? All this time?" Diego asked. "Why didn't you tell me?"

"I honestly don't know. By the time I thought to, it felt too late."

"So you sat around, what? Mocking me after every show. Laughing at the things I shared."

"No!"

"You kept dragging out the advice, getting me to call back in, when you could've told me exactly what I needed to hear the first day." With that, he turned and left, not giving me a chance to explain that I didn't know it was him at first. But he was right. If I had told him as soon as I discovered his identity that Alana liked him, he would have never had to call back. I wanted to chase after him, beg him to understand.

But as he walked away, I saw something that made my heart stop: the guy in the middle of the group about to fight in the parking lot had turned around, so his face was now visible. It was Max.

Instead of running after Diego, I ran toward the group of guys just in time to see Max shoved to the ground.

"Stop!" I called. "What are you doing?"

My brother picked himself up and wiped his nose with the backside of his wrist. Was he bleeding? Crying?

The boys in the circle laughed. They were bigger than my brother, and seemed older than him. I recognized one boy from the dunk tank line the other day.

"Are you proud of yourselves?" I asked them, my fury growing. "Oh, look at you, so tough that five of you can pick on one person."

"Who's this?" one of the boys asked Max. "Your little nerd girlfriend?"

I narrowed my eyes and faced the one who had spoken. He had a smirk on his face and he nodded at me like this was all a big game to him. "You did *not* just say that," I said.

"What are you going to do about it?" he asked, his smirk turning to a scowl. He took a step toward me. I had been running on instinct until then. But now, quite suddenly, I realized we were very outnumbered.

"Don't touch my sister," Max said.

"Oh, your sister? I should've guessed she was the only girl you knew." The guy shoved my shoulder.

I stumbled back, then took a step forward to knee him where he'd feel it, but Max beat me to it. Max punched the guy in the face, and he fell to the ground. My mouth dropped open. The other boys in the group shouted and all converged on Max at once.

I grabbed Max's arm and pulled him to retreat when I heard a loud, deep voice call out from behind us, "Get off of them!"

I turned to see Alana and Frank running our way. Frank flung one of the guys to the ground and turned to take care of another. The group scattered, realizing it was now a more even match.

"You mess with my friends, you mess with us!" Alana called after the boys as they ran away.

"You okay?" Frank asked me.

"I'm fine." I wasn't worried about me. I pulled Max in front of me. He was taller than me by a couple inches now so I had to look up at him to study his face. "Did they hurt you?"

He shook out of my hold. "I'm fine, Kate."

The range of emotions I'd experienced in the last ten minutes were catching up with me, creating a jittery mania inside my chest. "What were you thinking confronting five guys by yourself?" I demanded.

"I didn't confront. They approached me. I was just trying to show confidence so they'd leave me alone."

His words shook something loose in my brain. *Show confidence.* "You wrote the email, didn't you?" How had I not realized that before now? That email had totally sounded like Max. Liza was right; I had been too caught up in my own issues to notice things. I was so concerned about proving a point to my parents, to my friends, that I'd lost sight of everything else. My brother was getting bullied and I had no idea. "I'm sorry, Max. I'm so sorry," I said softly.

"Can you just take me home?" he asked, his eyes downcast.

"Where is Martinez?" Frank asked.

"He took off," I replied, my stomach clenching. "He found out that we knew it was him calling in to the podcast."

Alana's mouth dropped open. "And you didn't fix it?"

"I tried. I couldn't."

"So was the other thing Liza said to half the school true, too?" Alana asked me. "Are you in love with your best friend's guy?"

She had been there listening to the podcast after all. I didn't know what to say. My silence spoke volumes.

For the fourth time that night, I watched as someone I cared about turned away and left me behind.

# CHAPTER 33

I hitched a ride home with my parents since the way I'd gotten to the carnival (Frank's Beemer) was no longer an option. After my best friend had walked away from me, Frank had followed her and they'd driven off together in his car. Apparently Frank was mad at me, too. Or maybe not mad at me, but more invested in Alana.

I looked over at Max, who shared the back seat with me. He needed to tell my parents what had just happened.

*Later*, he mouthed.

I'd give him one day. I was done keeping quiet about this. That didn't help before.

My mom twisted in her seat to look back at me. "What happened with Liza?" she asked.

"I'll fix it."

She nodded slowly. "That Victoria is charming."

Was that her subtle way of saying that I wasn't? "Yes, she's good."

"You were good, too, baby," Dad said.

"Thanks," I mumbled.

Back at home, Mom followed me to my room, then hovered by the doorway when I went inside.

"I'm fine, Mom," I said, not sure what else she wanted to say but knowing I didn't want to talk about it tonight.

"You seemed miserable up there," she said.

"Up where?"

"Behind that microphone."

"I did?"

"Yes. Honey, if this class is killing you, you need to talk to Ms. Lyon about it. I can talk to her if you want. Maybe you can transfer out. Take something else as your elective. Take a business class or something that will help you run the marina one day."

I collapsed onto my bed. "No, Mom. It was fine until the whole Liza slipup. Normally I can make mistakes like that and not worry that they'll be damaging."

She gave a sympathetic hum. "I know I've been pushing you to try new things." Pity laced her voice. "I'm sorry if you feel like you had to do this for me."

"I didn't . . . I don't. I'm tired. I just want to sleep."

"Okay." She ran a hand down my cheek. "Let me know if you want me to talk to Ms. Lyon."

I nodded and she left. So much for proving a point.

* * *

Saturday morning, I lay in bed, feeling like someone had smashed me in the face with a hammer. My head pounded, my eyes hurt, my insides were in knots. I had stayed up most of the night thinking, trying to figure out a solution to everything, but I still had no answers. I'd spent the last month and a half doling out advice, and I had no idea what to do about the mess *my* life had suddenly become.

I rolled over with a groan and stared at my phone sitting there unassumingly on my nightstand. I held my breath and picked it up. No new messages. I sent off two texts of my own—apologies to Alana and Liza—then wondered why I had never gotten Diego's cell phone number. Probably because Alana liked him. I couldn't very well ask Alana for it now. I dropped my phone back down and rubbed my hands over my face.

I couldn't solve all my problems right that second, but I could try to at least solve one, the one inside my house. I forced myself out of bed and searched for my brother. He was sitting on the back porch staring at the sequoias in the distance. I sat in the patio chair next to him, pulling my knees up to my chest. In the light of day, I could see he had a small red mark by his left eye.

"So. What are we going to do?" I asked.

"I don't know," he said. "I told one of my teachers like you suggested and that just made it worse. They started calling me a narc."

"I'm sorry. How did this all start?" I put my legs down and turned to face him.

"I answered a question the first day of school. The teacher made too big a deal about how I must've done the reading over the summer."

"You read over the summer?"

"No. I just happened to know the answer."

"You *are* pretty smart."

"These guys started calling me kiss-up and nerd. It escalated from there, probably because I didn't react at all."

I sighed. "I wish you would've told me."

"I kind of did with the email."

I kicked his foot with mine. "That doesn't count."

He shrugged. "Maybe Mom will let me be homeschooled."

"Don't run away from this, Max. Unless you want to be homeschooled. Did you want to before all this?"

"No."

A ladybug landed on the wood railing in front of us and crawled along it. "I think some of what Victoria said on the podcast was true," I said slowly. "You need to surround yourself with people. Hang out with me or Liza and our friends. At least for a little while. Those guys are cowards. They only pick on you when you're alone." I paused for a moment, remembering something. "So that day I found your ripped shirt in your room? Did that really happen because you climbed the baseball fence?"

"Yes," he said. For a second I felt relieved. Then he added, "I climbed it because they were chasing me."

I tightened my hands into fists. "I can get Frank and Diego to give those guys a serious talking-to if you want." I actually wasn't sure if I could get Frank or Diego to do anything for me right now but I didn't mention that.

"Okay," Max said.

"Yeah?"

He swallowed hard, then nodded.

"I'm so sorry, Max. High school will get better. Not everyone is a jerk. You just have to meet your people."

His eyes were following the ladybug now, too.

"You totally punched a guy in the face for me last night," I said.

He laughed a little.

"It was a good punch, too."

"It hurt, but it felt pretty good," Max admitted.

"When did you turn into a superhero?"

"If only," he said.

"Speaking of which, I want to read your comic. You'll let me, right?"

"Sure."

* * *

I spent the weekend hanging out with Max and by Sunday, he had even worked up the nerve to talk to my parents about the bullying thing. They were sweet and supportive and concerned, and they told Max he could always come to them with his problems. He looked relieved.

I had almost deluded myself into thinking that all my problems had disappeared, too. (Even though nobody had answered my texts.) But everything would be fine. I'd arrive at school Monday morning and things would be back to normal.

My delusions were put officially to rest on Monday when I got into my car to find Max in the passenger seat as usual, but no Liza in the back seat.

"Where's Liza?" I asked Max.

"I think Aunt Marinn took her."

"Aunt Marinn drove her thirty minutes to school?"

"Yes?"

"Liza is still beyond mad at me." I had thought that maybe she had already paid me back with her declaration to Diego, but apparently not.

"What did you do to her?" Max asked.

"She didn't tell you?"

"She mumbled something about assumptions and ignorance."

"That about sums it up."

I turned the ignition and pulled out onto the road. "I really like your comic book. You've gotten so good at drawing. And the writing is clever, too."

"Liza helped me with the girl voice."

"That was nice of her but that wasn't even a tenth of the work. You're just supposed to say, thank you. Here, let's practice." I pulled up to a stoplight and looked over at him. "Max, your comic is awesome. You're super talented."

He rolled his eyes. "And people call me a nerd."

I playfully punched his arm. "Say 'thank you.'"

"The light is green."

"I'm not going until you say 'thank you.'"

The car behind us honked. I stayed where I was.

"Fine, thank you."

I laughed and applied the gas. "Now was that so hard?"

"Yes."

"It'll get easier." I sighed. "Everything will get easier." It had to. People would forgive me. We'd move forward. And we'd all be okay.

Max shifted in his seat and there was a sound of crinkling paper. He was stepping on something on the floor of the passenger seat. I glanced over to see the magazine Diego had given me. "Will you throw that on the back seat?" I asked. I didn't want it to get damaged.

Max reached down, picked it up, and Frisbeed it onto the back seat.

"That day out at the marina when all the WaveRunners got scattered . . ." Max started but trailed off.

"Yeah."

"I think it was those guys."

I opened then shut my mouth. I had accused Frank. "What makes you think that?"

"One of them . . . the guy I punched . . . Damon, he had come to the marina the weekend before, Labor Day weekend, with his family. He saw me. His family had rented a powerboat. The whole time Dad was going over rules with his parents, Damon was walking up and down the dock, looking at everything."

That punk kid not only picked on my brother at school but had to go and mess with our family's business as well. I gritted my teeth. "You're going to have to tell Dad."

Max nodded, but his eyes went down to his hands, which were resting in his lap.

"It's not your fault," I said. "That's on that Damon kid, Max."

"Maybe if I had reacted differently that very first time . . ."

I pulled off the road and parked against a curb. I shifted the car into park and faced my brother. "You can't think like that. *He* is the one who should be analyzing his mistakes, not you. Nothing justifies what he's been doing."

"Thanks." He looked out the windshield. "We're going to be late to school."

"This is more important to me." I squeezed his forearm. "You do know that, right?"

His eyes flashed to mine.

"Love you, Maxie."

"Okay, can we go to school now?" he asked, rolling his eyes.

I laughed and put the car in drive. After a few miles, he said, "Love you, too."

# CHAPTER 34

"Ms. Lyon?" I said, stepping inside the empty classroom.

"Yes?"

It was early, before first period, and Ms. Lyon sat at her desk with a laptop open in front of her. She was probably prepping for the other class she taught—computer programming.

"I have some editing requests from the live show on Friday." I placed a piece of paper down in front of her. I had made a list of everything I hoped could be cut from my less than stellar performance.

She read over the list. "This is a bit of overkill. I think taking out the word *cousin* would do the trick nicely. The exchange was very entertaining and will be good for the show and for you. It was some of your best work."

"Please." I didn't care about that. I cared about my cousin and how it made her feel.

Ms. Lyon nodded. "Okay."

"Thank you." I stood there, unable to move. Maybe now was the time to ask her about switching jobs again. Someone else would probably love the chance to host. If we kept Victoria the same, listeners probably wouldn't even notice.

"Did you need something else?" she asked.

"No." I left before I changed my mind.

* * *

It took Alana giving me the silent treatment through all of History for me to come to a realization. No matter what had happened over the weekend, we needed to talk about it.

So, at lunchtime, I found Alana at her locker and marched over to her. "Max needs us right now to walk with him from Spanish to the library."

She turned around. "Okay."

It shouldn't have surprised me that she would readily agree. It was Alana, and it was for my brother, but I was a little surprised. We walked down the hall together.

"Are you done giving me the silent treatment, then?" she asked.

"What? *You're* giving *me* the silent treatment. You didn't even answer my text yesterday."

"You didn't text me yesterday," she said.

Hadn't I? I brought out my phone. I'd texted Liza; I was almost certain I had texted Alana, too. But when I clicked on her name, there was my written-out text waiting to be sent. I handed her the phone.

"Aw," she said, reading it. "That's sweet."

I smiled, my spirits lifting a little.

Max was waiting outside his Spanish classroom and when he saw us, he looked relieved.

Alana hooked her arm through his, and we headed for the library. "You just need to walk around with me on your arm a few times, Max, and everyone will think you're cool."

"I don't care if people think I'm cool. My only goal is not to get punched."

"This will help with that goal as well," Alana assured him.

"You don't have to go to the library," I said. "Why don't you eat lunch with us?"

"I'm good in the library."

"Okay."

We dropped him off, then stood outside together.

The campus at lunch wasn't exactly the most private place for confessions. "Can we go sit in my car?" I asked Alana.

"That sounds ominous."

"It kind of is."

That shocked her silent and she took hold of my hand and we walked to the car together. We got inside; me in the driver's seat and Alana beside me in the passenger side. For once, Alana waited in silence while I tried to figure out what I needed to say. Finally I spoke.

"You kissed Frank, Alana."

"I knew you were still mad at me for that."

"Of course I'm mad at you. Diego is . . . Well, he's Diego. Why would you do that to him?"

She opened and shut my glove compartment. "I told you, Frank kissed me first."

"And it meant nothing to you?"

She squeezed her eyes shut. "I don't know! I like Diego . . . I think."

She was confused. Maybe if I told her how I felt, she'd be less confused. "What Liza said the other night at the podcast . . . it's true. I like Diego, too."

Alana took a deep breath and slid the *A* charm she had on her necklace back and forth along its chain a few times. "I don't think he likes either of us right now because of the whole Looking for Love thing."

"Yeah."

"I tried to talk to him this morning and he's not over it," Alana said. "You know Diego, he's really nice and polite. But all he gave me was a single hello and kept walking."

I ran my finger over the Toyota logo on my steering wheel. I hadn't seen Diego this morning, even though I'd looked for him as Max and I walked to class. "Why didn't you ever tell him you liked him, Alana?"

She bit her lip. "I've never had to tell a guy I liked him before. I flirt and they do the confessing. This was different and it made me question everything."

"It also made you like him more?" I asked.

She lifted one side of her mouth into a half smile. "Yes."

"And what about Frank?"

"Frank is a risk. He's not boyfriend material. He's the kind of guy you have a fling with, not a relationship."

So Frank scared her. That was a first.

"Plus," she continued, "I feel like I need to see things through with Diego first. I've invested all this time and energy into it, I'm not ready to walk away yet. I texted him yesterday and he never responded."

"What did you say in the text?"

"That I was sorry that we didn't tell him that we knew he was calling in."

Now was the time that I was supposed to step away. At least until Alana worked out her feelings. But I really didn't want to. I wasn't conflicted about Diego, like she obviously was. I knew exactly how I felt.

Even though it was a long shot, even though I was sure Diego had liked Alana for weeks and that he probably hadn't once thought of me as anything more than a friend, I wanted him to know how I felt. And I didn't want to lose Alana over this, either. Was that the very definition of having my cake and eating it, too? I didn't want to have to choose. I let my head fall back on the headrest.

"I want to tell Diego how I feel," I admitted. "And I don't want to lose you over it."

Her grip was back on the *A*, moving it back and forth over and over again along her chain. "And I can tell him how I feel and not lose you over it?"

I swallowed. The idea tightened across my chest, but I knew I had to say, "Of course."

"It will be weird. We'll create this awkward dynamic between the three of us."

I shook my head. "If he chooses you, I'll let him go. There will be nothing weird."

"We're going to make him choose? How horribly anti-feminist of us."

"The Woman Power part will be that his choice won't break us apart," I argued. "We'll still be best friends no matter what." I turned toward her, my eyes pleading. "Right?"

Alana looked thoughtful. "I've never had to compete with you for a guy."

"I know. What am I thinking, challenging the master?"

Alana smirked. "Is there a reality show about this yet? Two friends, one guy, death."

"Death?"

"Love, death, we'll see." Alana was joking, that was a good sign. She patted the console between us. "I'm not supposed to give up, am I? Was that what you were hoping would come of this?"

"No, actually. I was thinking *I* was supposed to give up."

"He's going to choose neither of us, mark my words. Because now we've turned him into some sort of competition."

"Not a competition. Just a prize," I teased.

Alana stuck out her hand and I shook it. "May the best woman win."

She seemed like she was being funny and lighthearted, but I heard an edge to the words. I sensed that no matter the outcome, I was going to lose someone at the end of this.

# CHAPTER 35

Tuesday morning, when I was all ready for school, I marched into my mom's bedroom. I was feeling so emboldened from my declaration to Alana the day before, I figured I might as well continue making declarations.

Mom looked up from where she was making her bed.

"I'm not going to quit," I announced.

"What?" she asked.

"I like the podcast."

"Okay," my mom said.

"And I'm actually good at it. I have fun. Victoria and I work well together. I've been working hard for this." Probably harder than I'd ever worked for anything, I realized. The marina, the lake, that was easy. It came naturally. The podcast was something I'd had to fight for. And there was a satisfaction in that.

"I know you have," Mom said, looking at me thoughtfully. "I just didn't want you doing something that was making you unhappy."

"It's not. And maybe because of it, I'm going to choose something different someday."

"Choose something different?" she asked.

"I thought at the beginning of the year that no matter what else I did, I'd always choose the lake. But now . . . I don't know. There seem to be more possibilities for the future. I want to try new things." As much as it killed me to say that out loud because it meant my parents were right, it was the truth. "I'll always love the lake, and maybe this is where I'll land in the end. The point is, I'm not sure anymore."

Mom smiled. "I know. And I'll always love *you*. And, Kate, you can try whatever you want to."

"Thanks, Mom." I pointed over my shoulder. "I better go. Don't want to be late for school."

On my way out the door, I grabbed my backpack and Max followed me to my car. My smile widened when I saw Liza in the back seat.

"I would've ridden with my mom," Liza snapped as Max and I got inside, "but she said that she refused to drive me a second day in a row."

"Are you going to hate me forever?" I asked. "What can I do to make this up to you? I made a mistake."

She gave a small grunt. For the rest of the trip, she read the *Lake Life* magazine that she'd picked up off the back seat. When we got to the school she asked, "Have you read this yet?"

"Now you're going to talk to me?" I asked.

She shook the magazine at me.

"No, I haven't, so you can't take it," I replied.

"Fine." She plopped it back down and got out of the car. Maybe I should've given her the magazine, extended some goodwill, but it was the only thing Diego had ever given me.

Max and Liza walked off together, and I saw Alana and Diego standing by his car. Really? She was already in the lead? Well, she was already in the lead before but she was just cementing it now. I steeled myself. If I was going to do this, I had to put myself out there.

I grabbed hold of my backpack straps and made my way to them. I could hear him holding a civil conversation with Alana, nothing overly friendly, but not bad, either. Had he forgiven her? If that was the case, he could forgive me, too.

I took one last breath for courage and slid up beside Alana. "Hi," I said, looking at the collar of his shirt first and then forcing my gaze up to his eyes. I missed those eyes. They instantly went cold.

"Good morning, Kate," Alana said. "Diego was just telling me a funny anecdote about a girl who brought her entire rock collection to tutoring yesterday."

"Oh yeah?"

"It wasn't that funny," he said. "I have to talk to one of my teachers before class. I better go."

"Diego," I said when he got one step away. "Can I talk to you for a minute?"

Alana widened her eyes at me as if saying, *You're going to do this now? Have I taught you nothing?* But it didn't matter because he said, "Not right now," and left. His voice seemed sad, not angry, and that just hurt even more.

"Ouch," Alana said.

"Yeah, I felt that one."

"I'm sorry," she said, and I knew she totally meant it. "This is going to end with us giving each other a speech about how we don't need no stinkin' boys, isn't it?"

"That doesn't sound like a bad ending right now," I said.

I hadn't seen Frank sneak up behind us, until he was between us, an arm around each of our shoulders.

"Good morning," he said, and kissed Alana's cheek.

"What did I tell you last night?" she said.

"That I should keep trying because I'm growing on you."

"I didn't say that!" Alana said.

"I was reading between the lines. Was I right?"

She laughed and shoved him away.

"I can work with that," he said.

I was impressed that he was still coming around at all. I would've thought that, in Frank's world, Alana liking another boy would mean Frank had to walk away and maintain his pride. But I was slowly learning Frank wasn't everything I had thought he was.

"Oh, Frank," I said. "While you're here. Remember when I accused you of sabotaging the marina?"

"No."

"Oh, I mean of posting pictures on the website."

"Yes, I remember that."

"Well, I was wrong."

"I actually did post pictures on the website," he said.

I patted his shoulder. "I was wrong about other things, Romeo. I'm sorry."

"That one actually sounded like you meant it."

"It was at least ninety-five percent sincere."

"We're going to change our parents' hearts yet, and it probably won't even take death, Juliet."

* * *

The next morning, the only glimpse I had of Diego was the back of his wavy hair as he disappeared into a crowded hallway.

"Don't worry," Alana said, obviously seeing him as well. "I haven't talked to him, either."

"I just never thought of him as a guy who held grudges."

"When pride is involved, people can hold on to a lot of things," Alana said wisely.

"How am I going to talk to him? At the very least I just want to explain to him why I didn't tell him."

"Why would I help you figure that out?" She winked my way. "Every woman for herself, remember?"

"I love you, too," I said.

"Good luck on the podcast today."

# CHAPTER 36

At this point, there was really only one way to get my message across to Diego. It would be embarrassing, it would involve letting more people into my personal life than I felt comfortable with, and it would make me more vulnerable than I'd ever been. But it was important. This wasn't a very good pep talk, I realized as I repeated the thoughts once again as I sat getting ready to record the podcast.

Alana was back on the production crew. This time, she and Frank sat at the phones.

"Good afternoon, Oak Court!" Victoria chirped into the microphone. "You're listening to *Not My Problem*, with Victoria and Kat."

"Today it needs to be Kate," I said.

"What?" Victoria asked, looking startled.

"I need to be Kate today because I have something to say, as Kate."

Victoria's eyebrows rose nearly to her hairline. "Okay, then, Kate. Take it away."

"I have a problem."

"And it's not that you hate people?"

I laughed a little. “No. Quite the opposite in this case actually.”

“You love someone?”

I thought about that for a moment. Was it love? It was on its way there, I knew that. “Maybe,” I said, my heart pounding. “I’m not sure he feels the same way. In fact, I’m pretty sure he is or was in love with my best friend.”

“Oh,” Victoria said. “You’re actually going to share.”

“Yes. See, I’m hoping he’ll give me a chance. I screwed up before I ever got to tell him how I felt. I kept a secret from him, and now he’s not speaking to me. And I miss him.”

“What do you miss about him?” Victoria asked.

Of course she would make me put everything out there. Make myself even more vulnerable. Drop some fronts I had up. But she was right, I needed to.

“I miss his attentive gaze,” I started, “and his insightful observations and his humor and our conversations and I miss his smile.” I caught my breath. “He hasn’t smiled at me in a while. That sounds so cheesy, I know it does. I’m not used to being this open.” I bit my lip. “I’m used to hiding behind sarcasm and indifference.”

“How does it feel to let it out?”

“Not good.”

Victoria laughed, obviously surprised by that answer. “I thought you’d say freeing.”

“No, it’s terrifying. But I have to do it. I have to do it

because if there is even a tiny chance that he returns any of these feelings, then it is worth it."

"Are you going to be vague and keep the guy anonymous or are you going to share with the listeners the name of your mystery love?" Victoria asked.

I hadn't prepared myself for that question. *Was* I going to be vague? What would be better? I didn't want to embarrass Diego or make him even angrier with me. But hadn't this whole thing started because we were keeping secrets?

A buzz sounded in my earphones, followed by Alana's voice. "We have a caller."

Victoria held up her hand. "Can we wait a few minutes on that? Kate is still sharing."

"I think you'll want to take this one . . . Kate." Alana met my eyes through the glass. She looked equal parts nervous and apprehensive.

"Let's take the call," I said, not sure what Alana was trying to convey with that look. It almost seemed like a bad thing. Was she trying to save Diego from my saying his name on the podcast? Was she trying to save *me* from further humiliation? Was she trying to help herself? Make it so she could tell him how she felt about him before I could?

"Hello," Victoria said, "You're on *Not My Problem*."

"Hi," the caller said. It seemed so strange that even from just that tiny, two-letter word, I could know who spoke it. But I did know. "Is Kate recording today?" the voice asked.

"Yes," I said. "I'm here."

"Hi, Kate."

"Oh!" Victoria said. "It's Looking For Love."

"It's Diego," he said. "My name is Diego Martinez, and I need to talk to Kate."

"Talk away, Diego," Victoria said. "She's listening."

"I'm sorry, Kate," Diego said. "I've been acting badly."

"I understand," I said, my heart racing. "You were blindsided. *I'm* sorry. I shouldn't have kept a secret from you. It wasn't for the show. I promise. I had no idea you'd keep calling."

"I know," he said quietly. "I shouldn't have accused you of that. I was hurt. And embarrassed. I felt like I'd been rejected both on air and in real life. I was trying to be a big person about it all. But in the end that one more piece of information I was told at the carnival pushed me over the edge."

"You don't need to be embarrassed," I said fervently. "You weren't rejected. She likes you. She's always liked you. I should've just told you. I was always just trying to help you tell . . ." I almost said *Alana*, but that wasn't my secret to broadcast. I'd already learned my lesson with Liza. ". . . your crush how you felt about her."

He let out a breathy laugh. "Why didn't you just read the magazine, Kate?"

The headphones slipped down the back of my head and I pushed them into place. "The magazine? Oh, the magazine . . ." Was something in the magazine? How did he know I hadn't read it? Had Liza told him?

"What just happened?" Victoria asked.

I met Alana's eyes through the glass and she shrugged.

"Read the magazine. And come find me if it changes anything," Diego said, and then he was gone.

"I'm so confused," Victoria said.

"I need to go."

"We're in the middle of recording."

My heart felt like it was going to beat out of my chest. Diego hadn't heard my confession, obviously, but he would when this all aired. For a moment, I thought I was going to be the embarrassed one, since he liked Alana. But he'd referenced the magazine that was sitting in the back of my car. He obviously hadn't just handed me a random magazine he thought I'd like. There was something I was supposed to see.

I ripped off the headphones and placed them on the floor. Into the microphone I said, "Sorry, Victoria, to leave you alone like this, but I know you can handle it and I can't wait one second longer." I really hoped Ms. Lyon wouldn't give me an F. But I had to do this.

"Good luck," Victoria said as I sprinted out the door. I snagged my backpack off the couch and didn't look back. I could hear someone, who I assumed was Alana, follow after me. I fumbled in the front pocket of my bag for my keys as we neared my car and pushed the unlock button. I opened the back door and snatched the magazine off the seat.

I turned back the cover. I noticed right away the red pen that had been taken to the first article. The headline had been manipulated, parts written over or letters and words crossed out and replaced. It went from saying: *Eight Ways to Stay Safe in the Water.* To saying: *Eight Ways to Say Yes to the Fall Festival.* Each of the eight tips were crossed out and now had various ways of saying yes—*I'd love to; of course; please, yes; sure; yes, thank you; I thought you'd never ask; no, I mean yes; yes!*

I swallowed hard. "Oh no."

I turned the page. The next article's headline had been doctored to read: *Have I been patient enough?*

Page after page was filled with festival references and different ways of asking me to go. The very last page, in black Sharpie, written over the face of a surfer said: *Will you go to the Fall Festival with me, Kate?*

I was a horrible person. Diego was right. I'd told him no in a subtle way. We'd stood behind the bleachers of the baseball stadium that night and he'd asked me if I'd read any of the articles in the magazine he'd given me and I'd said yes. He thought I had read this and was politely rejecting him. And yet he was still so sweet to me. So sweet until he found out I knew it was him calling in all along. And that had hurt him. He'd thought I was mocking him. Using him.

This whole time I thought he liked Alana and he really liked . . . me?

Alana, who had obviously been reading over my shoulder, said, "And the best woman won."

I met her soft stare. She smiled at me. "It's always been you, Kate," she said. "It was never me."

"I didn't know," I said. "I didn't know."

She took me by the shoulders and said, "I know. And we made a deal, right? We'd still be best friends no matter what."

I nodded. "Thank you."

"Why a magazine?" she asked.

"That first day I took Liza to the tutoring center, I tried to guess what magazines he read. Then after that, anytime there was a new magazine I noticed it and . . . no . . ." My mouth opened and closed.

"What?"

I laughed a little. "No, he was trying to guess my interests after that. He's the one who brought in the new magazines every Monday. I didn't realize it was him bringing them in until now."

"You two are going to be sickeningly sweet together." Alana picked up my keys from where I had apparently flung them onto the back seat of my car along with my backpack and handed them to me. "Go get your man."

"Are you going to be—"

"Of course I'll be okay. It will be fun to watch Frank try to win my affections. I'm ready for someone who's totally into me now."

I hugged her tight. "I love you."

"You too. Tell Diego I said hi."

I shut the back door and opened the one on the driver's side.

"Actually, never mind," Alana added. "Don't say anything to Diego about me. You should just kiss him. Wasn't that

Victoria's advice to *him* once? If he had taken that advice from the beginning and not your lame advice about patience, none of this would have ever happened."

I laughed. "Yes, Victoria gives much better advice than me. That was determined long ago."

Alana gave me a playful push into my car, and I pulled the door closed. Then I rolled down my window.

"Wait, I have no idea where to find him. I don't even have his cell number."

"I'll text it to you."

# CHAPTER 37

This is Kate. Where are you?

The hill behind the stadium, Diego texted back almost immediately.

"Thank you for not being too far," I whispered.

I drove over the single block and parked next to Diego's car. I carefully exited and stared up the hill. Sequoia trees blocked my view so I couldn't see him, but I started walking up, anyway. When I arrived, he was holding a golf club and a pile of golf balls were by his feet.

We locked eyes from forty feet away.

"Aren't you supposed to be in the middle of recording a podcast?" he asked.

"Yes, but I had a magazine to read," I said, inching my way forward.

"Did you like the articles?" he asked.

"So much. Even better than the originals."

"Yeah?" He twisted the golf club back and forth, perhaps a nervous reaction.

I finished my walk to him and held out my hand for his. With no hesitation, he placed his hand in mine. I smiled and drew the word *Valor* on the back of his hand. A shiver went through him, but then he tugged on my hand, bringing me closer to him.

I looked up, meeting his eyes. "I once got some advice that if I liked someone and wanted to know how that person felt about me, I should just kiss them," I said softly.

"Really? I got that same advice." He dropped my hand and the golf club at the same time and pulled me into a hug.

I pressed my cheek against his, savoring the feeling of being this close. Then I turned and kissed his cheek, then his jaw, then the spot right below his ear.

He let out a low hum. "I think I've run out of patience."

I smiled and finally let my lips meet his. He tasted like mint and smelled like pine. Or maybe that was the trees. It didn't matter. It was my favorite smell in the world, and this was my favorite feeling in the world. His hands traveled the length of my back and up into my hair. I stepped even closer to him and nearly tripped on the golf club that lay between our feet. He wrapped one arm tight around my waist, lifting me off the ground slightly, and kicked the golf club out of the way. We continued to kiss, soft at first and then the way we should've been kissing for weeks, urgently and holding back nothing.

He pulled away first and looked at me, slightly breathless. "Tell me everything."

It took my brain a second to catch up to what he'd said. "Everything?"

"From the first time I called in to the podcast until now." He pointed to a fallen tree nearby and we both walked to it, hand in hand, then sat down.

"Okay, the first time you called in, anonymity was kind of our selling point for the podcast and we planned to keep true to our word," I said. "We would keep the callers anonymous for the listeners. I didn't think it was a big deal. I didn't know any of the callers, anyway."

"Until me." He ran his finger up and down each one of mine in his hand.

"I wasn't sure it was you at first, either. You were disguising your voice. Alana didn't think it was you."

"Alana . . . so you assumed I was talking about her the whole time?"

"Yes, she liked you. And everything you said on the podcast made it seem like your crush was her."

"Like what? Because I was pretty sure everything I was saying made it seem like it was you . . ." He paused and smiled. "You know, since it *was* you."

"Like how she treated everyone the same, how she liked another guy." I paused, frowning. "What did you mean by liking another guy?"

"We talked about this. Your ex."

"Oh, right."

He smiled again. "Oh, right."

"You also talked about how she left when you invited her places and never stuck around when you were in places together."

"I talked about the fact that *you* did that."

"I did not."

He nodded. "You did. Always."

"I guess I didn't think about it."

"Because you didn't like me. I was right at first, when I worried you didn't like me back."

"Yes, I guess it's good I told you to have patience because if you'd told me right away I would've been too worried about Alana's feelings to even think about it."

"So I should take Frank out to dinner, then? As a thank-you?"

"Frank? Why?"

"Because she started liking him, and then you didn't have to worry about girl code."

"No, actually . . . I just started liking you too much. I talked to her about it. We came to an agreement."

He raised one eyebrow. "What kind of agreement?"

"The kind that lets me have both you and Alana in my life."

"I like that kind of agreement."

"Me too."

Diego was quiet for a moment. "So you're telling me that Alana doesn't like Frank? When Liza yelled out on Friday that you liked your best friend's guy, I thought maybe you had started liking Frank."

"What? No! I mean, Frank and I may be getting along better but that would be a jump. Alana liked *you*."

"I never thought of her that way."

"Not even when she asked you to my Cousins' Night?"

"I thought she had somehow figured out I liked you and was helping me out."

"Really?"

"Really."

"So when she asked you to the Fall Festival?" I pressed.

"I thought *you* were asking me. You were both standing by my car, if you remember. When I realized it was her, I was confused. But when she hung out with Frank most of the night I thought that maybe she knew Frank was going to ask you so she asked me so we could all hang out."

My head felt like it was spinning. I laid it on his shoulder. "I'm sorry it took me so long to realize I liked you."

"When did you realize?" he asked.

"The first time we stood here, actually, behind this stadium."

"*That* long?" he asked, his voice showing his surprise.

"Don't forget you were my best friend's crush. Totally off-limits. I'm glad I realized at all."

He laughed. "I should just count my blessings?"

"Yes. Totally." I squeezed his hand that was still in mine. "That's not when I started liking you, though. It's just when I realized it. I started liking you the day I hit my head on the locker."

"I guess that's a little closer to when I started liking you."

"When was that?" I asked, looking up at him.

"The first day you came to the tutoring center. You were so fun to talk to. We had a whole conversation about magazines. It had never been so easy for me to talk to a girl before. You found out more about me in that one meeting than I'd ever told most of my friends."

I pulled my knees up to my chest. "I feel the same about you," I admitted. "It's just easy. But I still haven't found out everything. You like to keep things inside."

"I know. I'm working on it."

"How are things going with your parents, anyway?" I asked. "Are they mad you're here right now and not studying?"

"It's still a struggle, but we talked about things, actually. Isn't that your motto?"

"Yes, it is. What did you talk about?" I asked.

"About how I should be able to go out, if I have all my other responsibilities done."

"So you didn't talk about how you want to travel?"

"One step at a time." He leaned over and brushed a soft kiss on my forehead. A shiver went through me.

"How did you know I hadn't read the magazine, by the way?" I asked.

"I didn't. For the longest time I thought you had. But then I guess Liza read through it in your car and she found me this morning and told me."

"She did?" I took a breath of relief. "She doesn't hate me after all."

"That girl adores you."

I couldn't help but smile. Then I nodded my head toward his pile of golf balls. "Hey. I know a guy who can hit a golf ball through the goalposts all the way over there." I pointed toward the football field.

Diego looked over. "Oh yeah? That would be hard to do. That's really far away. I don't know if I believe that."

"Well, he is pretty amazing."

He pulled me onto his lap. "*You're* pretty amazing."

My heart raced, and I traced my finger along the collar of his T-shirt. "I talked about you on the podcast today," I said.

"You did?"

"Right before you called."

"What did you say?" he asked.

"I guess you'll just have to listen."

"Should we listen together?"

I leaned over and kissed him, happy I could. "Yes. Friday."

# CHAPTER 38

That afternoon, when I got home, I went straight over to my aunt's house and smashed Liza in a hug.

"Stop," she said. "I'm still mad at you."

"You aren't. I know you aren't. You talked to Diego for me."

She smiled. "Fine, I'm not. Just don't ever talk about me on the podcast again."

"Never."

"Thanks for editing it out."

"Did Tommy find out, anyway?"

"Yes, but we laughed about it and I told him about how I liked Kurt so it worked out fine."

"Wait. You like Kurt?"

"Yes. But no, we're not talking about me right now. What happened with Diego? Did you guys finally spill your guts to each other?"

"We did."

"Good. I like Diego."

"Me too."

I left Liza's house feeling lighter, and I called Alana as I walked down to the marina. A guy answered her phone. "Hello."

"Um, did I call the wrong number?"

A loud mechanical noise sounded in the background.

"Nope. Alana is just in the middle of making smoothies."

"Frank?"

"Yep."

That was fast. "Tell her to call me when she's done."

"Is that Kate?" I heard Alana ask in the background. "Ask her if she finally caught her fish."

"Tell her yes," I said.

"Nice," Frank said. "Speaking of catching fish—me, Alana, you, and Diego, my boat, this Saturday."

"Okay." I sat down on the dock and dipped my feet in the water. The sun was low in the sky and sent a shimmery reflection off the lake and backlit a sailboat in the distance.

"Yeah?" Frank asked.

"Yes."

"Awesome."

"As long as you aren't a punk on the lake."

"I will try my hardest."

* * *

Friday, at lunch, Diego and I sat on a bench in the commons waiting for Alana. She'd told us she had a surprise.

Diego held my hand, like he had every time he'd seen me for the last two days. It still made me incredibly happy.

"You don't post a lot of updates online," Diego was saying. "Why not?"

I shrugged and tried to unwrap a burrito one-handed. Diego laughed but when I tried to take my hand back he wouldn't let me.

"You're a brat," I said.

"Yes, I am." He brushed a kiss to my knuckles.

"I don't know," I said, answering his social media question. "I'm private. You don't post a lot, either."

"I know." He set down his bag of chips and took his phone out of his pocket. "But I think we might need a picture of the two of us together. Since you have so many of you and Hunter."

I tilted my head his way. "Those pictures are like six months old. Have you been stalking my social media?"

"Yes," he said unapologetically. "How else was I supposed to see you when you were constantly ditching me?"

"I wouldn't say *constantly*."

"Constantly," he said. He held his phone out in front of us and pulled me up against his side.

"You know I take the world's most awkward pictures," I said.

"You're adorable." He kissed my cheek and snapped a picture.

"Awww," Alana said. "So cute."

Diego lowered the phone. Alana stood in front of us, with a group of about twenty people behind her.

"What's going on?" I asked.

"It's my surprise. A listening party."

"A listening party?" I repeated in shock.

She held up a wireless speaker. "The podcast was uploaded and we're all going to listen to it together."

My mouth dropped open. This was definitely a surprise, but not really the good kind.

Alana pointed to the grass in front of the bench and on cue, the group of twenty sat down.

"Did they rehearse that?" Diego mumbled next to me, and I smiled.

"Diego, you are in for a treat," Alana said. "This is Kate's best episode yet."

"I can't wait," he said.

My cheeks went hot. I usually hated listening to my own voice but this week would be particularly embarrassing. "Maybe we should listen to this later, when we're alone," I said to Diego.

"Or we can listen to it now," he offered.

So we did. And he heard me stumble through a very unpracticed and halting confession. Then I listened to *his* voice on the speakers tell all the listeners that he was Looking for Love. Several people in the listening group "awwed" and giggled.

Diego smiled my way when I told Victoria she needed to take over.

"Thank you," he whispered in my ear. "I know that was all really hard for you to say publicly."

"I had to."

He kissed my hand. "I did, too."

* * *

The rest of the day, people called Diego "Looking for Love" in the hallway, or stopped to ask us questions.

"Is this what fame feels like?" he asked.

"Don't let it go to your head."

We stopped at his locker before heading out to the parking lot. "Hey, can I store my history book in your locker? It's closer to my class," I asked, digging the textbook out of my bag.

"Already want to move into my locker?"

I laughed and handed it to him. He shoved it in and dug around his locker for a while, exchanging books and looking through papers.

I wrapped my arm around his waist. "Have I ever told you that you take an inordinately long amount of time at your locker?"

"You've timed me?"

"I don't have to."

"This coming from the girl who spent ten minutes at her locker the day she hit her head on it."

"I kept getting interrupted."

"I'm just saying."

I took a black marker out of my bag and wrote *D+K* on the inside of his locker door.

"Cute," he said. "People are going to think I did that."

I drew a heart around it. "Now they will."

He snatched the pen from my hand and beneath my heart wrote *Mi amor.*

My heart skipped a beat. I may not have remembered a lot of Spanish from class, but I knew what that meant: *my love*. I wasn't sure how to respond, though; it's not like he said it out loud. He didn't seem to expect a response; he just shut his locker door and took my hand again.

We headed for the parking lot. I could see my car in the distance, Max and Liza waiting for me there.

"Diego?" I asked.

"Yes?"

"I have a weird request."

"Okay?"

"My brother."

"Frank told me about the fight at the carnival. Who do you and I need to beat up?"

"No beating up. Maybe just a talking-to will do the trick. I'm going to suggest the next episode of the podcast be for people who have struggled with bullying to call in."

"Maybe I'll have to call in that day, then," Diego said.

"You've struggled with bullying?"

"My entire seventh-grade year. Some kids can be mean."

"They can."

"But then some can be really nice. Since then I've always hoped I could be the latter."

"I think you've succeeded."

We reached the car and Diego patted Max on the back. "I heard you defended my girlfriend the other night."

"Who?" Max asked.

Diego held his hand to the side of his mouth and loud-whispered, "Your sister."

Butterflies took flight in my stomach. Even though I figured as much, it was the first time he'd said the word *girlfriend* out loud and I liked the sound of it. A lot.

Diego turned to me and wrapped me up in a hug, kissing my cheek several times as I laughed.

"Right?" he asked.

"Absolutely."

"Ew," Liza said. "I'm going to call in to the podcast on Wednesday and ask how you politely tell friends that they are acting too cheesy."

I grinned at her. "And I will say, is there such a thing as too cheesy?"

* * *

"Have you ever wakeboarded?" I asked Diego as I climbed onto Frank's boat from the dock at the marina.

"No," Diego replied.

"Water-skied?"

"Nope."

"Tubed?" I asked, throwing my towel onto one of the chairs and turning to watch him hop into the boat. He joined me where I stood behind the driver's seat.

"I have sat on a WaveRunner one time."

My mouth dropped open. "You mean twice? Because you sat on one a couple weeks ago when you found our abandoned one in the cove."

"That was the one time I was referring to."

I took him by the shoulders and looked him in the eyes. With all the sincerity I could muster, I said, "I'm sorry."

"Yeah yeah."

"No, seriously. Your life has been so sad up until this point. What kind of friend have I been the last few months to not ask you these questions? To not have fixed this sooner!"

Alana added a six-pack of Diet Coke to the built-in ice chest under the bench seat along the back. "Kate is very passionate about the lake and everything that happens on it, in case you haven't learned by now. She actually suggested the entire podcast be dedicated to the lake at the beginning of the year."

Frank powered the boat on. "You did? I would've voted for that."

Alana hugged Frank from behind. "Then there would've been two whole votes."

"You wouldn't have voted for that?" Frank asked.

"No way," Alana said. "And since we're the only three lake kids in the class, you both would've been out of luck. Good thing she submitted *advice*."

"Because we all know how passionate I am about that," I said.

"I need some advice," Alana said.

I rolled my eyes. "Oh good. Just what I wanted to give out today."

"How do we make today not awkward when all the people on this boat were either on the giving or receiving end of being loved or hated in the last several weeks?"

"No comment," I said. "I'm off the clock."

Frank pointed to the dock we still hadn't pulled away from. "Max! Liza!" he called. "Do you want to join us?"

Max wasn't big on boating like I was, but who could resist the pull of a really nice boat? Not my brother.

"My advice to your question," Frank said to Alana, "is to invite people who weren't involved in the hate or love fest."

Max and Liza boarded the boat and Frank steered us away from the dock. I pulled the baseball cap I wore down lower on my head. I loved postseason Saturdays when it felt like we had the lake entirely to ourselves. Like it was ours for the taking.

Liza plopped down on the bench seat. "Hey, Alana. After this, maybe you can make us some of your famous chicken."

"My competition-winning chicken?" Alana winked at Diego and he let out a grumble.

"Where did you learn to make that anyway?" he asked.

"My mom, who learned it from her mom."

I wrapped my arms around Diego's waist and whispered, "Maybe she can teach you."

"Are you trying to say I have experts in my own backyard

that I can learn from before becoming a world traveler?" he asked teasingly.

"What? I didn't say that at all. I'm off the clock, remember?" I smirked and opened the middle section of the windshield to admit me into the bow of the boat. I sat on one of the forward-facing seats.

Diego joined me, taking the seat across the small aisle. "You look like you're in your happy place."

"You have no idea."

"I think this can be my new happy place, too," he said.

I was definitely happy. But I was learning that my happiness wasn't necessarily tied to one particular place or event, either. With Diego, I had the feeling I could be happy anywhere.

We passed the five-mile-per-hour buoy, and I heard Frank say, "Hold on!"

The boat picked up speed, and the air flowed over my face. I laughed, and Diego reached across the aisle for my hand. Now the air whipped against our hands and arms, seeping through the gaps between our fingers. Diego smiled over at me. I thought about what he had written on his locker door, how I hadn't responded, when I knew in my heart how I felt.

"My love," I said.

# ACKNOWLEDGMENTS

Book number ten. This was my number. The number of books I hoped I would be lucky enough to write and put out into the world. And here I am at my goal because of you readers. Thank you! Thank you for your support and encouragement. Thank you for reading my words and sending me fun notes and positive feedback and rooting for me. You are the best! I appreciate you all so much. I don't think I could keep writing without you. And apparently I'm not stopping at ten books, since I have several more under contract. So I hope you're ready to keep reading them!

I also want to thank my family. This isn't the easiest of career choices. There are lots of ups and downs. Lots of late nights, or times where I'm deep in my own head staring at walls. And they still love me! Good thing, because unrequited love is the worst. So to my husband, Jared, and my kids, Hannah, Autumn, Abby, and Donavan, I love you. You are my everything.

Next, I'd like to thank my agent, Michelle Wolfson. I may be biased, but I think she is the best agent in the entire universe. You may be saying to yourself, *but you haven't traveled the entire universe*. Regardless, I stand by this claim. Thanks for all you do, Michelle!

Thank you, Aimee Friedman, my amazing editor. You always have great ideas and suggestions and I know my books wouldn't be as good without you. You are awesome. And thanks to the rest of the Scholastic team for all you do: Yaffa Jaskoll, Rachel Gluckstern, Monica Palenzuela, Charisse Meloto, Rachel Feld, Isa Caban, Olivia Valcarce, David Levithan, Lizette Serrano, Emily Heddleson, and the entire Sales team and School Channels team.

I have some of the best friends ever. Friends who read my books and give me advice. Friends who get me out of my head. Friends who love me even when I'm grumpy. Those people in my life are: Stephanie Ryan, Candi Kennington, Rachel Whiting, Jenn Johansson, Renee Collins, Natalie Whipple, Michelle Argyle, Bree Despain, Elizabeth Minnick, Brittney Swift, Mandy Hillman, Jamie Lawrence, Emily Freeman, Misti Hamel, and Claudia Wadsworth.

And last, but not least, thanks to my family who have always supported me no matter what. Chris DeWoody, Heather Garza, Jared DeWoody, Spencer DeWoody, Stephanie Ryan, Dave Garza, Rachel DeWoody, Zita Konik, Kevin Ryan, Vance West, Karen West, Eric West, Michelle West, Sharlynn West, Rachel Braithwaite, Brian Braithwaite, Angie Stettler, Jim Stettler, Emily Hill, Rick Hill, and the twenty-five children that exist between all these people. I love you all so much.

# TAKE A SNEAK PEEK AT ANOTHER MUST-READ BY KASIE WEST!

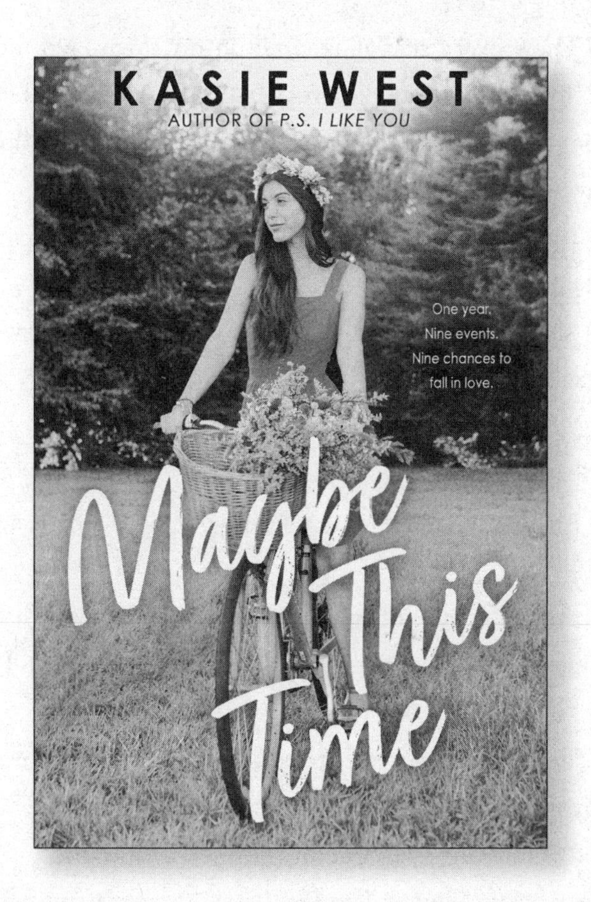


"Excuse me?"

I turned. A guy around my age, dressed in fitted jeans, a pastel collared shirt, and a tailored sport jacket stood there, a smile on his handsome face. He clearly wasn't from around here. He was citified.

I offered him a polite smile, hoping this wouldn't take long. "The event doesn't start for fifteen minutes," I said. "But you're welcome to wait in the lobby. Families are already gathering there."

I knew every school-aged kid in my town (and most of their living and dead relatives). So this guy had to be here visiting for the event. I tried to place him with a grandparent in my head—Betty or Carl or Leo or . . .

"You're not from around here," he said, as if voicing my thoughts.

I shifted the boxes in my arms. They weren't heavy but they were bulky. "What?"

"You're not from Rockside," he said.

"I am, actually. Born and raised."

"Ah. There it is. I didn't hear your Southern accent at first."

I straightened with a bit of pride. I worked very hard on making my accent as minimal as possible so that when I went away to college I wouldn't stick out like a sore thumb.

The guy took several steps forward and pulled his hand out from behind his back to reveal he'd been holding a pink tulip. "Something beautiful for someone beautiful."

My brows dipped down. *Seriously?* I wasn't sure what to make of such a brazen romantic gesture. If that's what he was going for. Was it?

I looked at the boxes in my arms, transferred them awkwardly to one hip, and reached out for the flower. With my hand halfway to its destination, I noticed a small green wire wrapped up the stem and supported the bulb.

I paused. "Where did you get that?"

The question seemed to surprise him, his smile faltered a bit, but he recovered with, "It doesn't matter where it came from, only where it's going." He extended his arm farther.

I set the boxes down on the floor and took the flower to inspect it. Sure enough, the wire was wrapped exactly the way I'd done it on over a hundred tulips that very morning. Hours and hours of my life were spent with that wire, in fact.

"You took this from one of the vases in the cafeteria?" I asked, incredulous.

He nodded. "Yes, I rescued it from its tacky prison. It looks happier already."

My mouth dropped open.

"No worries. There were hundreds of them. Nobody will be able to tell."

"No worries?" I turned and marched back to the cafeteria.

"I sense I've offended you," Mr. Obvious said, following me. Or Mr. Entitled? Maybe I'd go for a hyphenated last name since both applied.

I stood in the doorway and scanned the centerpieces.

"You're telling me that you're going to know which one of these flower arrangements I found *this* flower in," he said.

"*Found?* Yes, I'm going to tell you exactly which flower arrangement you *stole* this flower from, considering I've spent the last eight hours putting them together."